The Road Home

By

Pamela Klopfenstein

The Road Home

Copyright © 2012 Pamela Klopfenstein
ISBN: 978-0615722603

Cover Design: Ebooklaunch
Interior Design: www.e-SolutionsConsulting.com

www.pamelaklopfenstein.com

www.facebook.com/pamelaklopfenstein

Twitter: @writer_gurl

This baby might just be the miracle they need.

"The Road Home is a heart-touching story of loss and survival, and of a love strong enough to weather any storm. The well-developed characters struggle with problems the reader can identify with and the emotional conflict makes this a real page-turner with a strong faith message. I couldn't put it down."

Barbara Warren Author of:
The Gathering Storm
Murder At The Painted Lady

"The Road Home has all the makings of a memorable and heartwarming story, especially for mothers who have lost children or who have prodigal children."

Ann Tatlock Author of:
Travelers Rest
Promise to Keep
I'll Watch the Moon
All the Way Home

DEDICATION

I dedicate this book to my son, Jonathan, and all of the precious little
angels who have entered my life. You know who you are..
And I dedicate this book to mothers who have prodigal children.

CONTENTS

ACKNOWLEDGMENTS

To my husband, Kurt, thank you for all the times you took the role of
Mr. Mom and for all the times you lent your shoulder
for me to cry on.
Jeremy, Matthew, Da'laquan, and Da'oshia, I love you more than
chocolate almond ice cream smothered in Pepsi, books, and
the Tennessee Lady Vols.
A huge thank-you to my editor, Vicki McCollum, who endured the
verb-tense-change nightmare with me.
Thank-you, thank-you, to Annette Wilson who read the final
draft of this book.

CHAPTER ONE

On a chilly morning in March, Sarah Kiser tossed back the quilt on her bed. Since December, ghastly memories played in her mind every time she closed her eyes. She sighed in relief; thankful the phone call she'd received from Miss Johnson, caseworker at Child Protective Services, had interrupted her morning nightmare.

She dropped her feet over the edge of the bed and rubbed her eyes. They felt like a sandpit. It would be pointless to go back to sleep. Soon Josh and the boys would be getting up for work and school.

Miss Johnson's words replayed in her head. "We've taken a baby into custody. Will you consider fostering him?"

The moment she'd said it, Sarah felt excitement stir in her soul. It had been over a year since Jordan, her third child, had passed away. Since then she'd prayed fervently for God to send her another angel.

"Braxton was born at twenty-five weeks gestation. He currently weighs five pounds, and he's been in the neo-natal ICU for three months. I immediately thought of you because of your nursing background," Miss Johnson had said.

Sarah breathed deeply and exhaled, trying to digest all the information. She wanted to foster this baby, but she worried how her family would respond, especially Luke.

She climbed out of bed and paused to look at Josh. He worked extra hours to pay for Jordan's remaining medical bills, and when he returned home, he collapsed on the couch from exhaustion. A smile lit her face when she thought about the way he always placed the care of

1

his family in God's hands.

After Jordan died, Josh had thanked God for lending their family an angel, but Sarah knew he was still grieving. Every time they talked about the night of Jordan's death, tears pooled in his eyes. She had feared adding salt to Josh's open wound, so most days she withdrew from his comfort. Not physically, but mentally. She crawled somewhere deep inside herself and wept for her precious son, crying about the fifth birthday he would never have. For friends, high school graduation, and the wife he would never enjoy.

Sarah had been caught up in her own grief until she finally reached out for help. Her therapist, and friend, Toni, had taught her through many sessions that she could go on living without feeling guilty. She came to realize that grief is a process. She was beginning to heal, but she wondered if her family would be able to move forward without constantly hearing Jordan's footsteps behind them.

She slipped on her fuzzy house shoes and peeked out the bedroom window. A glint of light slipped through the midwestern sky. She tiptoed out of the room and gently closed the door behind her.

Downstairs she poured herself a cup of coffee and went into the living room. The fire in the wood-burning stove barely flickered. She turned the blowers to high, tucked herself into the plush sofa, and nursing her coffee, watched the flames dance in the stove while the heat from the blowers lulled her in a quiet relaxation.

The computer's screen saver caught her eye. Family pictures shifted across the monitor. Luke and Zack held stringers of fish, smiling. Her boys had their father's features—a rounded face, chocolate-chip colored eyes, and a warm complexion. The screen changed to vacation pictures. She laughed aloud at the first image: Luke had snapped a shot of Josh running from a horseshoe crab. The pictures continued their slide show. Games of Frisbee and beach volleyball, collecting seashells, swimming, and deep-sea fishing combined with outings to amusement parks. That was how they spent their holidays—leaving behind the painful memories of Jordan's death in Ohio to head south to the blazing Florida sun and bake like lobsters on the beach.

She lifted the Bible off the end table and leafed through the pages, skimming chapters and verses, searching for guidance. She paused at Matthew 19:14. "But Jesus said, suffer little children and forbid them not to come unto me, for of such is the kingdom of heaven." Closing her eyes she whispered, "Thank you, God, for answering my prayer to foster a child. If my family chooses to foster this baby boy, give us the strength we will need. I know we can give him the unconditional love that can only come from you, and teach him your ways, Lord. Please, protect my boys and my marriage." She wiped her eyes and whispered, "Amen."

"Mama? Are you asleep?" Luke had snuck into the living room and stood over her.

"No. I'm not asleep. I didn't hear you come down the steps." She picked up her coffee cup and grimaced when she took the first cold gulp.

Luke, her firstborn, now seventeen, stood five feet eleven and solidly built with broad shoulders. He had more energy than the energizer bunny, but at times his energy led to defiance. On the surface, he carried himself with a macho personality. Under that self-induced layer, Sarah saw something different—the baby she gave birth to and nourished, the years of watching him grow, maintaining straight A's, being in the all-star tournaments in baseball, and enjoying life. He had the world by the coattail and could achieve any dream in life he chased after, but now he lived life in the fast lane: cursing, fighting, drinking, and getting suspended from school.

She had watched him play and cuddle with Jordan through all hours of the night. He'd make his monkey sounds until Jordan squealed with excitement. They were like peas and carrots, but when Jordan left—Luke's world crumbled.

"Find what you were looking for?" He smirked.

She knew what he meant. In the past few months, he had refused to go to church, and she felt remorse for allowing him to have his way. She returned the Bible to the table. "Yes, I did."

"Well, did God tell you time heals all wounds?"

The comment stung, but she kept silent. Recently, he told her to butt out of his life; he'd work through his own problems.

"Would you mind bringing in another bag of wood?"

He rolled his eyes, as expected, then disappeared into the carport. She smiled because it wasn't often that Luke did something asked of him without having a smart remark.

His cheeks were rosy when he returned. "Wood!" he declared, with a bob of his head.

She grinned at his half curtsey. "Watch the carpet, your wood is shedding."

"Oops."

She waited for him to empty the bag of pellets into the hopper.

When he turned back to face her, she patted the sofa. "Sit down. We need to talk."

He didn't give her a chance to say anything; instead, he marched straight to the hallway closet.

"Do you have any plans tonight?" she asked, trailing him.

He snatched his backpack out of the closet. "Nope."

"Good. I'm taking you, your dad, and Zack out to supper."

"Why? So we can talk about my future?" he asked sarcastically.

Her stomach tightened. "Because I need to discuss something very important."

"I told you I'm through talking about Jordan's death." His gaze shifted toward the picture in a black wooden frame that hung on the staircase. Jordan wore his maroon-hibiscus swimming trunks, and Luke whirled him around the pool in his inflatable boat. A tear escaped his left eye, and she wanted to pull him into a hug, but she had learned from experience that you couldn't do that with a seventeen-year-old man-child, at least not Luke.

He latched onto the doorknob. "Are we finished?"

"Honey, if you'd allow God to help you with your pain, he would."

"Here we go again." Luke tugged at his baggy jeans. "Just stop, Mom, okay? I don't believe time heals all wounds like you say because it doesn't. At least, not for me."

"Would you at least consider going to supper with us?"

He dropped his backpack on the floor. "You know what I wish?"

"What?"

He lowered his head.

"I know, baby," she whispered, and this time she pulled him into a hug. "I'm sorry. I promise we'll talk about it tonight."

"Yeah, yeah." He pulled away. "I gotta run." He snatched his backpack off the floor, opened the door, and slammed it shut behind him without even saying good-bye or giving her a kiss. Did she expect one? Why would she? Since they had lost Jordan, Luke was afraid to open his heart to anyone for fear of being hurt again.

She leaned against the door and wiped at her tear-filled eyes with the neck of her nightgown. In the distance, a bedroom door closed.

Josh barreled down the stairs. "How's my lovely wife?"

"Fine. I'm going to get Zack up, or he'll be late for school."

She climbed the steps and went into Zack's recently made-over bedroom. She'd painted the walls gray, leaving a white strip in the

4

middle, where she'd stenciled OHIO STATE in scarlet. She'd carefully hand-sewn his white and black jersey curtains with a red button-down valance. Brutus, the Ohio State mascot, sat on the five by seven rug, and jerseys cluttered the walls like a sporting goods store. Zack's easel in the corner displayed his favorite player, Troy Smith, whom he had carefully hand painted. She tapped his shoulder. "Zack! Get up for school."

He tossed his pillow on the floor. "I don't want to go."

"I said *up*."

He rubbed his eyes. "Do I have to?"

"You're only fifteen. Don't rush your high school years. They're too precious," she said, then left his room.

Downstairs she poured cereal into a bowl and covered it with milk. She chose an apple from the fridge and located the sandwich she'd prepared the night before, PB and J.

Josh sipped his coffee at the dining room table. "What's on your agenda today?"

"We need to talk." She set the items on the counter.

"Mornin', Dad." Zack flopped into a chair.

"Hey, kid. How'd you sleep?"

"I'm still tired."

Sarah set Zack's bowl of cereal on the table. "Don't forget your inhaler."

"What's going on?" Josh asked.

"Let me finish packing Zack's lunch, and we'll talk while you get ready for work." She grabbed the Oreo cookies from under the kitchen sink. This was her hiding spot, so he wouldn't gobble them up in one sitting. She loaded five cookies on top of the sandwich and closed the brown paper bag. "There, champ. That should be a nice balanced meal."

Josh grinned. "Maybe without the cookies."

After she wiped down the countertops, she grazed her knuckles over Zack's scalp. "Have a good day, kiddo."

"Thanks for making me go," he teased.

Sarah looked at Josh. "You ready?"

He pushed back his chair. "Yep."

"Remember to get up slow," she added.

"Yeah, yeah..." Doctor Stevens diagnosed him with postural hypotension a month ago, and gave him direct orders to move slowly from a sitting or lying position to standing.

Upstairs, she waited for Josh to shower and dry off. When he finished, he ran a comb through his thinning hair. "So what's going on?"

She drew in a deep breath and exhaled, handing him his shirt and tie. "Miss Johnson called from Children Services. They want us to foster a baby."

He put on his white work shirt and buttoned it. "I thought we agreed to wait."

"It's been over a year since we got our license, and I know losing Jordan has been hard, but I'm beginning to heal." She handed him his black tie and his golden bars—his latest rank in the department of corrections, from lieutenant to captain, to place onto his shirt.

"*Err,*" he growled, glancing at his watch. "We'll talk about this later. I'm the only supervisor running shift today."

She settled onto the edge of the bed, placing her folded hands into her lap. "I told Luke we'd go to supper tonight and discuss it."

His face reddened. "You told him about the baby?"

"I told him I have something on my mind I need to talk about."

"Well, honey, I'm sorry I don't have more time, but I gotta run." He stretched the neck of her gown and kissed her collarbone. "Later."

"Bye," she whispered.

After she heard the front door shut, and Josh pull out of the drive, she wrapped her arms around her knees. *Please let them understand. We can't take more heartache. This baby just might be the miracle we need.*

CHAPTER TWO

Luke walked toward his friends at Community Park—the before-school gathering place—with his right hand tucked into his jeans pocket. He couldn't quit thinking about what his mama had said, and hoped she didn't expect him to talk about Jordan.

He approached his best friend, Mike, who crushed a cigarette beneath his heel.

"Hey, dude." Mike handed him a plastic bottle.

Luke grabbed hold of it, turned it up, and guzzled the Crown Royal as if it were water. The alcohol trickled down his chin and dripped onto his T-shirt.

Mike pulled out his lighter and lit another cigarette. He drew in a deep breath and blew a cloud of smoke into Luke's face.

Luke swatted at the air. "Watch it, dude. And I told you to throw those cancer sticks in the trash."

Mike stepped back. "What's up your craw? Yo mama?"

Luke wanted to tell him what was eating him; instead, he took another long, satisfying drink, then tossed the bottle into the aluminum trashcan. "Let's split."

When they reached the gray metal doors of the school entrance, Luke curled his fingers into his right palm and tapped Mike's left shoulder. "Later, dude."

In class, Luke felt a hint of remorse. He'd promised his mama a long time ago he wouldn't drink or do drugs, but his life had changed. The memories of his brother came flooding back and this time the alcohol offered no relief—he hadn't drank enough to pass out and forget.

"Luke Kiser, would you care to join the class for discussion?" asked his teacher.

"Huh?" He rolled his head in a loop.

The students snickered. Tim Mouser, the baseball team's relief pitcher, leaned back and whispered, "Coach said if you don't show up for conditioning tonight, he's cutting you from the team, loser."

If Luke was sure of anything in his messed-up life, he knew he wasn't a loser. Mouse was upset because Luke had made the all-star tournament round for baseball the past few years. He was among the top three pitchers Coach chose to help bring the team to victory. Mouse made no bones about letting him know his jealous rage. After every game, Mouse chatted with his clique in the shower stalls. At times he'd toss a bar of soap at Luke's head. The other jocks in his clique would laugh, but Luke was tired of being a doormat for anyone to stomp on.

Mouse antagonized him further, swinging his right elbow to knock Luke's book on the floor, causing papers to scatter. He turned around in his chair and snickered.

Luke felt his face flush when the other students started laughing. He retrieved his papers and book off the floor, feeling the sudden rush of adrenaline. "Jerk!"

Mouse jumped out of his seat, knocking his own book and papers onto the floor, and moved toward him.

"Get him, Luke! Beat the crap out of him!" shouted the students.

Luke got into a weaver stance, blocking the fist coming at him, and then came back at Mouse with a fist of his own, catching him squarely in the nose. Mouse staggered for a moment, swiping his hand across his face, and then fell backward, hitting his head on the tip of the desk before landing on his left side. Blood oozed out of his nostrils.

"Go to the principal's office and get some help!" Mrs. Jackson hollered to a student sitting near the door.

Jonathan, Mouse's best friend, helped him to his feet. Blood dripped onto his forearm as he wiped his nose with his hand. When he lunged forward to attempt another strike at Luke, Jonathan grabbed hold of his shirttail and held him back.

"This isn't over by a long shot, loser," Mouse said, pointing his finger.

The security officer entered the classroom and stopped in front of the two boys. "Get to the office *now*! One more episode on the way there, I'll call the police."

Luke tugged at his baggy jeans then threw his books into his backpack and walked toward the door, his heart ricocheting against his chest.

"Class is dismissed, temporarily. I need you to gather your belongings and go directly to the auditorium," Mrs. Jackson said.

He eased past the officer and ambled down the hallway until he came to the office door. The principal was waiting, his lips pressed tight, arms folded. "Luke and Tim, go into my office."

Before Mouse walked into the room, the school secretary handed him a wad of wet paper towels. He dabbed at the blood on his arm and took a seat in the corner.

"I want a detailed report on my desk by this afternoon," Principal Thompson told Mrs. Jackson. He shut the door and sat down. "So what happened, Luke?"

Does it matter? Does anyone care what I've been through? "Mouse called me a loser."

"You are," Mouse interrupted.

"Tim, keep quiet. And that gives you the right to bloody his nose, Luke?"

"I'm tired of being picked on." His gaze met the floor.

"Look at me when I speak to you," Mr. Thompson said. "You're on a five-day suspension starting now. And let me remind you that school policy says when a student strikes another, there'll be consequences. I don't know why you two are at odds, but you better get this resolved immediately. You have anything to say, Tim?"

Mouse shook his head. "No sir."

"And you're on a two-day suspension."

"Uh?" Luke's heart thumped. "He was coming after me."

"I'll have to wait on Mrs. Jackson's report to see if I need to implement any more action."

"So, it's okay if students badger other ones?"

"No, it's not okay. I'm sure that Tim had words with you. When there's a fight, as I've seen in the past, it takes two to tangle."

Someone knocked on the door.

"Come in," the principal said.

Mrs. Frenchie poked her head in the room. "If you're finished with Luke, I need to speak with him."

"I'm done."

Luke snatched up his belongings and trailed the counselor to her office. Easing himself into a plastic chair, he watched her shuffle papers on her desk. He didn't mind spending time with her even when she played the role of a shrink because she was attractive. Her dark auburn colored hair splayed on her shoulders, and her green eyes reminded him of the Emerald City on the *Wizard of Oz*.

Finally she sat down. "Are you okay? Any bruises or cuts?"

"Nope."

"That's good. Feel like talking about it?"

Inching his way down into his seat, he studied the hem of his frayed jeans. He knew where this conversation was headed. First they'd discuss the fight, then she'd ask if he'd gone back to counseling with his mom, and finally—did he feel like talking about Jordan's death? And the answer to the last two questions was always the same—No. So he stated the truth. "I really don't want to talk about it."

Mrs. Frenchie leaned back in her chair. "You realize this is your fifth suspension. Your English and trigonometry grades are tottering on the brink of *Ds*." She sighed. "If you keep getting suspended, you may not have the grades to graduate."

Like I need to be reminded. He clenched his teeth and moved to the edge of his chair. "What the heck am I supposed to do then? Tell me!"

"I would like for you to come to me when you feel like you're being threatened."

"So they can say I'm a rat?"

The counselor's eyes showed concern. "No. I want you to come to me so I can help you, especially before things get out of hand."

His jaw flinched. "So, now I'm the one with the issue."

"I'm trying to help you understand there are other options besides fighting. I want you to graduate." She cleared her throat. "You do want to graduate, right?"

Luke didn't hesitate. "Yeah. I wanta get out of this hole."

"Have you given anymore thought to what we discussed last month? About your brother?"

He flopped back in the chair. "I try not to think about Jordan, but no matter how hard I try, he keeps poppin' in my head. And I ain't going back to therapy."

"Do you feel like talking about it?"

He shifted uneasily, knowing full well what she was poking around for, and death was not a word he felt like discussing. Or better yet, a needless one. "No."

10

"Are you still angry with Zack?"

Luke *was* angry with Zack. Not because he didn't talk about Jordan anymore, but rather that he was able to move on. "Me and my family just have different ways of coping. They chose God. I chose booze. Guess they're comfortable with make-believe." His blood boiled. "Do you think a God who cares about people would actually let a doctor kill a kid?"

The counselor didn't respond.

Exactly. She's speechless. "Everyone thinks that God has an answer for everything."

She stared at him as if she was trying to see the depth of his soul. "Jordan's death no doubt has..." She paused to wipe absent crumbs from her desk. Luke could swear he spotted one teardrop lingering in the corner of her left eye, threatening to fall. But she blinked it back. "What do you want to do after graduation? I mean, I know that at one time you were thinking about being a mortician because your uncle worked in the field. Is that still your goal?"

"I've seen enough death to make me wanta puke, so now I'm undecided."

She titled her head, looked at him sympathetically. "I understand."

"It doesn't matter. No one gives a—" Luke shot out a four letter word.

"It matters to me. And I want to help, but you have to let me in."

He glanced down and drummed his fingers on his pant leg, refusing to talk anymore.

"Is that possible? Will you let me help you?"

Luke swallowed the emotions beginning to rise in his throat. "Whatever."

Mrs. Frenchie pushed away from her desk and walked over to where he sat, and placed her hand on his shoulder. "We'll take it slow. We'll work on graduation goals and take steps to improve your grades. And if you feel comfortable talking about Jordan, I'll help you with that too. Sound fair?"

He nodded.

"And when you return, I want you to come to me when you feel threatened by other students."

"Fine."

She leaned over and pulled a satchel from under her desk, fished around in it for a sec, then handed him a book.

Luke glanced down at the hardback cover long enough to see the title, then he glared at the counselor. "You want me to read a book called—" he glanced back down and said, *"Stand Still "?*

She smiled. "Do me a favor. Read one chapter at a time so you can absorb what the writer is saying."

"You're a nice lady," *and a total knockout,* "but I don't know if you can help me. I feel like I can trust you, but..."

"Let's just spend some time talking and see where it takes us. You never know. Sometimes, God puts people into our lives to help us."

Luke nodded, though still not buying the God thing.

"If there's nothing else you feel like discussing, you can wait in my office until your mother arrives."

Until your mother arrives took shape in his mind until he felt the weight of guilt. He didn't want to let her down. Getting suspended again would be one more burden for her to bear. "Did you call her?"

"Not yet, but I will." When the counselor disappeared, he opened the book she'd given him, and turned to page one.

In October 1984, a what-if presented itself with a terrifying probability. My husband, Frank, was diagnosed with an inoperable tumor. I was told he had only a few months to live.

Luke turned the book over, glanced at the back cover, and read—

In Stand Still, *the author will take you on a journey about her husband's life and death. She will teach you what the Lord taught her to do—"Be still, and know that I am God: I will be exalted among the heathen, I will be exalted in the earth." Learn how two words changed her life forever. It can change yours, too.*

He closed the book and put it into his backpack. Leaning back, he drew in a deep breath and clasped his hands behind his head. He was so angry; tears fell one after another, streaming down his cheeks like a hot river. What could he possibly say to his mama now? There was nothing more to do except wait for her arrival.

❧

Mrs. Frenchie watched Luke's gaze shift to the photograph on top of her desk when she'd talked to him earlier. In it, her husband's slender arm draped around her neck, and she held her baby, Abbey, close to her heart. The one that had been so utterly beautiful, like a brand new car with no dents or scratches, unexposed to pain. But all of that had changed on the drop of a dime. Her life had been stripped away, leaving her clinging to chains of grief and bitterness.

Since that day, two years after the death of her husband and child, she vowed to get out of the pit, go on with her life, and help others who might be drowning in a sea of despair. And she was glad she'd made that decision. Five years later, she accepted the job at Valley High and hadn't regretted her decision for one minute.

She counseled students with poor grades, helping them meet their graduation goals and admission to college. She gave them resources on how to submit applications, find a job, write reference letters, obtain scholarships and financial aid, but her greatest satisfaction was helping the ones who grieved. The ones who needed her to show them they were not alone—that someone in the world cared about what they were going through.

Luke was different. He had a family who cared, but he couldn't see through the pain. His heart was broken into a million little pieces as hers had once been, with a very faint heartbeat. Somehow she had to make him see that one day the sadness would subside, just as it had for her, and he'd find a drive to go on living and postmark the sadness for some other faraway place.

She leaned against the desk in a borrowed room, since Luke occupied hers, and turned her head toward the window. A hint of sunshine threatened to break through the clouds. *Everything is going to be alright,* she whispered.

And it is.

It always is.

CHAPTER THREE

Sarah wrapped a towel around her head and sat down at the vanity. In the mirror in the harsh morning light, she stared at herself—a grown woman with honey-blonde highlights in her hair. She opened the vanity drawer and pulled out the makeup she'd bought at Walgreens. Her therapist had told her to try things to lift her mood. Makeup definitely made her feel pretty; though Josh always said he preferred the natural look.

She opened the boxes, then finished her "makeover" with bronzing powder. "There." Her voice was a whisper. The effort to camouflage the past year brought a smile to her face.

The silence of the house started to press in on her. Pulling on a pair of jeans and layered T-shirts, she briefly considered her daily errands. Her thoughts shifted to Josh and the way he had rushed out of the house this morning. She hadn't had a chance to tell him everything about the baby. She hadn't wrapped her head around how to tell him. She needed more time. Downstairs she grabbed her leather satchel, keys, and coat, and headed out the door.

The sun had risen, creating an intense glare on the snow. She rushed to the protection of the tinted windows in the SUV. The Chinese elm cast a shadow on the house. Huge gray rocking chairs now sat idle. Three months before, she'd tried to add warmth by hanging a flag with a nautical scene on the front porch railing. It didn't fit with the snow and evergreens of the winter months, so she mentally added Wal-Mart to her daily errands. She put the SUV in reverse and backed out onto the wet street.

The store was too warm. She placed her coat into the shopping cart and moved to the store's garden section, hoping to find a small flag for Jordan's grave. She sorted through them when a flag scene of a sapphire blue ocean meeting with a soft chestnut beach, guarded by a squat of red and white lighthouses caught her eye. "Oh, Jordan." His name was past her lips before she realized she'd spoken. Next she found a scene to fit the season for her front porch.

Outside the cold air bit her cheeks as she headed toward her vehicle. She placed the bag in the backseat, turned the heat to high, then put the gearshift into drive and headed north, deciding to enjoy the drive. During the summer, the roads were lit with color and activity. The blue and gold wildflowers blended with rows of wheat in the fields. Children chased dogs through yards, big brothers taught little sisters how to ride two-wheelers, and families gathered for summer-time cookouts or simply sat on front porches, rocking. Winter changed the scene to a quiet peace. Smoke floated out of chimneys, multicolored lights stretched across acres of fence, and horses blew steam from their muzzles.

She came to the entrance of the cemetery, eased the SUV into the drive, and crossed over the bridge. From the opposite window, she could see the blueness of the pond. The winter hadn't been cold enough to freeze it, but snow had collected on the banks, and the water was motionless. She parked at section two and cut the ignition.

At Jordan's tombstone, she brushed the snow away and rearranged the toys—a fire truck, Teletubbies on blocks, and a plastic football. She took the flag out of the bag and placed it on the pole, then rubbed her numb hands together. "Jordan. How do I tell your daddy and brothers about the baby?" She paused, and drove the fire truck across his tombstone. She could hear his little voice saying vroom-vroom. She dabbed at her moist eyes, and said, "For the longest time, I wondered if God could suture my heart back together, but he did. After you died, it's like we ended up on this island where we don't belong, and Luke is drowning in a sea of despair. I just don't know . . . what to do to help him. Maybe this baby is what our family needs, you know, someone to care for like we cared for you." She swallowed hard, hoping to dissolve the lump forming in her throat, then continued. "I just hope people won't think I'm trying to replace you, because I'm not." She knelt to look at the picture of him on the front of the stone. "If I could have taken your place, I would have."

And just like every week, she placed a kiss on her fingertips and transplanted it to his chubby cheeks.

On the way home, her cell phone rang. She picked it up from the passenger seat. "Hello."

"Mrs. Kiser, this is Mrs. Frenchie. I need you to come to the school to pick up Luke."

"Is he okay?"

"He's been suspended."

❧

Sarah lifted the long-stem rose that served as a pen from the terra-cotta pot, signed in, and took a seat. Across the room Mrs. Frenchie filed papers in a cabinet painted yellow.

"Mrs. Kiser, I'll be with you in a minute." Mrs. Frenchie asked another employee if she could use the conference room next to the principal's office, then turned to Sarah. "Follow me."

Behind the closed door, Mrs. Frenchie sat down. "Please be seated. I have one more thing to finish."

Sarah sat on a brown cushioned chair, and crossed her legs. Her knees began to shake, so she uncrossed them.

Finally the counselor looked up. "I'm very worried about Luke, and I know you are, too."

Sarah forced a smile.

"His grades are suffering. I told him we'd work on post-grad goals, and I encouraged him to come to me when he feels threatened by other students."

Sarah sighed. "Thank you. Quite frankly, I don't know what else I can do."

"I also told him that if he felt like talking about Jordan's death, I'd be glad to help."

Sarah plucked a tissue out of the holder on the desk and blew her nose. "That'd be great. Maybe you could get through to him. I don't know what to do anymore, besides let him know I'm there."

"Sometimes that's all we can do. Let's just take one day at a time. When he returns from his suspension, I'll do my best to help."

Sarah sighed again. "Did he get into another fight with Mouse?"

"Yes. It seems they can't get along."

"That's true." Sarah stood and tossed the tissues in the wastepaper basket. "Can I see him now?"

"Yes, you may."

∾∾

Luke waited patiently for his mother's arrival. He had successfully drawn a baseball diamond, a pitcher's mound, and a dugout on his brown-paper book cover. The door swung open. His mother's face was the second one he saw. He stared at her, seeing the sadness in her eyes, the disappointment that pursed her lips, and he felt heartbreaking guilt. He wanted to get out of his seat, throw himself into her arms, and be swept up like a baby, but he couldn't move.

"Luke, I'll be in touch with you after you return from your suspension. Take care," the counselor said.

He nodded and walked to the door where his mom stood.

"Wait!" Mrs. Frenchie called.

Luke turned.

"Coach Spears said you've missed the last two conditioning practices. I hope when you return to school, you'll take the time to do the things you once enjoyed."

Luke and Sarah walked toward the SUV in silence. The late afternoon sunlight splashed their faces. Luke squinted at the brightness, cursing under his breath. They climbed into the SUV and headed home. He wished his mom would say something, but she kept silent; her knuckles were white from gripping the steering wheel. His thoughts shifted to what his counselor had said about him missing baseball conditioning. He loved the game, and claimed there was nothing more he wanted than a shot at being a professional ballplayer. But since Jordan died, even keeping his focus on that was something he couldn't do because he couldn't move past the pain.

His mother stopped at a red light, turned to him and opened her mouth to say something, but closed it again, like a fish. He didn't bother asking her what she was going to say; instead, he turned his head to stare out the smudged window, worrying how his dad would respond.

CHAPTER FOUR

Sarah went directly into the kitchen adjoining the dining room and hit BREW on the coffee pot. She rinsed out the coffee mugs, not bothering to use detergent and towel-dried them.

"Hey." Josh entered the kitchen and tossed his weighty key ring on the kitchen counter. "How was your day?"

"Fine." She added sugar and creamer to each cup. "And yours?"

"Long. Put two inmates in the hole, then got a big drug bust."

She sighed. "What now?"

"Marijuana. The State Highway Patrol said that if I keep it up, they'll give me a job."

She leaned against the countertop. "Luke's suspended again."

Josh squared his shoulders, narrowed his eyes. "For what?"

She flicked her head toward the dining room. "Ask him."

"Mouse called me a loser and knocked my stuff on the floor and was gonna hit me." Luke grinned. "But I used that block you taught me and punched his nose."

Josh folded his hands. "I showed you a self-defense technique to protect yourself when you're being attacked. Being called names and having your stuff knocked to the floor doesn't count. We only use it on out-of-control inmates."

Luke blew out a burst of air. "But Mouse was out of control."

"That's it, Luke. We're done. I'm not going to tolerate your actions anymore. You're grounded. No going to Mike's, no video games, no computer, no phone calls. Clear?"

"But, Dad."

"I hate to interrupt." Sarah set Josh's BEST DAD coffee mug on the table. "But—evidently Luke's grades are down. He's been skipping out on conditioning, too."

"I skipped because I had extra credit assignments, so even if get all *F's* for my suspension, I should manage to get a *C* or *D* in my classes."

"This isn't who you are! You have the potential to go to college and play baseball." Luke didn't respond so Josh continued. "As a matter of fact, starting this Sunday, you're going back to church."

Luke's hand smacked the table, jiggling the salt and pepper shakers. "I'm almost eighteen! You can't make me!"

Josh lowered his head, and Sarah knew exactly how he felt. How many prayers had they sent up to the Father, begging him to help Luke find stable ground? She lost track. Josh picked up his head and said, "As long as you're under my roof, you'll do as you're told."

"That's bull." Luke turned and stared out the patio glass door. "Are we done?"

"You haven't had any alcohol since the last incident, have you?"

"No, Dad."

"Good. Head on up to your room and study. I need to talk to your mom."

"I can't do anything right." Luke stood and shoved the chair back to the table, then bolted up to his room.

Sarah and Josh exchanged worried expressions. For the next few minutes, they sipped their coffee in silence. Finally, Josh said, "Tell me about the baby."

Sarah told him everything Miss Johnson had said. "Josh, he needs a home until his mom is able to take care of him. And . . . her first baby died."

Josh sat mutely, taking it all in.

"And I'm a trained nurse, and I have experience, so I should be able to help the baby and his mom." When Josh's eyes filled with tears, she stopped talking.

Josh cleared his throat, then pulled a napkin out of the holder and blew his nose. Finally, he said, "Honey, we, our family, lost Jordan. I mean, it hurt to lose him. What if this baby dies?"

"I don't know. I'm thinking God is sending him to us for a reason. So I don't think he'll die."

He took her hands into his. "Baby, for the past year, I've watched you grieve. And even though it hit you harder, I went through it, too, but you're coming to terms with what happened. I don't want to jeopardize that. I can't help it, I worry about my family."

She let go of his hands and crossed her arms over her chest. "I just want to help someone else. And . . ." She looked away.

"But you'll fall in love with this baby; never want to give him back." He sighed. "What's gonna happen when they send him home to his mom? Have you considered that?" When she didn't respond, he said, "I'm afraid your world will crumble again. That's all."

She ran her fingers through the top of her hair. "I know there'll be stress-filled days, and if he goes home with his mom, I'll pray for God to send me another angel." She hopped out of her seat and walked toward the living room.

"Don't walk away, Sarah."

"I'm going to get my Bible so I can show you a verse I found for guidance."

He sighed wearily. "You can't make a decision because you happened to find a verse."

She turned to face him. "True. But I can look to God for guidance. And if we take in this little baby, we can take him to church, and . . ."

"I'm not saying no."

"You're saying it'll be too hard."

He rested his hand on the back of the chair. "I resent that comment. If I wasn't worried about you, this wouldn't be an issue."

She stared at him for a long moment, then said. "What do you always tell me and the boys?"

He chuckled. "We're alive and we'll survive."

"My point exactly. Do you remember how we prayed for someone to help us when Jordan was alive? To guide us on what questions to ask?"

He nodded.

"I don't believe in coincidence, Josh. We received that call for a reason."

His left eyebrow raised. "And you think Luke will be receptive to this idea?"

She smiled. "Good question. I think Zack will open his arms wide for this baby. Luke might be a tough nail to hammer, but if he agrees, I think it'll do him good." She leaned against the doorframe. "I would never do anything to upset the kids. When we applied for our license, we thought it would be an exciting adventure for them."

Josh's cheeks puffed up like a blowfish as he considered this.

Finally, he blew out a burst of air and said, "I guess we'll find out how they feel later, but I do have a question."

"What?"

"Have you thought anymore about going back to work in the nursing homes, I mean, as a nurse?"

She shook her head. "I enjoy taking care of the elderly, but kids are my passion, and I can use my nursing skills with this baby. I feel this might be a new beginning."

He took two steps toward her and caught the tears on the tip of her nose with his finger. "You mean for Luke?"

She stammered into his chest. "For us. For Luke. We had Jordan four years, and now he's gone. It's our turn to give. I have faith this baby will bring our family joy."

He wrapped his arms around her chest and rested his chin on top of her head. "If this is something you feel strongly about, I'm in. But you have to promise that you'll keep going to therapy, so you won't get depressed."

"I will," she replied softly.

❧

Sarah stood under the porch awning and looked at her picket fence, debating whether she wanted to add cinnamon- or buttercup-colored roses to her collection this year, but her thoughts kept shifting to Luke. She wondered how he would respond to her quest to foster baby Braxton. He seemed to be hanging onto his world by a fraying hem, and that thought caused her to shiver.

Zack brushed past her and burst through the front door.

She trailed him. "Zack! Get your shoes off—you're dripping!"

He tossed them under the banister, shrugged out of his coat, and promptly dropped it on top of his soggy shoes. Then his bag hit the floor with a solid thud, propelling dust particles into the air.

She tousled his hair. "How was school?"

"Boring."

She didn't expect an actual answer. "Of course it was. Glad I drug you out of bed so you could go."

He went to the snack cupboard and opened it. "How was your day?"

"Exciting. We're going out for dinner."

He filled his arms with boxes of raisins and graham crackers. "Is Luke going?"

She tucked her head into her shoulder and hid a smile. The boys used to be best friends; they had recently switched roles to favored enemies. "Zack!" She flipped the dishtowel at him. "Yes, he's coming."

Arms full, he took off down the wooden hallway. "I'll be in my room."

"Zack! You forgot your bag!" He was already out of the "mom-zone" and couldn't hear, or at least he would claim he hadn't. She considered picking up his coat, but changed her mind.

Upstairs, while she reapplied her makeup, she heard Zack preaching from down the hall. This was his ritual almost every afternoon. Sometimes she perched herself outside his bedroom door and listened, but today his voice carried.

"Charity suffereth long, and is kind; charity envieth not; charity vaunteth not itself, is not puffed up. Doth not behave itself unseemly, seeketh not her own, is not easily provoked thinketh no evil. Rejoiceth not in inquity, but rejoiceth in the truth. Beareth all things, believeth all things, hopeth all things, endureth all things."

Sarah lifted her Bible from the desk and leafed through the pages, then settled on a verse. *"And now abideth faith, hope, charity, these three, but the greatest of all is charity."* She closed her Bible and sat in silence. *Charity,* she thought, is what her family would extend to the baby. "Lord, thank you for the opportunity to serve, and may your name be glorified in all that I do."

Thirty-five minutes later, she woke up Josh.

"Is Zack done with his homework?" he asked groggily.

"Yeah." She located the remote on top of the couch and silenced the weather channel. "He's done preaching."

They exchanged smiles.

"I'm sorry I fell asleep. I hardly ever nap."

"Nonsense." She folded the throw and placed it on the end of the couch.

"I'll get the boys." His face flushed as he stood.

"Remember to take it slow. Your blood pressure isn't stable enough to deal with quick changes in position."

"Yes, Dr. Kiser." He slowly walked toward the stairs.

"Zack! Luke!" he yelled "Zack! Luke!" He chuckled this time, but still no answer. "Hey, preacher boy? Could you bring your brother down with you?"

Zack appeared at the top of the steps. "Yeah, Dad. You call?"

"Only three times."

"Sorry I was busy . . . with homework." His face blushed at the lie.

"You were preaching, so you don't need to lie." Josh's smile tempered the severity of his tone.

"Sorry." Zack hung his head like a scolded puppy.

"It's all right. Grab your shoes, and don't forget your brother."

"I heard," Luke grumbled.

The boys thundered downstairs like a herd of cattle.

"Mom? Why didn't you hang up my coat?" Zack asked.

She tousled his hair on the way out the door. "Guess that'll teach you to hang it up, instead of dropping it on your wet shoes, huh, preacher?"

❧⋯❧

The restaurant was crowded, but they found a table in the back. At the buffet, Zack loaded his plate with stuffed mushrooms and garlic chicken. Josh and Luke opted for crab legs to start, and Sarah filled her plate with quiche, shrimp, and cantaloupe. Zack rushed to his seat and lowered his head to pray.

"Uh—um? Care to join us, Luke?" Josh asked.

Luke closed his eyes. Sarah and Josh hid their smiles.

". . . in Jesus' name. Amen."

Josh speared a mushroom from Zack's plate. "Thanks, kid."

"What's up? Why did you want to talk to us, Mama?" Luke talked around a mouth full of crab. Sarah couldn't believe he spoke civilly, and now wondered if she should even mention the baby for fear this would add more stress. And she'd been stressing all day on what to say and now that the moment had arrived, she wasn't so sure.

Josh's gaze met hers. "Go ahead."

She stirred the ice cubes in her glass. "Well . . . I'm not sure I want to talk about it."

"Your mom received a phone call this morning," Josh said. The boys leaned toward him. "We need your input, but first we need you to listen." He nodded, inviting Sarah to tell the story.

She took a deep breath and met Luke's eyes. *Just say it,* she thought. *Tell him how much this baby is like Jordan and how much it would mean to have him be a part of our family.*

"Children Services has a baby they want us to foster."

Luke's face clouded over. "What's wrong with it?"

23

"His name is Braxton. He's a lot like Jordan actually."

"Like?" Luke's tone was cold as he glared at his mom.

"Braxton was born a twenty-five week preemie and diagnosed with grade-three bleeds in his brain. He only weighed one-pound, thirteen-ounces at birth, just like Jordan."

"*Sheesh!* So he's gonna die, too." Luke's words were not a question.

"I hope not. I mean, I don't think he will."

"Is he cute?" Zack's face lit up.

"I don't know, sweetie. I haven't seen him."

"I say yes!"

Luke tossed his napkin on the table. "Shut up, Zack! You don't know what you're saying."

"Luke!" Josh spoke a single word, silencing the anger.

"Well Mom isn't thinking. She'll have to see the doctors who let Jordan die. And what if this baby gets sick?" He glowered at Sarah. "You gonna stay at the hospital and miss my games for a kid that isn't even yours?"

"*No,*" Sarah blurted. "If you don't want me to do this, I won't. I would never do anything to jeopardize your relationship with your father or me. Although, I wouldn't miss your games anyway. He has a mom who can help me."

Luke snapped the shell of his lobster-tail and dipped it in garlic butter. "Then why can't she take care of her own kid?"

"She's young and needs help. I'll nurse him until his mom can."

"Will you be training his mom?" Zack asked.

"Yes. I can teach her how to feed him. And things like proper use of oxygen, the apnea-heart monitor, range of motion exercises so his extremities don't get stiff. Stuff like that."

"I don't know," Luke said.

"Sweetie, I know you're angry about Jordan. However, that is not an excuse to run from another child. I mean, wouldn't it be nice to help someone who needs you?"

"You don't even know what you're asking of us."

"Come on, Luke!" Zack interrupted. "It's not Mom's fault Jordan died."

"I didn't say it was. But we don't need to bring a sick baby that isn't family into our house. Even if he lives, he'll go home. One way or another—we'll lose him, too."

Zack swiveled his head between Luke and Sarah, waiting for the next verbal spar. When no one spoke, tears welled up in his eyes. "I miss Jordan. It would be fun to have a baby brother again."

"Don't you get it, Zack? He isn't gonna to be our brother—he's gonna be one of Mama's projects."

"Luke." Josh spoke his name as a warning.

Luke wiped his hands with a lemon-scented towelette. "Sorry, Dad, but our family has been through enough."

Josh twirled cold pasta on is fork. "There's no doubt that Jordan's death changed us, but just listen to what your mom has to say."

Sarah wiped her eyes with a napkin. "I feel like God is giving me a chance to help someone else. Didn't Jordan teach us that?"

"You mean, you need them," Luke said.

"Maybe I do. Is it wrong to help a family and gain satisfaction from the experience?"

"Even if you help them, you can't fix what happened to Jordan. He isn't ever coming back. And you're trying to replace him."

Not exactly, she thought, *but she did owe them an explanation. The truth. For her family.* She looked away for a moment, then looked back.

"I know that helping Braxton won't bring Jordan back." She drew in a deep breath and exhaled. "I would rather choose faith over fear, meaning, I believe this baby will . . ."

"That sounds like a bunch of bull," Luke said.

For the second time, in less than five minutes, she was stunned. She was positive Luke would eventually agree, knowing how much he loved Jordan. *Tell him the truth.*

No one spoke. Zack pushed congealed mushrooms around on his plate, causing the fork to squeal.

"And then?"

"Then what, Luke?" Sarah asked.

"What if?"

"Say it, honey."

"He dies?"

"I don't believe he will. And I don't know how to explain it, but I want to feel needed again."

"You are," Zack piped in. "We need you, Mom."

"I know, sweetie. It's just I want to care for a fragile baby that I can nourish and . . ."

Josh leaned across the table and squeezed her hand. "What?"

"And protect him." She felt surprised by her response, but it was the truth.

Luke pushed his plate to the middle of the table. "You can't protect every sick kid."

"No, but I can protect this one. And this baby is exactly what our family needs." *There the truth was out.*

"And why would that be?" Luke asked.

"I think God is trying to mend our hearts, at least yours. I mean, Luke, you haven't been the same since Jordan died." She swallowed hard. "I mean, ever since he died, you're getting into trouble. You've lost sight of your dreams. You . . ."

"So you think God put Jordan's soul in this baby's. Kind of like reincarnation?"

Sarah smiled. "Of course not." She gazed into Luke's eyes. "Before Jordan died you had the biggest heart of anyone I ever knew."

Luke shrugged. "So now I don't?"

"I didn't say that. I'm just asking to give a little bit of yourself. I know it's asking a lot."

This baby could fit seamlessly in her life in a way that mattered most—to her family. And even though Sarah knew Luke's heart was broken beyond repair, at least for the time being, she knew this baby was exactly what they, he, needed.

"When's he coming?" Luke finally asked.

Sarah smiled at Josh. "In a day or so. He needs to get a little stronger before they discharge him, and I need to get his room ready."

"Which room?" Luke asked.

"Jordan's," she said, hoping to get his stamp of approval. Instead, he rolled his eyes. "I guess he could sleep in yours." Her attempt at humor failed.

"What do you think boys? This responsibility will be your moms and mine, but we'll need your support. Are you in?"

"I am." Zack spoke without hesitation.

"Luke?"

"I don't want to bring more baggage into our family, but if it'll help Mom, I'm in. But if it gets to be too much . . ."

"We'll make other arrangements," Sarah said.

"So we've agreed to try?" Josh asked.

Luke pushed back his chair and waved both hands, signaling that the conversation—at least his part, was over. "I'm going to get some dirt cake."

"Me, too," Zack chimed in.

"And me three," Josh added.

Sarah watched her family move to the dessert bar. She breathed deeply, then exhaled, now that the intense moment had passed. *Just you wait and see Luke Kiser. Eventually that boulder in your heart will be moved,* she thought. And once it happened, she was sure he'd feel the faintest glow of hope, and finally, peace that could come only from above.

CHAPTER FIVE

Red paint splotched across Sarah's cheek, onto her shirt collar. She'd spent the past three hours painting an apple-farm canvas for her kitchen. Glancing at the clock on her workbench, she felt immediate guilt at deferring her regular duties. "Fine," she said, cleaning her brushes, "so I work when I'm stressed."

The phone rang, causing her to jump and drop the paint-can lid. She raced to answer it. "Hello?"

"Sarah? This is Alberta Johnson. Has your family made a decision?"

She laughed nervously and picked up the lid. "Yes. We've decided to take Braxton."

"Sarah! I'm thrilled! I know this is short notice, but is there any way you and Josh could meet his mother and grandmother this afternoon?"

"What?" she gasped. "You want us to meet them today?"

"If that's okay."

"What time?"

"The grandmother is coming from work, so is five o'clock okay?"

"We might be cutting it close because Josh will be coming from work also. Where are we meeting?"

"In the conference room beside the graduate nursery on the fifth floor."

"Do I need to bring our foster license and my nursing license or driver's license?" Her nervousness escaped in a tight laugh.

"Just bring an infant car seat and your ID."

"He's coming home today?"

"Yes. Your caseworker will meet with you after I introduce you to the family. Sarah, relax. This is a done deal—we just have to work out the logistics."

Sarah clicked off the phone, then called Josh with the news. At first, when she told him the baby was coming home *today*, she thought he sounded upset. When she questioned him about it, he told her not to worry that pretty little head of hers because he was just busy handling an office matter. Before he hung up, he promised to be home in time to go to the hospital with her.

She sat down on the canyon-colored hearth in her living room and glanced around. Heirloom quilts and family pictures formed a cozy and inviting room. Even though she lived in a suburb, she had added her own taste of country living by painting the room warm rust colors.

I can't believe this is actually going to happen. Although her family had shared a tragic event that would forever color their past, this could be a new beginning. With a smile, she went upstairs to shower. An hour later, she entered Jordan's room, lifted his bank-phone from his dresser, and picked up the receiver. Her throat tightened when the notes played: "I just called to say I love you."

"Mama?" Luke stood in the doorway. "Whatcha doin?"

Her eyes scanned the room—Jordan's CD player, his Beanie Babies crouched atop the entertainment center, the colorful floor mat used for therapy, and braces set like trophies on the floor waiting to be filled—Braxton would definitely benefit. "I was thinking."

"Are you getting rid of Jordan's stuff?"

"Never." She placed the phone back on the dresser.

"I can't believe you watched the *Titanic* with him sixty-four times." Luke pointed to the painting on the wall, which Thomas, the boyfriend of Jordan's nurse, had painted. Rose and Jack stood on the ship gazing into each other's eyes.

"He never tired of it, did he?" She smiled at the memory.

"Nope."

Sarah couldn't believe he was being civil and sharing. He eased himself onto Jordan's bed and placed the stuffed golden retriever in his lap. She sat down next to him and patted his back, surprised he allowed her. "Sometimes, disasters can bring out the worst in people or they can bring out the most humble and heroic part of them. I want you to think about that."

He grinned. "I don't see myself as being a hero. I'm not afraid of a challenge, but a hero, no way."

"Why would you say that?"

"Jordan was a hero. He fought his own battles just to survive, and when he should've cried, he laughed. He was the happiest person I've ever met."

She swallowed hard, but kept silent, hoping he'd keep sharing.

"Remember when he shook his pelvis to the beat of Elvis?"

Tears stung her eyes, but she refused them. "I do. It's times like those you need to think about."

"Someday, you're gonna tell me how he died. I wanta know every detail." He rested his head on top of the retriever.

"Oh, Luke." She patted his back. "Why would you want to know? Just be happy he's with Jesus."

"Maybe you're happy, but I'm not. I want him back." He cradled the dog to his chest. "And I wanted to say good-bye."

"You should go to his grave and talk to him. Maybe you'd feel better."

"No way! Mike said when he went to visit his family, it felt like it was final or something."

"But you were there the day we buried him. Sooner or later you've got to come to terms with his death."

"Sometimes . . ."

"What?"

"Sometimes when you and Dad are asleep, I sneak downstairs and cuddle with his bears. And it's like I can see his smile, you know, like he's lying right beside me." He sniffled.

"Honey, you're as normal as the day is long. We grieve differently. Look at your dad and Zack. They miss Jordan, but they cast their cares on the Lord. By doing so it's helped them to cope immensely."

Luke chuckled. "Zack's definitely in cahoots with God."

"He loves God. That's for sure." She hopped off the bed when she spotted him coming up the drive. "At five, your dad and I are going to the hospital to bring Braxton home. We'll only be gone a couple of hours. I'll have my cell on me if anything happens, and please don't argue with your brother."

Luke sighed. "I'll make pizza for supper."

"Are you sure? I don't mind putting them in the oven."

"I'm used to it. Did you forget?"

How could she? Her boys learned to fend for themselves when

Jordan was alive. "Of course not."

In the kitchen, she nudged Luke playfully in the side when she saw Zack's backside sticking out of the pantry. "Uh . . . Um . . ."

Zack emerged, both hands stuffed with raisins. "Hey."

"How was school?" she asked.

"Boring." He popped a handful of raisins in his mouth. "Watch it!" He shouted when Luke sprinted past him and knocked him off balance, causing raisins to fall out of his mouth and tumble to the floor.

Luke didn't respond, but Sarah did. "Apologize, Luke."

"Sorry," he shouted from the living room.

"He's so mean." Zack stooped to pick up the raisins.

"Let it go," she said, bending over to help. "Tonight, we're bringing the baby home. Please, please, try to get along with your brother. And by the way, how're your grades?" She dropped a handful of raisins into his hand.

"Straight A's and B's." He straightened, and kissed her on the cheek. "I gotta go study. Big test in science tomorrow."

"Way to go, kid."

⊱⊰

Luke clicked the television remote to the off position and dashed up to his room. He opened his English book, and then tossed it on his football-shaped beanbag. At his footlocker, he lifted the lid, grabbed the bottle of Crown, and unscrewed the cap. Then turning it up, he finished it and placed the empty bottle under his mattress.

"Whew!" He grabbed the monkey from the canvas chair and stretched out on his bed, remembering every time he had made the monkey sounds that sent Jordan into fits of giggles. He wished Jordan was still here—not in a vague I-wish-you-were-still-here way, but the pit of his stomach sensed the loss, and he didn't want to feel the pain anymore. The only thing that made the pain disappear was alcohol.

The song in his head, "Somewhere over the rainbow," wouldn't stop playing. Frustrated, he went to the door and opened it with a sticky *pop*. Zack was hooting and hollering about how he loved Jesus. *Thought he had homework.*

Wondering where his mom was, he made his way downstairs. He looked through the kitchen window and spotted her adding chemicals to the Jacuzzi. He picked up her cell phone and punched in the numbers to call Mike. While he waited for Mike to answer, a tune he'd never heard before played. "Come on, pick up."

"Hey, bro. Waz up?" Mike asked.

"I'm grounded." Luke lowered his voice. "Can you bring me another bottle of Crown at six?"

"What if I get caught?"

"My parents won't be here. Just stick it under the blue tarp in the carport. I gotta run, Mom's coming." He clicked off the phone, laid it back on the counter, sneaked through the family room and up the stairs. He landed on the top step when he heard the front door open and close.

CHAPTER SIX

Sarah drew in a deep breath and exhaled while Josh looked for a parking slot. He turned off the ignition and grabbed her hand. "You nervous?"

"Some."

He leaned over the center console and planted a kiss on her lips. "I love you."

"Ditto," she said, and forced a smile.

At the hospital elevator, he gave her hand a light squeeze. "Don't worry."

She pushed the UP button. "I don't like meeting new people, that's all."

Arrows on the fifth-floor wall pointed the way to the graduate nursery—a step down from the NICU. "This way," she said, latching on to his hand and leading him down the hall. When they rounded the corner, they found Miss Johnson standing by the conference room door.

"I'm so glad you could come on short notice." Her gold tooth glinted when she smiled.

"Thanks. We are, too." Josh's voice exuded confidence and ease.

"I'm sure you're anxious to get started. Braxton's family is waiting." She opened the door to the conference room.

A young African-American woman, whom Sarah guessed to be around eighteen, sat in the corner of the couch, her posture indicating her lack of interest in meeting the family who would be taking her baby home. Her eyelids were red and swollen. A woman stood next to Miss Johnson, her posture erect and stiff. The room was warm, but their attitudes, icy.

"Hi. I'm Sarah." She offered her hand to the young woman, who quickly shifted her gaze downward, refusing to acknowledge Sarah.

"And I'm Josh."

Silence.

Miss Johnson shuffled the papers on her desk, then pointed toward the standing woman. "This is Shirley, Braxton's grandmother."

The woman, dressed in lavender scrubs, nodded in their direction as she brushed at the tip of gray hair that fell onto her brow. "Nice to meet you."

"And this is Georgia, Braxton's mother." Miss Johnson said, but Georgia still refused to make eye contact. Miss Johnson pointed to the fake-leather furniture. "Please be seated."

"The point of this meeting is to get acquainted and discuss a plan of action for Braxton. Any questions?" Miss Johnson's eyes scanned the room.

Josh put his arm around Sarah's shoulder. "How's he doing?"

"He's doing well. They moved him from ICU to the graduate nursery three days ago."

Georgia cleared her throat. "You takin' my boy?" she asked Sarah.

"I'll be watching over him until you get him back."

"Humph!"

Sarah studied Georgia's face. Her brown skin glowed, her chubby-cheeks doused with a dark-burgundy blush, and two strands of hair looped down in front of her ears. The rest of her hair lay piled on top, secured with bobby pins. Tweety Bird earrings dangled against her neck.

Shirley moved to the edge of her seat. "Can I come see my grandson whenever I want?"

"You have to talk to your caseworker. There are certain rules we have to follow as foster parents," Josh said.

"Humph! I can't believe they're takin' my boy!" The coldness in Georgia's voice turned to tears. Her brown eyes blazed as her words gushed out. "I made the mistake of tellin' the social worker if I had to take my baby home with all his issues—I'd have a breakdown. I only wanted some financial help. Some help. Humph!"

"We're trying to help. There are many things happening in your life that need to be addressed, and then we'll consider sending him home." Miss Johnson spoke firmly, as if she'd said the words before.

"I'm sorry, Georgia." Sarah could only imagine how it would feel losing her child to the system. "I lost my little boy too, but . . ."

"But what?" Georgia blurted out. "Ya'll still got your other kids. Do you know how it feels when someone just takes your baby?"

Sarah considered that. "I'm only a foster parent, but I promise with my whole heart, I'll do everything in my power to protect your son as if he were my own." She wondered if she'd added more flame to the blazing fire when Georgia shot her a look. Her stomach churned.

"I know it ain't your alls fault." Georgia folded her arms across her chest and lowered her head.

"How come your son died?" Shirley asked.

Sarah hated answering that same question for the zillionth time, but she had promised Jordan as he lay dying in her arms that if anyone cared to hear the truth about why he died, she'd be more than happy to tell the truth. "A doctor came to our state and practiced for one year. He obviously didn't know what he was doing. He injured several kids, including the three who died."

"Mmm . . . I'm so sorry." Shirley replied. "Did they fire the doctor?"

Sarah feared discussing too much of Jordan's death in front of Miss Johnson. Children Services knew he died, but they didn't know the details. "It's a long story. I just want to help your daughter."

Shirley smiled, and for the first time Sarah felt a glimmer of approval stemming from her.

Sarah cleared her throat. "Georgia, I want to help you. Is that possible?"

Georgia pulled at her loose shoestring. "Help? I've done heard that fore. Look where it done got me, but ya'll can help me get my boy back." She looked at her mom. "I gotta get out of here. I feel sick."

Shirley extended her hand, "Very nice to meet you two. I'm gonna see if I can rearrange my work schedule so I can visit my grandson at your house on Wednesday, since I can't make it to his doctor appointment Monday."

Sarah swallowed hard. "At my home?"

"We were going to ask if we could have the visits at your home since Braxton is on so much equipment," Miss Johnson said.

"That'll be fine," Sarah replied, though not thrilled about having strangers in her home.

Shirley held onto Georgia's arm as they left.

"Are you ready to meet the little guy?" Miss Johnson asked.

Sarah's heart fluttered. "Yes."

Miss Johnson led them to a small room that held a metal sink and a cart fully stacked with gowns, gloves, and masks. "You'll need to scrub in. This is standard procedure for all visitors. And I have to go, but your caseworker should be here soon. Thanks for everything."

After she left, Josh looked at Sarah over his green paper mask. "You okay?"

She nodded, her throat as dry as cotton balls. The hospital gown, masks, and hand washing reminded her of Jordan's hospital stay.

A nurse wearing Elmo scrubs approached them. "Are you ready?"

They followed her down the hall, passing dimly lit rooms. Each room held its own tragedy, yet an opportunity for a miracle. Passing by the nurse's station, Sarah's nerves jumped. The hum of the hospital stopped for Sarah when the nurse led them into a small corner.

"Here he is," the nurse said.

Sarah's heart thumped when she saw the little baby who lay on a plastic bed curled in a ball. She steadied her hand to brush his cheek. "Hey there, little guy."

"He's a fighter," the nurse said, and grinned. "While you two get acquainted, I'll go get his meds."

"We're sure going to miss him." Sarah turned toward the voice. A mother tucked in a rocking chair held her baby. "I'm Victoria. This," she gestured with her head to the child asleep in her arms, "is Mabel. We've been Braxton's roommate for a couple of days. I'm glad they found him a family."

Sarah wondered if Victoria had spoken with Georgia. "I bet you and his mom had time to bond?"

"I feel sorry for her, actually."

"What a cutie." Sarah knelt beside the rocking chair and latched hold of Mabel's little finger.

"I wanted a boy but got a girl. I'm okay with whatever God wants, as long as she gets better."

Sarah sensed the worry stemming from this mother. She appeared tired and dark smudges underlined her eyes. Her baby, Mabel, had a naso-gastric tube pumping formula into her stomach.

"Anyway," Victoria continued, "Georgia loves Braxton. She comes to sit with him every day, but mostly she talks about her son who died. I suppose I would, too. If something happened to my Mabel, they'd have to lock me up in a nut house."

Sarah shivered. "Do you think Georgia could care for Braxton long term?"

"I can't say. I know the nurse tried to teach her things, but she couldn't grasp it. Then one day she blurts out, 'I can't take care of him. I done lost one son.'"

"Do you know if she actually gave Braxton up, or did Children's Services take him?"

"I think it was a combination of both."

Sarah stood, her knees felt weak. "It was nice to meet you, Victoria." When she turned back to Braxton's bed, Josh had his hands tucked into his jean pockets.

"I'll be right back," he said.

Sarah knew exactly where he was going. From previous experience, he could only tolerate the nursery for roughly fifteen minutes. The beeping monitors turned his stomach.

"What do you think?" the nurse asked, coming to stand beside her.

Sarah smiled, latching onto Braxton's tiny finger. "He's a doll baby."

The nurse tossed her latex gloves into the trash. "You can change his sleeper while I finish writing up his discharge orders, and then we'll complete the training."

While Sarah undressed Braxton, she sang softly, "Hush little baby, don't say a word." When she stopped, his droopy eyes popped open. They were darker than her mascara. She grinned as she pulled the apnea-wires through the front opening of his sleeper. Before fastening the snaps, she said, "You're so tiny; this sleeper would fit a doll baby."

Josh returned and stood by the bed.

Sarah frowned. "You okay?"

"I'll be fine." He turned away from the bed to load Braxton's diapers, wipes, knitted caps, and sleepers into the diaper bag.

The nurse returned and handed Sarah two vials of medication. "Take your time, honey."

While Sarah demonstrated to the nurse how to give the medication and operate the apnea-heart monitor, a loud voice from behind caused her to jump. "Isn't she a gem?" She turned to see a woman, slightly taller than herself, who held a car seat. "I'm Sheila. Braxton's case manager." she extended her tanned hand. "Well, momentarily. And yes, I was talking about you."

"Thanks, but I'm not all that."

"Sure you are. We don't have many foster parents who take in medically fragile babies." Sheila placed the car seat next to the rocker. "I brought this in case yours didn't pass the test, which it turns out, didn't."

Sarah laughed. "Boy, times have changed, and so have car seats."

Sheila moved to Braxton's bed and patted him on the arm. "I can't believe he's almost three months. I'm so glad he has a home, now. Thanks." She smiled and her blue eyes twinkled. "Sorry to rush out of here, but I have to take my daughter to dance. I'll see you Monday, if I'm still assigned to the case."

"Thanks for the car seat, and taking him home is our pleasure."

After the caseworker left, Sarah drew in a long deep breath, realizing how tiny and helpless Braxton was. *We can do this, we'll be just fine.*

While she continued repeating her mantra, Josh wrapped his arms around her waist. "Wow," he whispered against her ear, "he is a lot like Jordan."

Sarah briefly smiled at the memories—Jordan's sleepers were too big, just like Braxton's. His blood pressure cuff could wrap one time around an adult thumb, and his cap the volunteers had knitted, rested just above his eyelids. "Yes, he is."

"You ready?" Josh asked.

She put Braxton's tiny coat on him, placed him in his car seat dotted with rabbits and, covered his face with a lightweight blanket. "Ready."

Josh hoisted the diaper bag, apnea-monitor bag, and portable oxygen onto his shoulder. "Let's go."

After they said good-bye to the nurses, they made their way outside. Inside the SUV, Josh pushed the button to lock the doors, and then patted Sarah's hand. "Don't worry, everything will be fine."

Even though he spoke those words of comfort, she worried how Luke would respond. "I hope so."

CHAPTER SEVEN

Luke sat at the computer, downloading songs to his iPod. He cringed when Zack maneuvered him back to the painful subject, like a mouse through a maze, when he said, "They're here."

"Chill-lax," Luke shouted, as Zack ran to open the door.

Sarah set the car seat on the floor. "Any fights while we were gone?"

Zack grinned. "Nope."

"Luke, could you please go help your dad?" Sarah lifted the blanket off Braxton's face.

"I got it." Josh shrugged off the bags onto the floor.

"He's a cutie pie," Zack said, hovering over the baby.

Luke knew it was time to move, but he couldn't make himself get up. He had only agreed to take the baby to make his mama happy. It took a supreme act of will to force a smile. He walked over to see what in the world Zack was making a fuss over. "He's black?"

Sarah tossed her coat on top of her purse. "Does it matter?"

He didn't want to answer that question because it did matter. The minute Mouse found out they were taking care of a black kid, he'd be dead meat. "Mike isn't one-hundred percent white, but yeah, it could be a problem if Mouse finds out."

"He's tellin' the truth," Zack interrupted. "Two weeks ago, Mouse's brother Tommy beat up a kid at school because he wasn't white. BAM!" Zack smacked his fist into his left hand. "And the kid got a black eye."

"I'm sure the school officials will handle them if there's a problem." Josh said.

"The way Tommy and Mouse get into fights all the time, it seems to me they have issues with more than just people who aren't white." Sarah responded, tracing her fingertips over Braxton's tiny nose.

Luke couldn't argue either response, but his parents were wrong. "Mama?" He tagged behind her to tell her she was wrong, but the phone rang. He picked it up and handed it to his mom.

She pinned the phone between her ear and shoulder, put the baby's supplies in the cupboard, and spoke with the oxygen company. She placed Braxton's bottle into the warmer. "Thank you," she finally said.

"What'd they say?" Josh asked.

"They're going to deliver the oxygen supplies later this evening." Sarah slid into a chair beside Luke, "Honey, I'm sure this will be another hurdle for you if Mouse is as racist as you say, but you have a lot of repressed anger. And you use machismo as a shield."

Luke drummed his fingers on the table. "Get to your point."

"People can say cruel things, but you have to let it go."

He leaned back in his chair and locked his elbows behind his head. "I'm just sick of the same ole garbage, and I'm not puttin' up with any more bull even if it causes me to flunk my senior year."

She sighed. "Please use this time off from school constructively, perhaps thinking of ways to avoid Mouse. You can't afford another suspension."

"Braxton's bottle is warm," Josh interrupted. "Want me to feed him?"

"Yes, thanks." Sarah cupped Luke's face with her hands. "I want you to be happy."

He considered this as he stared into her eyes, wondering how she managed to get on with everyday life. *Maybe she's just lying to herself. Is that what adults do? Just pretend nothing happened?* To him, that was even scarier. Finally, he pushed her hands aside and said, "I wanta know everything about the night my brother died."

She rubbed her hands nervously, then said softly, "When I feel you're ready, I'll tell you."

"See." His face reddened as he smacked the tabletop. "You try to protect everybody and that's not fair!" He jumped out of his seat and fled up the steps.

⧽⧼

Sarah hadn't wanted her boys to watch Jordan die. His death had been too much for her to bear. She wished there was a script for healing, or an instruction book for putting the broken pieces of a life back together.

Josh patted the baby's back in a rhythmic motion. "Honey, don't beat up on yourself for trying to protect our kids."

"I don't understand why he needs to know. I want him to focus on the good times."

"You know as well as I do about human curiosity. Why don't you run out and get the diapers, some clothes, and a baby bed, while I finish feeding him?"

She laughed and went to get her keys from off the kitchen counter. "Ugh! I forgot about dirty diapers."

"Where you goin', Mom?" Zack asked.

"To the store. Wanta come?"

"Will you buy me a wrestler or video game?"

"Only one. Deal or no deal?"

A smile lit his face. "Deal."

⧽⧼

Luke peeked out his bedroom window and watched his mom pull out of the driveway. Making his way into the bathroom adjacent to his room, he stared at the image in the mirror. *Who are you?*

Forcing away the thought, he pulled his fake-diamond earrings from the box and pushed them into his ears. He was going out for a walk. He galloped down the steps, halted on the landing, and stared through the wooden-box window of the staircase. He thought his dad was engrossed in the baby until he heard, "What you up to?"

He knew if he took one step toward the door that Mr. Snoop Dog would come barreling off the couch and scold him. *Better to ask.* He walked into the living room and sat down. "I'm bored."

"Got your studies caught up?"

"Yep."

"I was sitting here thinking about the all-star tournament last year." Josh shifted the baby to his other shoulder.

"Remember when Bryan threw that curveball and struck that guy out? He was so mad." Luke grinned. "I thought he'd break the bat."

"That was a good season." Josh put Braxton in his infant carrier. "When you were in third grade we had you tested, and the teachers told us that you're gifted."

Luke raised an eyebrow. "I never knew that."

"You probably don't remember. My point is that I want you to start channeling some of your grief into baseball and bringing your grades up."

Luke nodded. "Would you care if I walked around the block?"

Josh hesitated for a sec, then said, "I'll expect you home in twenty minutes, and no going to Mike's."

Luke got up and tugged at his baggy jeans. "See ya in twenty." He snatched his jacket out of the closet, put it on and zipped it up. Outside, he walked into the carport and stuffed the bottle of Crown into his jacket— the one Mike had left under the blue tarp. Then he headed toward Community Park, kicking at the concreted walkway. *No going to Mikes. Yeah right. And who in the heck is mom trying to save now?* He shook his head. *She takes responsibility for the whole world's happiness even at the expense of mine.*

❧◈❧

Sarah returned home and found Josh lying on the floor next to Braxton. She pointed at a stack of quilts three layers high. "What's this?"

"A make-shift bed."

Braxton lay on the quilts, a lightweight blanket covering his tiny body, and at times, his left upper lip turned up and quivered.

"Think he'll be warm enough?"

"I think so. The stove puts off enough heat to warm the entire house. How many packs of diapers did you get?"

"Five." She unzipped her purse, pulled out her bankbook and receipts, then she sat down and proceeded to put her spending into the bankbook.

"Dad?" Zack stepped into the room. "Did Luke go play basketball?"

"He was bored, so I told him he could go for a walk, but to be home in twenty-minutes."

No way was he going for a walk because he was bored, Sarah thought. "What time did he leave?"

Josh's face reddened as if he had just been caught with his hand in the cookie jar. "Uh . . ." He looked at his wristwatch. "I'm not sure."

Her cheeks flushed. "He's suspended from school, Josh."

"Honey, he's only taking a walk. It's not like he's on house arrest."

"And you trust him?" She didn't mean for the words to spill out harsh, but she couldn't help it.

"It's only a walk. We can't keep him locked in his room like an inmate."

"I realize that." Her tone softened.

He jumped up from the floor like a jack-n-the-box and went to get his shoes from under the banister.

"Where are you going?" she asked.

"To find Luke."

CHAPTER EIGHT

Luke had seen his dad pull into Community. He'd pushed Mike behind the bushes, causing his unopened Budweiser to tumble to the ground. There they stayed until his dad's taillights faded. Exhaling steadily, Luke picked up the Budweiser, opened the tab with his teeth, and quickly sipped the rising foam.

"How'd you know where to find me?" Mike stood and brushed at his backside.

"You're pretty predictable."

"Did you find the Crown?"

"Yeah, thanks." Luke handed Mike his beer, then opened his jacket and pulled out the bottle.

Mike sighed. "I'm worried about ya. Since Jordan died, you're getting into fights all the time, your grades are worse than mine, and you're drinkin' like a fish. I'm here if ya need to vent."

Luke almost laughed. "As the old saying goes, 'if that ain't callin' the kettle black,' and you drink all the time."

"I just meant that if you need to vent, I'm here."

Luke knew he could be macho, and when he guzzled he could even be rebellious, but he also knew that Mike cared about him. "I'm sorry. I'm just ticked because Mama won't tell me how Jordan died."

"I'm sure she's only trying to protect you." Mike finished off the beer and threw the can in the bush.

Luke puckered and spat onto the ground. "I wanta know."

Mike pulled the chewed silver-colored pick out of his bushy-hair and scratched his scalp. "Why? So you can go psycho?"

A silence slipped between them. Mike pulled a Winston out of his jacket, clamped it between his teeth and struck a match, waiting.

"Jordan was my best friend, besides you and Zack." Luke tilted the bottle, took a swig of Crown and swallowed. "I'm just ticked because Zack got over his death way too fast."

"How would you know? You barely talk to him." Mike took a long drag off his cigarette. When he exhaled, the smoke snaked through the air.

Luke couldn't help but laugh. The night air was so thick with fog and cigarette smoke; he could reach out and play tic-tac-toe in it. "I try to talk to him, but he's so bent on staying close to God." When Mike didn't respond, Luke leaned against the tree and continued. "Jordan had this smile that radiated a kind of magic. You remember?"

Mike grinned.

"Why did God take him away? I mean . . . come on Mike . . . he was just a kid. And you know what?"

Mike tilted his head. "What?"

"If I could go to heaven right now, I'd kidnap him and bring him back."

Mike traced his cigarette along the barren elm tree. The ashes tumbled to the ground. "Just don't get so caught up in the past that you forget you have two brothers."

Luke knew his best friend was only trying to give him good advice. *You ain't never lost a sibling,* he wanted to shout at him, but he stayed his words and nodded. "I'll try."

"Are we cool?"

Luke turned the bottle upside down, took a long swig, screwed the cap back on and slipped the bottle into his jacket. "Yeah, bro, we cool. See ya at school after I'm released."

❧

Sarah sat at the edge of the couch; her bare feet pressed together, her hands locked in her lap. Inside, she felt jittery and afraid. She worried about Luke, but the Lord had seen her through many storms and this one was no different.

She heard the door open and close. "Luke?"

He came into the living room. "Yeah."

"It's past twenty-minutes. Where've you been?"

"Takin' a walk."

Josh lowered the volume on the television. "I went to Community, Dustin's house, and you were nowhere in sight."

"If you'd gone down Texas Street, you'd a seen me." Luke dug into his pockets and stuffed a jolly rancher into his mouth.

"I expect to know your whereabouts. Your mother and I were worried sick. If we have this conversation again, you won't even be able to take a walk. Is that clear?"

"Clear. I'm going to bed."

After he went up the steps, Josh rested his head on Sarah's shoulder. "Everything will be fine."

She pulled a pillow from behind her back, bopped it on top of his head. "You said things would be fine when our kitchen ceiling sat on the countertop for a week."

He chuckled. "I can't help it if the pipes burst in the bathroom, but I do worry about my family."

She nudged him playfully. "I know that."

And she did. Even though Josh wasn't as open about his emotions, he had told her many times, "I want my boys to go to college, so they don't have to work as hard as I have. And I want them to live a Christian life."

"Did you check to see if you had any plans for Wednesday?" he asked, interrupting her thoughts.

"No plans, but I'm uncomfortable having strangers in our home, but if it will help out Children Services . . ."

"I didn't like the idea either, but what else can we do? And I wouldn't worry about Georgia. You know if that was you, you'd be upset."

"I know."

Josh yawned. "I'll put the crib together tomorrow. Try and get some rest before Braxton wakes up."

"Did you put the coffee in a thermos?"

"Yes, but don't drink too much. With a newborn, you're going to need sleep."

Josh went to lie down, and Sarah flopped down on the opposite couch, fished the remote control out from the cushions, turned on the TV, and tried to rest. But her racing thoughts kept her turning. *What can I do to help Luke? How will Georgia respond when I see her Monday?*

Ugh . . . She wished she had a keyboard in her brain, so she could hit the delete button. She gazed at the wrought iron clock—at least an hour before the baby would awaken. She counted backwards. "One hundred, ninety-nine, ninety-eight . . ."

Beep, beep, beep. Sarah sat up. Through gritty eyes, she glanced at the red button on the apnea-monitor screen. Her hands trembled as she raced to pick up Braxton. "Breathe, baby," she said, holding him close to her chest. She exhaled a sob when he rattled out a burst of air.

"Is he okay?" Josh rubbed his eyes.

"He's fine. I'm not sure how many pauses in breathing he had, but he's fine," she cried.

Josh rolled off the couch and crawled to her. "And you?" The tenderness in her his voice brushed her heart.

"What if I hadn't woken up? What if he hadn't taken a breath?"

"Honey, you can't "what if" yourself to death. He's fine."

"Mmmg hmm." Braxton agreed.

"Did you hear that?" He stretched his hands toward the baby. "Give him here. I'll feed him and get him back to sleep."

"No. I'll be awake listening for every breath he takes, and you have to be up in four hours for work. But thanks."

"As for you, little man," he patted Braxton's thigh, "no more excitement."

After Sarah fed and burped the baby, she laid him back in his bed and glanced at the monitor. She noted even green beeps. Then she lay down and flipped through the television channels. A late night talk show caught her eye. The show featured a little boy who had survived fifty shunt-surgeries. "Fifty." She whispered the word in the dark. *You should still be here Jordan. Why did that doctor neglect you?* As usual, no answer came.

❧

The next morning, Sarah nursed her coffee, her eyes fixed on the big-screen TV. Authoritative voices filled the room with recent updates from the War on Terror. Luke mocked her on a regular basis because she didn't know how to pronounce *Al Qaeda*, and she didn't even know the difference between Iraq and Iran. She regretted she hadn't been more open to World History when she was in school. She clicked off the TV, then lifted the baby carrier and moved it to the entrance of the living room, so she could keep an eye on Braxton while she made dinner early—something her mother had taught her as a teen. 'If you ever get married and have children, Sarah, always make dinner early, that way you're not beating feet at the last minute when the kids get home, trying to cook and help them with homework.' Sarah had taken her mother's advice the day she tied the knot with Josh.

In the kitchen, she plopped a handful of potatoes into the sink and rinsed them. She heard Luke's heavy footsteps stomp down the stairs.

"Mama?" he hollered.

"I'm in the kitchen."

He thrust himself down on the barstool.

She grabbed a chef's knife from out of the drawer. "How'd you sleep?"

"So-so."

She noted the bags under his eyes. He edged himself off the barstool and walked over to the fridge, opened it, then grabbed a package of hard cookie dough. "When you gonna buy me a car?"

"You have to prove to me and your Dad that you can be responsible."

"I am." He ripped the package open with his teeth.

"Getting suspended for the fifth time doesn't prove to me that you're responsible." She located the cutting board in the lower cupboard and placed in on the counter.

He sat down on the edge of the barstool and took a bite of raw cookie dough. "That's bull."

"Your Dad and I are very concerned." She sliced the potatoes in wedges and put them into a bowl filled with cold water.

"Whatever. I can't do anything right." He swallowed. "Dad says I'm too aggressive."

"And you get into fights," she reminded him.

"Whatever. Dad says I'll be a bad driver. 'You're too volatile, Son.'" He mocked his dad's voice, and Sarah smiled in spite of herself.

"He worries about you."

Luke rolled his eyes. "Dad's just nuts."

"That's enough."

"I'm not going to change."

She set the knife down and walked around the edge of the counter. Their eyes locked. The sparkle she longed to see in his eyes had long ago turned dull. She wanted to make everything better for him, the way she'd done a thousand times in her life. But how? Her therapist had told her that everyone had to work through their own grief. And

48

it could take *years*. Sarah didn't know if Luke had years, especially with the way he was dealing with grief.

"No one is asking you to change. Just to get a little more control," she finally said.

"That's not true. You and Dad want to be in control of everything."

"We don't want to bury another child."

"So why'd you take another sick kid?" He flicked his head toward Braxton's carrier.

"He has nothing to do with you." She hunched forward, resting her elbows on the counter.

"Yeah, but why did . . . I mean come on, Mama." He ran his hands through his bed-head hair. "I want my own life."

"And how does the baby intrude on that?"

"You don't get it. Do you remember what Zack said after Jordan died? He said, 'I got my mommy back.'" Luke lowered his head as if shocked by his own outburst.

Quickly, Sarah turned her head. She saw her mother's picture hanging on a small wooden ladder attached to her apple valance. *What should I do, Mama?*

"Mama?"

"What?"

"He doesn't . . . It's just—" Luke fumbled for an explanation.

She knew what he meant, but the words came out all wrong. "He takes attention off you?" She said, turning back to face him.

"No. I just don't want to fall in love again and . . ."

"Honey, last night we talked about pain."

"Right, Mom. We did. And what about it? Huh?"

A tiny headache pricked her eyes, and she rubbed her temples. "If I make you an appointment with Toni, will you go? I really believe she could help."

Luke's eyes filled with tears. She lifted her thumbs to wipe at them, but he pushed her hand away.

"Don't. Just forget it."

A tiny voice screamed. She went to pick up Braxton from his carrier. She felt Luke's gaze penetrate her as if she'd committed a crime when the baby nestled against her cheek. She wanted to ask him to hold the baby, but knew better. He needed time.

"Do you think you could take me driving soon?" He asked softly.

She was surprised he could just change the subject so quickly. One minute he's hurting, and the next, worrying about driving.

"You can drive us to Braxton's doctor's appointment on Monday, if you drive safely." She waited for a negative response as she placed the baby's bottle into the warmer.

"Just don't tell Dad."

She lifted the bottle out of the warmer, and offered it to the baby. "You know me and your Dad don't have any secrets."

"Why can't he lay flat and drink?" Luke immediately changed the subject. Again.

"Because he could aspirate." She sat down on a dining room chair.

He rolled his eyes. "English, Mom."

"Aspirating is bad. The formula could go down into his lungs and cause them to collapse." She stopped when his eyes glazed over again.

"Is that what happened to Jordan? When his lungs collapsed?"

"Yes," she replied softly.

"Do you remember when I was a baby?"

"Of course, but I'm sure you wouldn't want to hear it because you couldn't drive then either, so I'm sure it would be boring." She set the half-empty bottle on the table.

He grinned. "You stink at comedy. Was I as handsome then as I am now?" He stood up and raised his shirtsleeve, showing off his bicep.

Why doesn't he stop clowning around and open up?

She forced a smile. "You wouldn't go to sleep at night until I waltzed you around the floor to gospel music."

"Gospel?"

"It wasn't rap, but it put you to sleep," she teased, leaning over to put the now sleeping baby back in his carrier and securing the latches.

"Enough of my babyhood. Can I ask you a question?"

Sarah picked at the fuzzy balls on her shirt. "I'll answer if I can."

He joined her at the table. "Do you ever wonder where you'll be twenty years from now?"

She pondered his question for a few minutes. Finally, she said, "I try not to think that far ahead. I mean, right out of high school, I joined the Army, got out, married your Dad, then had kids. I went to nursing school, not knowing that someday I'd use those skills for my own experiences, meaning, you know, caring for your brother, and now Braxton. But I believe God helps us with unexpected challenges."

He glowered at her. "God didn't prepare you for Jordan's death, did he?"

She tried to smile, but failed. "Nothing prepares us for losing someone we love. But leaning on God does make their absence more bearable." She fought back the tears. "After Jordan died, my mind was set that doctors used preemies for guinea pigs, and they decided who lived and who died. But then I realized something."

"What?"

"I realized that everything in life happens for a reason. And that doesn't mean it won't tear you apart, but if we allow God to stitch our wounds, he will."

Luke gritted his teeth. "I'm sorry, Mama, but I can't forgive Doctor Aspen. He was a jerk!"

"Our faith says we must forgive, Luke, like God forgives us."

"How can you when he caused Jordan's death?" His voice rose on the last word, giving it emphasis.

She drew in a deep breath. *God please help him understand.* "It's been tough, Luke. I forgive. I didn't say I forgot."

"How did he even manage to get a license to practice?"

Sarah frowned. "Maybe he got lucky when he opened a box of Cracker Jacks."

Luke snickered. "You remind me of Gregory House."

"Who?"

"Come on, Mama. Surely you've seen *House*? Oops. I forgot, you don't do TV."

"Sometimes."

Luke chuckled. "I love this guy. He's always trying to figure out the patient's symptoms, and he's so sarcastic. I mean, he's got like the worst bedside manners ever, but," Luke paused to catch a breath, "at least he goes to bat for the patient, even if he lacks bedside manners 'cause he's the BOMB! And this one time, he even got drunk with one of his patients that got admitted, you know, to the hospital from death row. How cool is that?"

Sarah leaned back in her chair, actually surprised to see Luke grinning. Narrowing her eyes, she said, "You haven't been drinking again have you?"

"Nah. I just love this doctor because he knows a lot about the medical field, kind of like you. And Mom, if he was a real-life-doctor, and we could've taken Jordan to him, you can bet your last dollar this dude would've saved his life."

She finally smiled. "He sounds like an amazing—" Before she could say, doctor, Luke interrupted.

"Did you get a medical dictionary and memorize it?" His smirk told her he was kidding.

"No, I learned what I needed to. Then I built on that knowledge. It's a process, but times change, people change, and you've got to be open minded enough to accept that, or you'll get left behind wondering where everyone else went. But there's one thing that I will never change."

Luke's eyebrows scrunched. "What?"

"My trust in God."

He immediately changed the subject. "Sometimes I forget you know stuff."

"What?"

"Well sometimes I forget that you're more than just me and Zack's Mom."

"Oh, yeah?"

"Sometimes I think the only stuff you think about is what time my curfew should be and whether you packed enough cookies for Zack."

"Come on Luke—you know there are never enough cookies for Zack."

They laughed, and Braxton squirmed, cracking open his eyes. Sarah hoped Luke would respond to him; instead, he looked the other way and rubbed his temple. "I still can't believe a so called intelligent doctor made a fatal mistake."

Sarah's face flushed. "It was no mistake. The doctor's pride got in the way. And the worst part is that even when doctors mess up, they usually get to keep their jobs. Unless, they have a ton of lawsuits and can't afford medical malpractice insurance."

"I hope Dr. Aspen can never afford medical malpractice insurance."

Sarah sighed. Luke was too young to understand these issues in life. Teenagers should be dreaming about their future, going to dances, and having a good time with their peers. He'd spent so many evenings listening to his parent's talk about medical issues; he'd etched them into his brain. Or maybe he'd spent too much time watching *House*.

"Has the medical board disciplined him yet?"

"Nope. They keep telling me the records are out for review," she replied.

"They're probably crooked, too."

Sarah ached for her son. She wanted to help him through the pain, to give him something to believe in that would make life easier to bear. *But what?* Hadn't she said enough already? She slumped down into her chair. The silence between them widened. Finally she said, "You know

I'll always be there for you."

Wordlessly, he nodded, and then left the room.

CHAPTER NINE

Luke woke up to a trail of weak sunlight. He had fallen asleep reading the book Mrs. Frenchie had lent him. He reread page fifty-eight, paragraph three, aloud. "On the Isle of Faith, you'll never be alone because I'll always be by your side. Many people never reach this Isle because of unbelief."

Then he read the bottom of page fifty-nine aloud, "Some of us have carried around wounds so long we are no longer able to see them because they become a part of who we are. We hide behind our pain."

Frustrated, he shut the book and tossed it on top of his English book, unable to deny the statement made about hiding behind pain. He placed his elbows on his knees, then cupped his face with his hands. *Who is going to help me with my pain?*

He opened his bedroom door, made his way down the steps. He slid open the patio door and stepped out onto the deck. His dad was cooking on the grill; the scent of charcoal filled his nostrils, reminding him of family camping trips.

"Hey, bud. Ya hungry?" Josh asked.

"Starving." Luke grinned when he saw the apron his dad wore. In big bold red print it said, *COMPLAINTS TO THE COOK MAYBE HAZARODOUS TO YOUR HEALTH.*

"Think you'll make do till dinner?" Josh asked.

"If you hurry."

The air shifted, causing the hot coals from the charcoal grill to warm him. He glanced at Zack sitting in the Jacuzzi, sipping a Pepsi as if he didn't have a care in the world. "Ain't you cold, dude?"

Zack snickered. "Why are you being nice?"

"I'm not. I asked if you were cold?"

"Hardly." Zack picked up the rubber duck, glanced at the mercury. "It's one-hundred and two degrees in here."

"Ain't ya got a sermon today?"

Sarah stepped out onto the deck and, handed a platter to Josh. "That's enough, Luke."

"Sorry, I was just . . ."

"Antagonizing your brother," Josh finished the sentence.

Sarah put her finger to her lips. "Shh . . .don't yell. The baby's asleep."

Josh closed the lid on the grill. "Got your studies caught up, Luke?"

Like it's going to matter. "I'm suspended. Remember?"

"I take it you're being sarcastic."

Luke couldn't be like his dad. Mr. I-work-at-the-prison-full-time. *What kind of pain isn't he dealing with?* He could hear his dad's words echo in his head—you need to grow up son and take responsibility for your own actions. If you ever need to talk—talk to me. I know how painful pre-adolescence can be.

You never lost your brother, did ya? He wanted to scream the words at his dad, but held back for fear of heaping more pain to his already messed up family. Gazing over, he saw his dad for what seemed like the first time since Jordan died. His hair had receded, creases carved his forehead, and it looked as if someone sprinkled his hair with salt and pepper.

He lost his son, Luke. A little voice inside said.

Shut up, he said back. *He's in denial.*

"Let me know when supper's ready." Luke slid the patio door open and went back inside.

In Zack's room, a Bible lay open on his walnut stained desk. The Bible pages were worn, and Zack's favorite passage highlighted in orange. "Then they cry unto the Lord in their trouble, and he bringeth them out of their distresses."

Luke ran to his room. *Why did you take my brother, God? Who gave you the right?* He put his fist in the air. *Mama said you'd be there for me, but you're not.* He stifled his wretched sobs and headed for his locker. *Did I forget to put the lock back on?* He opened the trunk lid and found no bottle. Frantically he sped to the wastebasket, his jacket, and under his bed. "What in the heck," he said, then stopped. His mother entered his room, holding the bottle.

"Looking for this?"

He wanted to run and hide from Mrs. Holier-than-thou. He sat down, bent his knees, and hid his face in his folded arms. "What?"

Sarah perched herself on his bed. "I asked you a question."

He lifted his head.

"Care to explain why I found this in your locker when I was cleaning?"

"I'm holding it for a friend."

Boy you're getting good at telling lies, the voice chided.

Now he felt worse. He had told more lies in the past year than he had in a lifetime.

"I wasn't born yesterday. Have you been drinking?"

When he stood up, his rebellious side kicked in. "You're miserable. That's why you took that baby to cover up your pain. And that's why Dad works all the time."

Color crept up his mother's neck and splotched on her face. She wiped her tears with a shaking hand, then sat down and patted the mattress. "Sit. I need to share something with you."

Luke hesitated.

"Please?"

He didn't like to see his mother cry. "Make it fast, I'm hungry."

"When I was a senior in high school my parents divorced."

"I already heard this story."

She continued even though Luke rolled his eyes. "I got a full time job and helped raise my brother and sister, but when graduation day approached, they got back together." She paused a minute as if reflecting, then said, "Uncle Dan told me the only reason they did was to make me happy. So I didn't go to my graduation."

He cleared his throat. "Why not?"

"I wasn't happy about the situation. I was depressed and . . ." He watched his Mom tug at her sweater. "I'm not as holy as you think."

Luke grinned. "Did you get drunk?"

"I didn't intend to. My aunt bought me a bottle of wine, and I was so depressed, I drank the whole thing, you know, and missed my graduation, but the point is this," she pointed a finger at him, "I learned a lesson. There's nothing we can take externally that will ease the inner pain, but talking to others who are going through something similar helps. Do you understand?"

Yeah. Drink to silence the rage within. "Don't worry about it."

"Promise me you won't drink anymore."

Luke sighed. "I can't promise anything right now. I'm living minute by minute."

"You will stop drinking or . . ." Sarah brought her hands to her chest.

"Or what?" *Just like her to share and then spoil it.* "You're telling Dad?"

"Why wouldn't I? You've been suspended, and now this?" She pointed to the empty bottle. "Your father will be so hurt. I don't know what to think. You're like Dr. Jekyll and Mr. Hyde."

"Who's Dr. Jekyll and Mr. Hyde?"

"Look them up on the Internet. Maybe that will give you something to do in your down time to keep you out of trouble."

"Mama!"

"Get cleaned up so we can eat. After supper, we'll talk."

∾∾

Everyone seated around the dining room table in their usual spot. Sarah glanced at the food Josh had prepared. Ears of corn sat in gold plastic trays, oven baked potatoes, still lined with foil and heavily salted at the rims, rested on each plate beside a steak.

She decided to break the news about Luke's drinking after dinner.

"Let's pray," Josh said.

They lowered their heads. "Thank you, Dear Heavenly Father, for your mercy, grace, and the food we're about to eat. Let it be nourishment for our body. Amen," Josh said.

When they lifted their heads, Luke eyed the food with a lost-my-appetite look.

"Can you pass the butter?" Sarah said.

Luke woodenly passed the tiny platter filled with chips of butter to Sarah, then picked at his food.

Josh smothered his potato with sour cream. "Thought you were hungry?"

Luke didn't respond. Sarah knew that soon Josh would sense something was wrong. It wasn't like his family to eat in silence. Normally he'd have to quiet the combativeness of Luke's actions toward Zack, or she would chatter on about how she'd talked to the medical board or share the events of her day.

Nothing.

"Want to tell me what's going on?" Josh finally asked.

Luke pushed his plate forward, making the table shake.

"Watch it! You spilled my pop," Zack scolded.

Before Sarah could say we'll talk about it after supper, Luke blurted out, "I've been drinking."

Josh exhaled steadily, laying his knife on his napkin. "How long?"

"Wha—huh?" Luke stammered.

"How long?"

"I'm almost eighteen!"

"And you're still in school, under my roof. You refuse to go to therapy, and you won't let us help you. I'm at wit's end, Son."

"Dad? I don't mean to hurt you."

Josh pointed his finger. "You just earned yourself another month of going nowhere. I'm driving you to school, and you are to get right home."

Luke barked out a laugh. "Yeah, right."

Josh's eyes narrowed. "You heard what I said."

"I wanta know if Jordan suffered," Luke shouted.

"So you can have nightmares the rest of your life?" Sarah said.

Luke wrenched his gaze away.

"You couldn't handle the news. Since your brother died, you've gone down the path of self-destruction. I'm afraid of what you'll do next," Josh said.

Luke blinked and a tear escaped his eye. "So he did suffer. Isn't that right, Dad? And you and Mom and Zack all pretend like you're fine. You think prayer is the answer to everything."

"Every one of us has suffered, but we're not the ones choosing a life of despair. And we're still a family." Josh leaned across the table to touch Luke's hand. "We're in this together."

Luke pulled his hand back. "I wanta know if he suffered?"

"We already told you he died of a brain stem herniation."

"That's not what I mean."

A tear slid down Sarah's cheek. She whisked it aside with her fingers, wiped her nose with a paper napkin. If Luke learned the truth—that Jordan had fought for his last breath, she feared he'd drown his sorrows in another bottle of booze.

"When I turn eighteen . . ."

Josh leaned back into his chair, crossed his arms over his chest. "What? Quit school? Drink until your liver fails?"

Luke's face flushed. "You won't even let me drive."

"You think I'm going to let you drive since I know you're

drinking?"

"Mom said I could drive her to Braxton's doctor's appointment on Monday."

"If he drives safely." Sarah suddenly lost her appetite and pushed her plate to the side.

Josh sighed heavily. "If you want to get your license, you better get your act together."

Luke fell silent for a moment and exhaled a long sigh. At last he said, "I'm not hungry. I'm gonna go study. Maybe God will make me a math genius."

After he pushed in his chair, Josh said, "I love you, Son."

"Love you, too, Dad."

Sarah knew they weren't exactly all the words Josh wanted to hear, but what else did he expect from a teen at odds with his parents?

❧∽

Luke threw himself on his bed. Tears squeezed past his eyelids and streaked down his cheeks. *You want me to quit drinking? Give my brother back.*

Zack appeared in the doorway, a beach towel wrapped around his hips. "Wanta talk?"

"What the heck could you teach me?"

Zack came in and flopped on the beanbag. "Remember when Jordan was in the hospital? It was just you and me."

Luke threw his football pillow in the air, up and down, catching it. *Blah, blah, blah.* He listened to Zack drone on about how close they used to be, how they had learned to make French toast, baked macaroni and cheese, and oven baked pizzas when their Mom was at the hospital with Jordan. When he couldn't take it anymore, he shielded his ears with his hands. For the next five minutes or longer, Zack's lips flapped like a flag in the wind. Finally, Luke uncovered his ears and set straight up. "Okay, preacher. If hell is the hereafter, then why am I suffering on earth?"

Zack lowered his head and tears slipped down his cheeks, absorbing into his towel.

Luke hopped up off the bed. Sure, he was at odds with his brother, but he didn't like to see him cry. He knelt beside him and patted his hand. "I didn't mean to hurt you."

Zack let out a sob. "I know we're different. I just happen to find comfort . . ." He forcefully coughed, holding his throat.

Luke sprinted to Zack's room and grabbed the portable nebulizer. Back in his room, he plugged in the machine and dumped the small plastic tube of albuterol into the plastic cylinder, and covered Zack's face with the mask. He steadied his shaky hands. "Breathe nice and slow, buddy."

When the misting stopped, Luke noted the blueness of Zack's lips had faded. Zack rubbed his chest, drew in a deep breath, and exhaled. Finally he said, "You're not the only one hurting. I miss Jordan, too. And when I made that comment after he died about getting Mommy back, I didn't want him to die for that to happen, so I blame myself. And, you're lucky."

Luke chuckled. "Lucky?"

"Yeah. I feel guilty because I didn't spend a lot of time with him." Zack lowered his head. "Guess that's why I spend a lot of time with Braxton."

Luke rubbed the stubbles on his chin. "Why can't I be like you? You never get angry. And you always smile."

"That doesn't mean I'm not hurting."

"I don't know about that."

"It's true." Zack's lower lip quivered. "I actually considered joining the EMO's at school, you know, slash myself to make my heart stop hurting."

"You wouldn't dare." Luke hopped up. "You'd hurt Mom and Dad."

"I'm not. Just thought about it." Zack flicked his damp hair out of his eyes, and patted down the cowlick that looked like a broken bedspring farther back on his head.

"Good, because you scared me." Luke knew full well his brother would never do anything like that anyway. Or would he? Did he even know Zack anymore?

"Do you remember when Mocha broke his leg in the fence-post hole Dad just dug?"

Luke went to his dresser and rearranged his trophies. "That crazy dog was never the same after that. All he did was lay around the house, and his farts stunk like raw sewage."

"Do you know why he laid around?"

"Probably because he was getting old."

"I think it's because he remembered the pain."

Luke turned. "Your point is?"

"When we hurt, we find something else to replace our pain."

"So you think I drink to forget?"

"I think you're afraid to love again. That's why you didn't want Mom and Dad to take Braxton."

"So you're not only a preacher, you're a psychiatrist, too? *Sheesh!* Zack! You're only fifteen. And don't start this babble-bull with me about depression or time heals all wounds or you drink alcohol to cover up your pain."

Zack's forehead creased. "Do you?"

"I ain't playin' psycho-therapy with you, dude." Luke kicked his footlocker. "If I ever see Dr. Aspen, I'll stick his head in a vice-grip and make him plead for his life."

Silence.

"You think I wouldn't do it?"

"I think you should go back to counseling."

Luke punched his dresser. "Ouch! Zack! I'm so ticked off, I don't know what to do."

"You better not let Mom see you punch anything, or she'll blow her stack."

Luke massaged his fist. "Remember when Mama cracked her wrist?" Zack opened his mouth to speak, but Luke put his hands in the air. "Don't—Let me finish. One night when I went downstairs to grab my notepad, I saw Mama punch the countertop. You wanta know why I think she did it?"

Zack chewed his thumbnail, listening.

"Because she was hurting. So if God is indeed a loving God, then why do bad things keep happening to his so-called people? Huh? Did you ever ask yourself that question?"

Zack sighed. "Mom and Dad raised you in church. You should know better."

"At one point I did, but now, I've tried to pray, and it's like my prayer—" Luke pointed upward— "gets as far as that ceiling."

"God understands."

"Then why doesn't he fix it?"

Silence.

"Come on. You read your Bible all the time, but you don't have an answer."

"Would it matter if I did? You're mad at God, so nothing I say is gonna matter." Zack went to his room and slammed shut the door. Within minutes, Luke could hear him hooting and hollering about a dude named Daniel, who survived a den of lions. *Yeah, right.* Sure, he'd heard the story in Sunday school, but to be honest, to him it seemed like the guy had a death wish.

Frustrated, he flopped on the bed and turned to face the wall, not giving his English book another thought.

CHAPTER TEN

Sarah placed the baby's head against her chest, and patted his back. Her nostrils filled with the scent of undigested formula. When Braxton's hand accidentally brushed her other cheek, she realized the magnetic attraction that drew her to him—unconditional love. Within minutes, his eyes closed. She placed him in his crib and pulled up the lightweight quilt to cover his tiny shoulders.

She peeked in on Zack, who lay like a corpse, flat on his back, mouth slightly parted, hands clasped on his torso. He appeared to be taking in shallow breaths. She watched the rise and fall of his chest before glancing at his recent Bible study, Jeremiah. She was proud of him for climbing to the top of his class with straight A's, and proud of the fact that he loved the Lord.

She passed from Zack's room to Luke's, who appeared to have had a fight with the devil. His pillow was barely under his head, two others tossed on the floor, and his sheets were halfway up the bed. He rested with a peace she was certain he'd fought to obtain. Surely, there was hope for saving Luke from his agony. Her mother had told her for years, nothing was ever lost. She'd taken that memory and tucked it into her heart.

In the kitchen, she took a cast iron skillet out of the stove's bottom drawer to make sausage gravy. She placed biscuits on the rounded stoneware, popped them into the oven, and hummed "How Great Thou Art" while nursing her coffee.

She worried about how opposed Luke was about going to church.

Three years ago, he played Joseph in the Christmas play. Jordan was baby Jesus. Back then, Luke loved church just as Zack did now.

When the oven beeped, she removed the biscuits and placed them in the lined woven basket Josh had bought for her two Christmas's ago, then poured the gravy into a bowl. At the sliding glass door, she slid her feet into Josh's steel-toed boots, slipped on his heavy quilted jacket, and stepped out on the deck.

She smiled at the blades of grass that poked through the last of the melting snow, reminding her of porcupine quills. Five weeks ago, the groundhog hadn't seen his shadow; a good sign spring was right around the corner.

Gazing out into her barren gardens, the memories of when she and Josh had created a triangular butterfly garden in memory of Jordan flooded her mind. "These dwarf daylilies will remind us of Jordan's sunshine smile," Josh had said, sprinkling soil around the base of each plant.

Spring couldn't come soon enough. Gardening was her haven—a place where she could lose herself. She'd carefully prepare each garden bed, getting it ready to burst forth with color—turning over the dirt while taking care not to disturb the roots of the other selected plants. She would remove the twisted dead canes and seal the tips with clear nail polish. She wondered if she'd have enough energy to tend to them now, since most nights were spent tending to Braxton.

She stepped off the deck and, walked toward Jordan's garden. Glancing down she read the cemented stone. *If tears could build a stairway and memories a lane, I'd walk right up to heaven and bring you home again.* The wind made her shiver. She pulled the collar of Josh's quilted jacket around her ears. *I'd bring you home again.*

Back inside, she kicked off Josh's boots and placed his jacket right where he'd left it, draped over a dining room chair. She started for the kitchen when loud voices trailed down the steps.

"I said, I'm going," Luke said, trailing Josh into the kitchen, "but I'm not participating. And I'm taking my iPod."

Zack rubbed his eyes, stumbling into the kitchen. "Some people are trying to sleep."

"Sorry, bud," Josh said. "You're brother is being stubborn. And you're not taking your iPod into the church. That's disrespecting the Lord's house."

"Fine." Luke put a spoonful of gravy in his mouth, then threw the spoon back in the bowl, causing some of it to splatter on the stove.

"Yuk," Zack complained.

Luke wiped at the corner of his mouth. "Every time I go, that preacher, what's his name?"

Zack flopped on the barstool. "Truman."

"He stares at me."

Zack snickered. "So you say."

"God said, 'Brother, ha—the only way to get to me is to accept my son who I sent, ha." Luke mocked Truman.

"He says *ha* so he can breathe," Zack piped in.

"Can't he talk a little slower? Then maybe he wouldn't be so winded?" He shook his head. "I don't even know why I agreed to go."

Zack snickered. "God ain't gonna bite you."

Sarah set the biscuits and gravy on the table. "Let's eat, boys."

"I'm makin' me a bowl of cereal," Zack said.

Josh pointed to the bowl. "There's plenty of gravy."

Zack wrinkled his nose. "But Luke ate out of the bowl."

"I only did a taste test." Luke plunked down into a chair, piled three biscuits on his plate, and covered them with gravy. "Truman stares at me like I'm the devil or something." He paused to take a drink of his OJ, then he said, "And he acts like he's in paradise."

Zack joined him at the table. "He is."

Luke rolled his eyes. "No nerd-herd, paradise is the Bahamas."

"Enough you two. Finish eating so you can get dressed." Josh wiped his mouth with a napkin.

Luke couldn't keep from talking. "Who's that woman that shouts Praise the Lawrd?"

Sarah nursed her coffee. "For heaven sakes, Luke."

"Well, she scares the he-be-je-be out of me when she shouts."

"Enough boys. Zack wipe your mouth and go get dressed," Josh said. To Luke, "Finish eating."

Thirty minutes later, they were getting ready to leave for church when Luke stomped down the stairs.

"Dad's gonna have a cow when he sees what you're wearing," Zack said.

Sarah darted around the corner.

"Don't worry, honey. They'll understand," Josh said.

How could she not worry? Luke's jeans were so baggy the crotch almost met his knees, and the shirt he wore read: ANGER IS MERELY DEPRESSION WITHOUT THE GUSTO.

Sarah sighed. "Where'd you get that shirt?"

A smile toasted Luke's face. "Mike. He said it was totally me."

Zack snickered as he ran a comb through his hair. "That's for sure."

Sarah zipped up her black boots. "Did you get Braxton's diaper bag?"

"Done. And the SUV is warming up," Josh replied.

They put on their coats and filed out the door.

They drove along Route 202. Josh braked and skidded to the red light.

"Irresponsible driver," Luke said.

"Let it go." Sarah opened her purse to find her lipstick. She could understand that Luke was suffering from the loss of his brother, but she couldn't understand his sarcasm. Turning around in her seat, she spotted Zack tapping Luke's leg.

"What's so funny?" Zack asked.

Luke grinned. "That woman back there at the church. Did you see her?"

Josh glanced in the rearview mirror. "The one kneeling beside the Virgin Mary?"

"Yeah. I bet her knees are cold."

The smile left Zack's face. "What?"

"She seemed lost in a trance, kind-a-like the statue might come to life and solve her problems."

"Enough, Luke!" Sarah slid the lipstick back into her purse. "There's nothing wrong with that woman praying."

"But not to the Virgin Mary, Mama."

"You don't know what she's praying about, so keep quiet." She drew in a deep breath, trying to stifle the anger that was starting to emerge.

"Your mom's right. And you might want to pay attention to the preacher today. Maybe he'll say something that will benefit you."

"I seriously doubt it, but I do hope church is as interesting as the ride's been." Luke chuckled and plugged the earphones back into his ears. Then he cranked up the volume to "Brains" loud enough for everyone to hear.

Josh backed the vehicle into a slot beside the one that read: RESERVED FOR THE PREACHER. He jammed the shifter into park. They scrambled out of the car and filed into the church.

❧❧

In the sanctuary, Luke took a seat next to Margie, a retired schoolteacher, on the last pew. He felt a rush of wind snake up his pant leg and turned to see one of the deacons open the door for an elderly woman as if he was the gatekeeper.

Turning back toward the front, his eyes scanned the crowd. His mama had taken a seat three pews ahead behind the preacher's mother, her friend, Pauline. Zack sat on the "amen bench" next to his dad. Now he wished he hadn't come. There were other places he could be: Mike's house or Dustin's, boozing it up to the beat of the music while Dustin laid tracks.

"Nice to see you, Luke," Margie said.

He loved how she dyed her hair the way his grandmother had before she passed away at the age of fifty-three—born-blonde. "You, too." *Yeah right. Since Jordan died, nothing mattered, especially church.*

Leroy, the song leader, stepped up to the platform. He waved his hands in the air, signaling the choir to come. Luke watched his dad, who sang bass, file in beside the preacher's wife.

"Let's all turn to page three hundred and sixty." Leroy's voice was loud.

Luke plucked the blue songbook out of the pocketed bench. The voices began to blend as they sang, "I've found a better way."

Luke scooted himself down into his seat, closed the book. *I've found a better path for my feet, too.* He smiled at the congregation who stood before him, singing their praises to the King. After the singing ended, Brother Matt asked if anyone had a prayer request or testimony.

"Pray for our troops," Birdie said.

Luke considered that. *Hmm, I think I'll join the Army, and when I do, I'll track down the enemy and wring their necks.*

"Pray for me," Sandy began. Sniffle. "I had to put my grandmother into a nursing home. She broke her hip, and until I can recover from my shoulder surgery, she'll have to stay there, so she's upset with me."

I bet she is, he thought, remembering the commercial he'd seen on TV. *Checking into a nursing home is like checking into a roach motel. You might never check out.*

"Remember the lost and my family," Josh said.

Oh great. Just like dad to bring attention to me. Luke tugged at his jeans and raised his head. First, it began with the musician, Benny, who starred at him over the top of the piano. Then Joe turned to stare and almost tripped over his cane. Finally, they all turned to give Luke the once-over.

"Let's remember that," Matt said, "anyone else?"

Silence stirred the air. When no one spoke, Matt said, "Brother Jimmy, would you lead us in prayer?"

After they prayed, the congregation seated themselves on the blue-padded pews. After the testimonies were given and the special songs were sung, the preacher stood in the pulpit.

Luke thought he'd seen Truman's angular face shift his way. He lowered himself farther into his seat.

"I'm just gonna testify." Truman began. "I gotta wait on the Lord."

Luke glanced up. *Hopefully it won't be too long.*

". . . . we're just pilgrims on a journey, but Praise God, when these troubles and trials are over, I'm goin' to my eternal home to be with our Lord."

"Amen," Brother Jimmy said.

Troubles and trials? For a preacher who wears a smile ninety-eight percent of the time, what trials could he have? I lost my brother. Preach something to me about grief and maybe you'll get my undivided attention.

Truman made his way down the aisle. "Brother, when we got the Holy Ghost to comfort us, we don't need the spirits in the bottle."

Spirits in a bottle? Now that's something I can relate to. The minute he'd thought it, Luke felt a pang of remorse. He'd promised his mama many times that he would never drink, and that was a promise he'd intended to keep until Jordan died. *But the Holy Ghost?* Of all the times he'd watched *Ghost Hunters* he'd never heard anyone mention a Holy Ghost. He recalled hearing about it in church, but was it something he could feel or see?

Truman turned his head toward Luke. "Maybe today is your appointment with God. He made his plan so simple that even a child can understand."

Luke grinned. The preacher had hollered and jumped around the pulpit, and at one time almost galloped up the aisle, but not one silvery gray hair was out of place. *Probably from all the grease, he poured in it.*

When Truman finished his sermon he said, "Let's have the song leader come, and have everyone stand to their feet." He paused long enough to scan the crowd. "Is he calling to you today? Do you feel burdened down with a contrite spirit and broken heart? You don't have to be. Christ will give you rest."

Luke's heart ricocheted against his chest. He felt bad for the way his life was headed, but he brushed away the thought.

"God wants you to trust in what his son did for you at the cross," the preacher said.

Luke swiped at the bead of perspiration on his forehead, wiped his sweaty palms on his jeans.

"Please come." Truman cried.

Luke couldn't take it anymore. He felt like such a lowlife, and he longed to be like Zack, the brother who stood at the left of the altar, giving his troubles to the Lord. He wrenched his gaze from the preacher and turned to Margie. "Let me out."

Roger and Margie filed out of their pews, made a way for Luke. He went directly to the bathroom, tried to turn the knob, but it was locked. Nervously, he paced the hall. Slowly, the door cracked open and out walked Brother Paul. Luke strutted past him without making eye contact.

In the bathroom, he splashed his face with cool water. When he exited, he spotted Paul slurping water from the drinking fountain. Luke made a beeline for the side door that Margie's husband, Roger, left cracked, so the ones who skipped out of Sunday school could sneak in unnoticed.

"I'm glad you came today," Paul said, causing Luke to stop dead in his tracks.

Luke held tight to the door handle, breathing heavily, almost to the point to where he thought he'd pass out. "I've enjoyed being here."

Liar. Now he felt more guilt. When Paul turned to go back into the sanctuary, Luke heard, "Praise the Lawrd." He didn't have to be in the service to know whose voice that was. It was Sister Shirley. She'd shout the roof off the housetop.

Releasing a big breath, he thrust the door open and stepped outside. The cool air bit his cheeks as he walked to the SUV.

In the distance, he heard Truman saying goodbye to every blessed soul who took the time to show up. He couldn't understand why in the world this preacher couldn't get enough of shaking people's hands, but he was starting to realize that there was something a little different about this man he'd known for many years. *But what?*

When his dad stopped to chat with Truman, suddenly Luke felt the preacher shift his gaze toward him. In the distance he heard his dad say, "I'll tell him."

His mama approached, wiping her tears with a tissue.

Luke shivered. "You got the spare set of keys?"

Sarah dug through her purse, handed them to him.

"Everything okay?"

"Yes, honey. It's just I find comfort in God's word."

If there's so much comfort, then why is she crying?

Zack placed Braxton into the SUV and strapped him in.

"Zack, go get Dad and tell him to quit talking. My stomach's growling. And how did you sleep through all that commotion?" Luke said to the baby.

Josh opened the door, slid into his seat. "Good service. Boy, if I didn't have the Holy Ghost to comfort me, I would've thrown in the towel a long time ago."

Luke punched Zack's shoulder. "You've watched that ghost hunting show with me. How's come they never mention a Holy Ghost?"

"Because they ain't gonna spot the Holy Ghost on TV," Zack replied, rubbing his bicep. "He's in your heart."

Luke's tone turned serious. "I thought Jesus was?"

Josh looked at him in the rearview mirror. "When you get saved you get the whole package. The Father, the Son, and the Holy Ghost."

"Mama? Why do you cry in church?"

"Honey, God comforts us through his word. Sometimes we laugh, we cry, but we were really crying tears of joy."

Luke considered that. *If she found her way out of the pit then why can't I?* "And didn't I hear the preacher say that even when we try to do good that evil is always present?"

"That doesn't mean we shouldn't try to be good people," Zack said.

Josh put the SUV into drive, then pulled out onto the street. "Zack meant we ought to try to live the best we can so others can see Christ living in us."

"And what if our best isn't good enough?"

"We're just a bunch of sinners saved by grace," Zack advised.

Sinner saved by grace. "What's grace?"

"In a nutshell, grace is unmerited favor, and mercy is what Christ extended to us when he went to the cross and died for our sins," Josh replied.

Sarah asked the dreaded question. "What did you think of the service, Luke?"

"No prob."

Josh put his turn signal on and stopped at the red light. "Oh by the way, Truman told me to tell you that he was happy to see you today."

"Okay." *I'd be happy, too, if . . . Oh well. It doesn't matter. Nothing does since Jordan died.*

CHAPTER ELEVEN

Sarah waited in the doctor's office for the nurse to call Braxton's name. "There's your mommy," she cooed to Braxton. This was his first visit with Dr. Bleu, the pediatrician. She sighed, wishing they could've been alone, but no, they had to be accompanied by a posse—the nurse, Georgia, and the newly assigned caseworker were due to arrive.

Georgia strolled in. Shatter-free glass doors sporting iron bars closed behind her. Josh had warned Sarah about this section of town. *Hold tight to your purse and don't lollygag in the parking lot. As soon as we can, we'll find a new doctor. But where?* Not many on the list the county had given her took medically fragile children.

"Hi, Georgia." Sarah had decided to be civil even though she was irritated.

"Give me Fat Boy." Georgia didn't speak to Sarah, she spoke at her.

Sarah felt a twinge of jealousy when she put Braxton into her arms. In the middle of her self-pity, she took a seat beside Luke, who was engrossed in a sports magazine, and draped her Eskimo-style coat over the baby's carrier. "You drove well today. Your dad would be proud."

"Why'd you wear that thing for? I told you it makes you look like a miniature elf."

She didn't respond. Josh had told her to choose her battles. She picked up a copy of *Country* magazine, thumbed through the pages, jotted down a sausage-egg casserole recipe, and stuffed it in her purse.

Luke nudged her in the side. "What's up her craw?"

Sarah hid her smile behind the magazine. Even though Luke could be a thorn in her side, he definitely was in tune with his surroundings.

She put her finger to her lips and mouthed. "Quiet."

"She should just be grateful you're taking care of her kid." He lowered his voice, but he could still be heard.

Sarah glanced over the top of her magazine. Georgia shot her a dirty look. *Strike two for me.*

The door swished open. A black woman of about fifty checked in with the receptionist. Her hair, highlighted in earthy shades of copper, extended to her shoulders, and her long teal jacket accented her slender form.

The receptionist nodded in their direction and the woman turned toward them. "I'm Miss Bond." Her fingers glinted when she extended her hand. "Are you Sarah?"

Sarah stood and returned the gesture. "I am."

"Braxton Toliver?" A nurse in pink scrubs called.

As they paraded into the exam room, Miss Bond said, "Miss Davis couldn't make it. She had an emergency."

Within minutes, the doctor entered with Braxton's chart and sat down. He read for a brief moment, then turned on his stool. "I'm Doctor Bleu." His eyes scanned the room."

Miss Bond introduced everyone, concluding with Braxton's mother, Georgia.

"Okay," Dr. Bleu said, then looked at Georgia. "Tell me about Braxton's medical history. What is his diagnosis? What medications is he taking?"

"Don't ask me 'bout nuttin'." Georgia pointed to Sarah. "There's the woman takin' care of him."

Dr. Bleu took Braxton's hand. "You certainly are a popular little guy. Has he rolled over yet?"

"Not yet," Sarah replied.

"Since he was so premature, you do realize he'll have to be seen by quite a few specialists?

Sarah nodded.

Dr. Bleu listened to Braxton's bowel sounds with the round silver end of a stethoscope. When he finished, he placed it around his neck like a necklace. "I'll write the referrals and my nurse will schedule the appointments. Is that okay with you, Mrs. Kiser?"

"Fine."

It wasn't fine, but she couldn't tell them her feelings about Jordan's experience and that this was the hospital where he had spent his last days.

Dr. Bleu handed his card to Sarah. "Call me if you have any questions." And then he slipped out the door.

For a moment, the silence gained weight. Sarah felt the lump forming in the back of her throat.

Finally, Miss Bond spoke. "Do you mind if I make a home visit this Wednesday?"

Sarah swallowed hard, hoping the lump would melt away. "That'll be fine."

"Do you know if Shirley will be coming?" Miss Bond asked.

Georgia leaned over to pick up Braxton's bottle that had dropped onto the floor, refusing to make eye contact with the caseworker. "I guess."

Miss Bond walked toward the door and flicked her head, indicating for Sarah to follow.

"I'll be back, Georgia." Sarah closed the door behind her and drew in a breath.

"It's a little tense in there," Miss Bond said.

"Georgia's not a happy camper."

Miss Bond smiled gently and Sarah felt her nervousness subside. "She agreed to put her baby into care until she could obtain a stable job and housing. And she was afraid to care for him since he has so many needs." She frowned. "I hope for her sake she can get the help she needs. Poor girl's been through a lot."

"I heard that her first baby died."

"Yes, that's true."

"How did he die?"

"We'll talk about it some other time, but Shirley said Georgia hasn't been the same since it happened."

"I see." Sarah smiled weakly. *What happened to this girl and her baby?*

"The agency is demanding that she go to therapy. Our psychiatrist plans to do a psychological evaluation this month, and depending on her test results, we may take temporary custody of the baby."

Sarah contemplated that for a moment. "What about his dad?"

"He's in prison." Miss Bond fidgeted with her files as she spoke.

"In prison? Why? What happened?"

"I don't have the answer to that question." Miss Bond shrugged. "And I'm not sure Braxton's grandmother, Shirley, can juggle her work schedule to care for him. Although we haven't ruled her out." Miss Bond closed the file. "How're things going?"

"Great. Braxton's very easy to love."

"I don't doubt that for a minute. He lives in your home; you feed him, clothe him, and take care of him—he's becoming part of your family."

Miss Bond's words were not enough to make Sarah hopeful. Her eyes tightened. "If his dad is in prison, and his mom can't take care of him, and the grandmother says no to taking him, is there a remote possibility I could keep him?"

"You know that the majority of the kids go home. Don't get your hopes up." Miss Bond's eyes were tender.

"You're right." Sarah cracked open the door and poked her head in the exam room. Georgia sat by the window, rocking Braxton. *What would the psyche evaluation prove? Could Georgia care for him long term? Sometimes life doesn't seem fair*, she thought, easing the door shut.

"Here you go." The office nurse handed her a pile of prescriptions and appointment cards. "The first appointment is at the pulmonary clinic at nine o'clock tomorrow morning. Do you know how to get there?"

"Um . . . unfortunately." When both women turned to stare at her, Sarah felt the blood surge to her face. She rubbed her cheeks.

"Are you okay?" Miss Bond asked.

"Maybe I'm getting the flu."

"Hope not," the nurse said. "If you have any problems, feel free to give us a call."

Miss Bond opened the door to Braxton's exam room. "We're ready."

After Georgia put Braxton's coat on him, they filed out of the room and down the hall. In the waiting room, Sarah stopped to gather her coat and Braxton's carrier.

"Mama?" Luke walked out of the bathroom, wiping his hands on his jeans. "Can I drive home?"

"Take Braxton's carrier with you. I'll be along in a minute." She handed him the keys.

Outside she felt a whirlwind of emotions begin to stir, just thinking about going back to River Stone Hospital. She pulled her gloves out of her coat pocket, wiggled her fingers into them, and walked to her SUV.

"Sarah? Wait!"

She stopped to face Miss Bond.

"Are you okay?"

"Yes. Why do you ask?"

"I get the feeling that something is wrong with the appointment at the pulmonary clinic."

"Oh." Sarah's voice choked with panic.

"I'm referring to the look you gave me and the nurse when you said that you 'unfortunately' know where the clinic is.' Your face turned as red as Rudolph's nose."

Sarah giggled, even though she felt jittery. Right then, she wanted to spill her guts and tell Miss Bond everything about Jordan's death. "I'm fine, really."

"Are you sure?" Miss Bond's voice was compassionate.

"Maybe we can discuss this during the home visit." Sarah knew one thing for sure, if she had to talk about Jordan, she didn't want to do it in a doctor's parking lot.

"Okay. I'll see you on Wednesday." Miss Bond turned toward her PT Cruiser.

"Miss Bond," Sarah called.

She turned. "Yes?"

"Are you coming to the appointment in the morning?" The mere thought of seeing the doctors who'd had Jordan's "utmost care at heart" made her stomach churn.

"I'll be there." Miss Bond hit the button on her key ring to unlock her Cruiser. "I normally attend the first few visits to get a feel for the case. Is that okay?"

Sarah felt a smile beginning to take form. "That'd be great."

By the time Sarah reached her vehicle, Luke had sat himself in the driver's seat and had the stereo cranked up to "What You Know" by *T.I.* His head swayed to the rap.

"Turn it down."

"Why? Braxton likes the thumpin'," Georgia interrupted, buckling Braxton's safety seat. "You old enough to drive, boy?"

"You old enough to have a baby?" Luke responded sarcastically.

Sarah wanted to say, "Keep your mouth shut," but the words didn't come out.

Georgia grinned. "What's your name, boy?"

"Luke. You got an issue with that, too?"

"Nah. I like men with attitudes. Stay cool whip."

Georgia leaned over, her full lips meeting Braxton's cheek. "Thanks for letting me warm up and take care of Fat Boy."

"Don't worry. I won't do anything to let you down." Sarah smiled.

Georgia snapped the car door shut and walked to the bus hub, her long braids swaying in a rhythmic motion with her hips, and Sarah stood in the breeze, collecting herself.

"There's that Bond woman." Luke turned down the volume.

Sarah opened her eyes to see Miss Bond leaning out of her car window. "Sarah? Did Georgia say something to upset you?"

"No,"—she exhaled a shaky laugh—"I'm fine." She hated stretching the truth, but hated more that she was deceiving herself.

"Okay. See you tomorrow." Miss Bond rolled up her window and drove away.

"Luke! You almost hit the curb, pay attention! And quit fumbling with the radio."

"Have a cow, why don't ya?" Luke plunged a hand through his hair. "She's pretty cool, Mama."

"Georgia?"

Luke grinned. "Yeah."

"I suspected you would like her. Two wanta-be adults with devastating pasts."

"Why'd you say that? Just 'cause I think she's cool?"

"You have a lot in common. She lost her son to death, just as you lost your brother, and now she's lost Braxton to the system. And she definitely has an attitude."

"No. She's nothing like me." Luke turned the corner. "Don't put me in the same classification with anyone. I know I have an attitude, but not like hers, no way. She has an attitude even I can't contend with."

"Let it go. I didn't mean it."

She did mean it. *Two strangers, two teens, two devastating bonds. Of course they would connect.* She wanted to help Luke, but once he found out that she'd been the one who decided to not have Jordan brought back to life with CPR, she feared he'd blame her for his brother's death. Would he understand that she'd stood by his bedside for eight months, watching the doctors' probe him until there was not one vein left to stick? Or would he cast his darts, assuming she'd given up? And she worried whether she'd be able to connect with Georgia.

"Don't I turn here?"

"At the next light. And what's up with cool whip?"

Luke grinned. "You gotta be up on the terms. It means to act cool." Luke whipped the SUV into the driveway, making a sudden stop before hitting the house.

"You have to ease into a driveway slow," Sarah scolded. "You almost hit your Dad's motorcycle."

"I'm fine. Take a chill pill." He cut the engine and sped out of the car before she could ask for help.

Sarah didn't budge; instead, she gazed out the cracked, smudged window, thinking about how much her world had changed in the past week. She lowered her head onto the headrest and her mind went back to her teens—a girl who knew only sunshine and laugher. Now, she had emerged as a "serious caretaker" and "super mom." A neighbor's voice broke into her thoughts.

"Just keep pedaling, honey," he called. But instead of pedaling, the girl let her Barbie bike coast down the driveway. Then the front wheel turned sharply, causing the bike to wobble. Her dad steadied the bike as he wrapped his arms around his daughter's waist. When she whimpered, he said, "Oh, sweetie, it's okay. If you fall off, just get back on and keep pedaling."

Sarah sighed and wondered wearily if Luke and Georgia could come to terms with what had happened in their lives. If they kept pedaling, would they, too, eventually get there?

Josh opened the driver's door. Before he uttered a word, she hid her face in the curve of his neck. Her tears fell onto his warm skin and mascara burned her eyes. He kissed the top of her head. "We better take Braxton inside before he gets chilly."

"Yeah, and me, too." She said between a sob and a laugh.

"Then we can talk. "Josh maneuvered Braxton out of his car seat, shouldered the diaper bag, apnea-heart monitor, portable oxygen, and walked into the house.

In the living room, Sarah lifted the fleece blanket off the couch, fanned it on the floor, and sat down. Josh lowered the baby into her arms.

"Can you grab his keys out of the diaper bag?" She sat Braxton between her legs and supported his back with her stomach, then placed the keys in his right hand. Immediately they went to his mouth. "Silly." She tickled his ribcage, causing him to squirm.

"Sarah, I know you're a chronic worrier. What happened? Is it Braxton? Did Georgia treat you bad?"

"No." She leaned back slightly, pulled the appointment card out of her jeans pocket, and handed it to him.

He glanced down to read it. "I see."

Exactly. The last place on earth I want to go. She blew raspberries on the baby's short neck. "Bubble, bubble," she said between kisses.

"Babe, you knew you'd have to go there, and now that you have an appointment, it's tormenting you. So I'll take him."

She pressed her lips hard, shook her head. "No. You can't miss work, and I'll have to face them again someday, anyway."

Josh copped a squat beside her and patted her thigh. "When you walk into that hospital, hold your head up high."

She nodded, her throat too dry to talk.

"You have a good mommy, Brax." Josh tickled his right foot, causing him to squirm again. This time his little hand opened and he dropped the keys. "Anything else going on?"

"Luke thinks Georgia is way cool."

"Did you expect anything less? They're both rebels."

"I just wish I could . . ." Sarah wanted to finish her sentence, but she choked.

"Fix their broken hearts. You can't keep doing this to yourself. They're teenagers, or at least I think Georgia is. She looked to be about seventeen or eighteen."

"Nineteen. I saw it on Braxton's chart."

"Okay. So now you have two teenagers that have to come to terms with what has gone on in their lives. Even if you could, you can't fix it for them."

There was truth in his words. She'd fix the war on terror if she could.

When the baby's eyelids started to droop, Josh said, "I'll lay him down. You relax."

Instead of relaxing, Sarah sat in the puddle of light streaming through the window. Maybe Josh was right. She had to believe that if she held tight to her faith, as she'd done in the past, she could definitely weather another hurricane.

CHAPTER TWELVE

On the drive to the hospital, Sarah felt a wave of panic sweep through her. Most people that traveled Route 210 thought of stopping off at Gabby's Garden or Grandma's Café for a down-home cooked meal. There were other places, too, that brought the route to life—the bowling alley, chains of restaurants, and Wally World.

"Wally World would be fun," she said aloud, trying to pull away from her panic, and making a mental note to stop on the way home to get more diapers. Then her thoughts shifted to Braxton. She thought about the joy that he was already bringing to her family. Everyone was content, except for Luke.

In the hospital parking lot, she shouldered the diaper bag, portable oxygen and monitor, then picked up the car seat with the baby tucked inside, and walked toward the sliding glass doors.

"Wait!"

She turned to see Georgia approaching with her freshly braided weaves and overstuffed jacket.

"How's Fat Boy?" Georgia asked, then added, "Girl, you looked zonked."

"I managed to get some sleep." Sarah yawned and went inside the hospital.

"I don't understand why ya'll gotta be getting' my boy up all night."

How in the world can I make her understand? "I have to follow the doctor's orders." Sarah explained the three-hour feeding schedule, the beeping monitor that kept her up at night. By the end of the speech, they had reached the registration desk. She sat the car seat on the floor, looked at Georgia and said, "Do you understand?" Georgia didn't acknowledge understanding of anything. She was too busy checking out her newly manicured nails.

After Sarah registered Braxton, a nurse escorted them to a small exam room. "Who wants to hold him while I get his blood pressure?"

"I will." Sarah unzipped his jacket and lifted him into her arms.

The nurse wrapped the blood pressure cuff around his ankle and pressed the button on the machine. The cuff deflated and the nurse wrote the recording in his chart. Before closing the door, she said, "The doctor will be in soon," and left them all alone.

Sarah hoped the doctor wouldn't take too long before he examined Braxton because she didn't feel comfortable with Georgia, and now wondered if she should've even agreed to let her come to her home.

Someone knocked, and the door swung open. "Sarah, good to see you," Dr. Mustar said.

She forced a smile. "You, too."

"I understand you're Braxton's foster mother?"

"Yes." The only thing that had changed since she'd last seen him was he'd gotten wire- rimmed glasses.

He peered over his glasses at Georgia. "And you're his mother?"

"Duh." Georgia propped her elbow on the edge of the sink, resting her forefinger above her right eyebrow.

The doctor didn't react to Georgia's inappropriate behavior. Before he opened the baby's chart, the nurse reentered. "The grandmother and caseworker are here."

Miss Bond extended her hand to the doctor. "I'm Tina Bond, and this is Shirley, the baby's grandmother."

"Any kin to James Bond?" the doctor teased.

"Yes. That's my brother." She laughed. "Wouldn't that be nice?"

The doctor opened the baby's file and studied it. Finally he said, "Braxton has bronchopulmonary dysplasia. Most premature babies develop this disease because their lungs were immature at birth." He glanced at Georgia. "In simple terms, it's scarring of the lungs. Most times, they require breathing treatments. Has he needed any?"

"Only a few," Sarah replied.

"That's good."

Sarah didn't mind seeing this doctor. It was the monster across the hallway she feared bumping into.

"Can you place the baby up here?" The doctor patted the exam table, then took the stethoscope off his neck and listened to Braxton's heart and lungs. Next, he unsnapped the baby's sleeper and tapped his fingers like a drum on Braxton's tummy. When he finished, he looked at Sarah. "His lungs are clear, and I'm going to discontinue his oxygen since his saturations are one-hundred percent."

When the doctor said this, Sarah glanced at Georgia, who sat with a blank stare. She had hoped that Georgia would come to terms with the unfortunate situation and partake in the care of her baby.

The doctor continued his exam—checking the baby's ears, nose, and throat, then he snapped his sleeper and handed him to Sarah. This warmed her heart to see how passionate the doctor felt about his patients. How many times had he missed having supper with his own family to care for sick children? And why couldn't all doctors be like him? He jotted a few notes in Braxton's chart then closed it. "I'll see him back for follow-up in three months. Sarah, can I speak with you privately?"

Sarah handed the baby to Shirley and followed him out the door to the desk. He pulled her to the side and whispered, "I admire you for being able to come back here."

She took Josh's advice and kept her head held high.

"I heard some awful things about Dr. Aspen after he left the hospital."

She gulped in air, accidentally swallowing her gum, then coughed. "Y—yes, he definitely made a mess of things."

"You're not alone. He messed up a lot of lives." He handed the chart to the nurse. "You know Braxton's at a high risk for aspiration pneumonia?"

"I realize that."

"I'm ordering a suction machine and writing a referral for a gastroenterologist. He weighs eight pounds, but he needs a doctor to monitor his weight and reflux medications."

"I appreciate the extra effort." Even as she said those words, she felt the panic sweep through her. A gastroenterologist meant she'd have to face the monster.

"I'll have my nurse schedule the appointment," he said and walked to the nurse's station.

Sarah stared across the hall. Residents stood in their white coats, forming a circle. Her eyes scanned each face, looking for Dr. Porfor. It bothered her that the doctor kept sending Jordan home when the doctor should've admitted him to the hospital. And it angered her that when Dr. Porfor had discovered Dr. Aspen's undeniable medical neglect,--that the shunt needed to be replaced in the ventricle of Jordan's brain—he didn't bother to tell her. His gaze locked with Sarah's, and immediately he broke away from the circle and escaped into his office.

Sarah's heart fluttered. She felt as if she'd just run the hundred-yard dash in less than ten seconds. At that moment, she wanted to go after him and say, "Why didn't you tell me Jordan's brain was under pressure so I could've transferred him to another hospital?" Instead she did nothing. She didn't want to feel like a bird with a broken wing again. She'd only recently begun to fly. Abruptly she turned, almost colliding with the nurse. "I'll call you to schedule Braxton's appointment when I get home."

"Are you sure? This will only take a minute."

"I have to check my calendar." Sarah was sure of one thing—she had to leave *now*. Sure she'd begun to fly again, but when she'd seen Dr. Porfor, the anger had rekindled. She hurried back to the room and thrust open the door. "Georgia! We need to go."

"Is everything okay?" Miss Bond asked.

"Yes. I . . ." Sarah pressed her hands to her flushed cheeks.

Shirley intervened. "Are you sick, dear?" Then she proceeded to put the baby's coat on.

"No. I'm fine." Sarah shook her head, fought against the tears, waiting while Shirley buckled Braxton in the car seat. Then hoisting the bags to her shoulders, she said, "I'll see you all on Wednesday." She hurried out the door.

"Wait up," Georgia called.

Sarah didn't lose pace. She fled out the sliding glass door and went straight to her SUV. After she strapped in the baby, she closed the door, and then found Georgia staring at her.

"Wanta tell me waz up?"

Sarah stared at the sliding glass doors of the hospital where Miss Bond and Shirley stood talking. "No."

"I get the feelin' that hospital gives you the creeps 'cause of Jordan."

Sarah felt surprised by Georgia's interest. "It's nothing."

Georgia brushed past her and opened the door. She planted her glossed lips onto Braxton's cheek and clipped shut the door. "You ain't foolin' me, girl. I'll see you Wednesday."

On the drive home, the rain was so heavy the wipers barely kept up. She turned on her hazard lights, and even thought about pulling to the side of the road to let the rain pass like other responsible drivers, but changed her mind. *Oh well, Josh can go get the diapers.* By the time she turned onto her street, the rain beat down even harder, if that were possible. She parked in the driveway, and through the downpour, ran inside the house. "Luke," she shouted, "can you help me?"

Silence.

❧✣❧

Luke would be eighteen soon and there was nothing his dad could say to him that would make him walk the straight and narrow. He strutted through the yard to the school. When he came to Stucco Hall, he caught a glimpse of Mike. "Hey ya, Mike."

Mike grinned. "Dude, you're grounded and suspended, remember?"

"What my dad doesn't know won't hurt him."

"How'd you escape?"

"Mama's at the hospital with that kid, so she'll be stressed by the time she leaves, and you know what that means."

"*Shopping.*" Mike laughed, showing off his million-watt smile.

"Any chance you could skip out early?"

"I never thought you'd ask. Wait at Community. If I don't show in twenty, go home."

Luke crossed the street to Community and stood outside the gazebo. Bunches of kids were huddled by the old metal bleachers, joking around and smoking cigarettes. Eleven minutes passed, and Mike hadn't shown. Luke cocked his head to see him finally crossing the street between the parallel yellow lines, but Mike wasn't the only thing he saw. *What the heck is he up to?* he wondered, as his dad whipped his truck into the parking lot.

"Holy smoke, it's your dad," a girl said, wearing more makeup than Gene Simmons.

"I didn't know your dad was an officer." A student jerked at his leather jacket and tossed his cigarette butt. "Let's split."

"He's not," Luke replied, "he works in a prison."

"Too much for me, dude." The student with three nose piercings said.

Josh climbed out of his truck and closed the door behind him. "Mike? Why aren't you in school?"

Mike's eyes widened. "Umm . . . I'm sick."

"You are? Does your aunt know that you skipped out?"

"I bet she will now," Luke smarted off. "Let the lecture begin."

Josh took four steps toward Luke, then pointed his finger at him. "And you snuck out when your mother went to the hospital. Didn't you?"

"Dad! Why don't you just beat me with a cane and get it over with?"

"Excuse me! When did you plan to come home? After you got drunk?"

"I wasn't drinking."

Josh gave him a stern look. "But you weren't following the house rules either." Luke couldn't help but notice every time his dad said those words his index finger inched closer to his face.

"I only wanted to see Mike."

"But you're grounded!" Josh lectured.

Luke didn't respond.

"Mike, you best get home or back to school," Josh said. "Luke, get in the truck, *now*."

Just like a parent to screw everything up, Luke thought. He gave Mike a high five, then joined his dad in the truck.

Josh drove to the school parking lot and cut the engine. For a moment, the only sound came from the cars racing up and down the road, even though the posted speed limit was twenty-miles per hour. Finally Josh said, "I want you to hit me, hard."

"What?" *He's lost his mind.*

"Hit. Me. Luke." Josh gritted his teeth.

"Why?"

"Because I've obviously done something wrong."

"No, Dad. Stop. You're a good parent."

"Obviously not." Josh stared out at the baseball diamond. "Do you realize my whole identity is wrapped up in being yours and Zack's dad, and your mom's husband?"

See what you're doing? The little voice inside chided him.

It's God's fault I'm messed up, so shut up.

"You're a good parent, Dad."

"Then why do bad things keep happening?"

Luke's gaze met the floor. "I'm stupid."

"No, you're not." Josh leaned over the console and lifted Luke's head. "Look out there and tell me what you see."

"A ball field."

"And what else?"

Luke swallowed hard. "Coach said the scouts are coming to the tournaments this year. 'They'll be impressed with your pitching and batting average, and your grades will get you the scholarship you deserve.'" Luke mocked Coach Spear's words. "Then he patted me on the back for pitching a seven-inning game two times that week—with two shut outs. I know if I try, I can land a career pitching in the majors, but . . ."

"What do you see now?" Josh put his hand on top of Luke's.

Luke pushed away his dad's hand. "Nothing, I don't see a thing."

"You don't? Where're you going to be five years from now?"

Five years. I can't see past today. Luke shrugged.

"You going to quit school? Quit ball?"

Luke didn't know. His life felt like a jigsaw puzzle with half the pieces missing. "You think just because you work in a prison you know everything. You're not perfect! Not by a long shot!"

"I never said I was. Everyone has moments in their lives that carve pictures, good or bad— heartache, pain, loneliness. The list could go on, but you don't want to get so far out there that you land a stay in jail, or worse. You're a good kid. You can't control what's happened. None of us can."

Luke sighed. "I have to find my own way, Dad."

"I want what's best for you, Son."

"I know, Dad," he said, and finally surrendered to his father's warm embrace.

CHAPTER THIRTEEN

Luke lay on his bed, staring at the ceiling fan, watching it whirl round and round. He drew in a deep breath then exhaled, trying to squash his anger. Earlier he passed by Zack's room. Through the door, he'd heard Zack asking God to forgive him for being selfish. That annoyed Luke.

Selfish? Ha. Luke gritted his teeth and clenched his fist. "You're the one that's selfish, God. Just had to have Jordan, didn't ya?"

He waited, but no response came. He sat up in his bed and stared at the one-eyed stuffed monkey—the one he and Jordan had played with. The monkey looked as if it were staring back. Luke chuckled. He wasn't sure how the monkey lost its eye, but he guessed it'd happened on Jordan's last hospital stay. He recalled waving it above Jordan's head, then the monkey flew out of his hand and whacked its head on the metal bed rail. A day later his dad said, "This monkey only has one eye." The eye never turned up. Everyone assumed— since the eye was amber in color—the housekeeper must've thought it was a broken vial of medication, swept it up, and tossed it into the trash. Not that it really mattered.

Zack appeared in the doorway. "Can I come in?"

Luke pulled the monkey into his lap. "Why?"

"I don't have to. It's just . . ."

Don't forget you have another brother, Mike had said. Luke rubbed his finger over the monkey's peach-colored face. "Come in."

"What'd you do today?"

"Nothin'."

Zack sprawled out on his floor. "I heard you yelling at God."

"And?"

"Do you ever wonder if Mom and Dad asked God if he cared that Jordan was sick?"

"Nope. Guess I never really thought of it that way."

Zack sighed. "Everyone wants to blame God, but it's not his fault."

For a few minutes, neither one of them spoke. Finally, Luke said, "I think God gave up on me and is busy trying to convert others. And if he is a compassionate God, he wouldn't have taken Jordan."

Zack positioned himself Indian style. "When Jesus was told that Lazarus had been dead four days, he cried because he felt sorry for what Mary and Martha were going through."

"But he could get over it, because he's God."

Silence.

"The day we buried Jordan, I literally wanted to scream, but I had to be strong. I even told Mama that Jordan's death would get easier, but you know what I was wishing?"

Zack bit down on his lip, listening.

"I was wishing God would shrink me to the size of a leaf and let me float right on up into heaven with Jordan."

"I know you miss him," Zack said. "It hurt me to watch Mom and Dad cry." His lowered lip quivered. "There's something I haven't even told them."

Luke waited for Zack to get better control, then he said, "What?"

"I write him a letter once a month."

Luke raised his eyebrows. "About?"

"I keep him informed about our family." Zack chewed his thumbnail.

"Quit bitin' your nails. You're gonna get an appendicitis attack." Luke drummed his finger on the side of his bed. "Can I read one?"

Zack nodded, then went to his room.

"Boys! Pizza's here!" Josh hollered up the steps.

"Just a minute, Dad," Luke shouted.

Zack returned with the letter. His hands trembled as he handed it to Luke.

Luke slowly unfolded the letter and read silently,

Dear Jordan,

I was selfish for wanting mommy back. I didn't want you to die for that to happen. Tell Jesus Luke needs him 'cause he's drowning. Luv, Zack

Luke refolded the letter and handed it back to Zack, his hands shaking. If he cut loose, his tears would fill their fish tank. Yet still, they fell. He mustered enough strength to take a deep breath and latch hold of Zack's hand. "Are you gonna be a preacher someday?"

Zack chuckled and tucked the letter into his jeans pocket. "If I get a scholarship, I'm heading to Ohio State."

"Go to Michigan." Luke punched him in the left shoulder.

"Ouch! That hurt." Zack rubbed his bicep, grinning. "I'm an Ohio State fan till death do us part."

"I still think you're going to be a preacher."

"I'm only fifteen. I think right now God just wants me to graduate and find a job."

Luke chuckled. "I think your official office is set before you, buddy."

"Amazing." Zack shook his head. "You do pay attention in church."

Luke grinned.

"Busted," they spoke at once.

Zack turned to leave the room.

"Hey, Zack?"

"Yeah?"

"Thanks for loving me."

"Who said I love you?" Zack teased.

❧

Sarah set the table with leftover paper plates from Luke's sixteenth birthday party, while Josh finished feeding Braxton. The boys thundered down the stairs.

"How many pizzas did you order?" Zack plopped into a chair.

"Three. We know you can eat one by yourself," Josh teased, placing the baby in his bouncy seat.

"He eats all that food and don't gain a pound. It's not fair I got stuck with Mom's genes," Luke complained.

"What's wrong with my genes?" Sarah put her hands on her hips.

Luke grinned. "Because you're stacked like the Campbell's Soup Kid."

Josh chuckled at that.

"It's not like I sit around eating bonbons all day."

"Honey, no one is saying you're fat."

"Just a happy magic marker," Zack chimed in, causing Sarah to grin.

Luke loaded his plate with pizza and sat down. "Hurry up. I'm starved."

The rest of them joined Luke and bowed their heads. When Zack finished saying the blessing, he snatched three pieces of pizza from the cardboard box. "What movie did you get?"

Josh sprinkled red peppers on his pizza. "*Remember The Titans.*"

Luke grinned. "Slam dunkin'. That movie's tight."

"But it's been out for eons," Zack said.

Sarah sprinkled grated cheese on her pizza. "How was school today, Zack?"

"Okay."

"You haven't told Chad about Braxton have you?" Luke asked.

"He lives up the street, so I'm pretty sure he's already seen him. And he is my best friend, in case you forgot."

Luke let out a dramatic huff. "Great. Now I'm gonna be dead meat when Mouse finds out we're raising a black kid."

"Like I said before, there's nothing wrong with a white family raising a black child," Sarah said.

Luke rolled his eyes. "So you say."

"So I say."

The phone's shrill ring caused Sarah to jump. She raced to answer it before it woke up the baby. "Hello."

"How's Fat Boy?" Georgia asked.

Sarah grinned. "He's doing well. How're you?"

"I got a letter from Braxton's daddy. He's bustin' early."

"As in going AWOL?"

Georgia laughed. "Nah. Girl, he busted up his ex-girl's face, that's why he got put in, but he's gettin' out early. Ain't that off the hook?"

"Wow."

"Just thought you'd wanta know. That Bond woman called today, and we're havin' a meeting at the agency when he's out."

Sarah wondered if she'd have to attend.

"Tell Fat Boy I love him."

"I will." Sarah placed the phone into the cradle. "That's wild," she said, going back into the dining room.

"What?" Josh tossed his paper plate into the trashcan.

"Braxton's dad is getting out of prison early."

Luke's ears perked up. "What's he in for?"

"He battered his ex-girlfriend again and broke parole."

"And they're letting him out early? I hope Braxton never goes home," Luke said.

Sarah and Josh exchanged smiles.

"We better hurry up and watch this movie because we got school tomorrow." Zack dropped his plate in the trash.

Halfway into the movie, Luke said, "See what I mean? People can be so racist, but look at the Titans. They overcame. Why can't everyone be like that?"

Sarah sighed. She knew how Luke felt after watching the movie. *Will some people ever realize that it's the soul of a man that really matters?*

CHAPTER FOURTEEN

Luke spotted Jonathan, Mouse's friend, through his dad's truck window in front of the Adrian Hall entrance. *Now they'll tease me because my dad drives me to school.*

"Later, Dad." He opened the passenger's door.

"Steer clear of trouble."

"Yeah." Luke snapped the door shut behind him, watched his dad's taillights fade. Then he crossed the street to Community, strutting through the grass, and kicking the yellow cigarette butts that cluttered the ground.

"Well if it isn't the loser." Mouse clamped a cigarette between his teeth.

Luke shrunk back to the rebel he'd created—everyone expected a bad mouth and a just-mess-with-me attitude. *Go ahead. I'll waylay you again,* he thought.

"Luke, over here!" Mike shouted.

Luke strutted past Mouse, hoping he would run his mouth. Luke hadn't had any alcohol this morning, and he wanted to hit something hard to calm his nerves. When he came to the tree where Mike stood, he tugged at the sleeves on his jersey and stared back at Mouse, unblinking, almost smiling.

"Keep your cool, dude," Mike said when Mouse went to join his want-to-be-jocks at the gazebo.

"Hey, Luke! Ready for round two?" Mouse sneered.

"Get out of here, Mouse," Mike intervened.

"Get out of here, Mouse. What's he going to do, beat me up?" Mouse covered his mouth and fake-laughed.

"Grow up, Mouse," Mike spouted back.

Mouse walked away, holding his hand to the small of his back, middle finger up.

"Let's split before I bust him up," Mike said.

At the school entrance, Mike tapped Luke's left shoulder. "Stay cool. I miss having ya at school, bro."

Luke threw his backpack over his left shoulder. "Personally, I can't wait till these days are long gone."

He scurried to his trigonometry class before the bell rang. He had just pulled his book from his backpack when Mr. Pierce told him Mrs. Frenchie wanted to see him in her office.

He didn't feel like talking to her today. *Why do adults try and probe your head like a scientist with a microscope?* When he came to her office door, he knocked.

"Come in."

He opened the door and seated himself in front of his counselor. While he waited for her to close a file, he studied the picture on her desk, sitting in a silver frame with glistening teardrops glued to its outer edges. Luke wondered, if the guy with his arm slung around his counselor's shoulder was her boyfriend or husband. If the baby she held was her niece or her kid. Regardless, the three of them were smiling.

Ain't life just a bowl of cherries?

He watched her shuffle the papers around on her desk, and noticed the dark circles under her eyes. *Man she's hot.* The minute he thought it, he knew it wasn't right. He didn't want to be accused of fortification, or whatever God's people called it. And besides, now days a student and a counselor having an affair would get her locked up. He needed her here, maybe because she cared, probably because she was as good looking as *Kristen Stewart.*

She looked up. "How's it going?"

"Considering it's my first day back, it's all good."

She smiled. "Did you have a restful night's sleep?"

"Yep. I slept like a baby." Even though he had used that phrase, he couldn't help but wonder why, because a baby woke up every four hours wanting to be fed, or in Braxton's case, every two or three.

"Are you planning to go to conditioning this week?"

"Depends on my grades."

"I spoke with your teachers, and from what I gather, if you did all the extra credit assignments, then your grades should be more than sufficient." She smiled, tapping her pen on a folder. "Coach Spears reports that you are one of the finest pitchers he's ever seen in our school district. I'm proud of you."

He nodded.

"Have you seen Tim Mouser today?"

"Nope." He couldn't tell her of the morning incident. His dad would flip out if he found out he'd been to Community.

"If you do and he says one word, please tell me."

"Yep." He shifted in his seat uneasily.

"Do you have any thoughts about what you want to do after graduation?"

He shrugged. "Still undecided."

"I understand that right now you feel lost, but you'll find your way. I don't mean to prod, but do you feel like talking about Jordan?"

He hesitated for a moment, then he said, "I just want to know if he suffered. Do you think that's too much to ask?"

She paused, as if searching for the right words. Finally she said, "No. But I've told you in the past, I think your parents are only trying to protect you." She wrote something on the inner flap of the folder then continued. "I learned from your mom a couple months back that he died from the neglect of a doctor."

"Yep." Luke shifted again.

"And you didn't get to say good-bye. That bothers you a lot."

He nodded, feeling the knot in his gut tighten. "Yep. I wanta know what happened before he . . ." Luke couldn't finish. The images of Jordan giggling resurfaced. *I deserve to know. He was my brother.*

"Talk to your mom about this. Tell her you want to know."

"I have. She won't tell me. I mean, I know it had to be bad, but I just feel that if she'd tell me, I could move on."

Mrs. Frenchie sighed. "Will it bring him back?"

He shook his head. "No. But . . ."

"Could you handle whatever it is she's not sharing?"

He shrugged. "Don't know."

"Then let me give you a word of caution. Before you ask for something you're not positive you can handle, make sure you can first. I know it's hard, Luke. And I can't tell you how to feel. But I'm here for you."

"Okay." He smothered a grin.

"Are you reading the book I gave to you?"

"I'm almost done."

She smiled, flashing her pearly whites. "Good. There's something else I want to give to you." She handed him a packet. "Just something to think about."

Luke glanced briefly at the packet. "Armed Forces? Me?"

"It's another option for you to think about. A lot of students I've counseled have opted for the military, and they've done well."

"Thanks." He stood up and swiped his backpack off the floor in one motion. "See you later." Outside the door he paused. *How did she know I was thinking about joining the Army?*

The school bell rang. He pushed his way through the cluster of kids to the outside. One more class and the day would be over. The sun broke through the clouds, causing Luke to squint. Shielding his eyes, he gazed upward, wondering if God had put his counselor in his life to help him. *But why? I'm not a saint like Zack. Sinner, yeah.* Today his mama was gonna tell him every detail of his brother's death. He was ready to hear the truth. And no matter what she had to say, it couldn't be worse than losing him.

⤜✦⤛

Mrs. Frenchie leaned back in her chair, replaying the conversation with Luke in her mind. She was glad her parents had been there to help her when her life, just like a snow globe turned upside down, had been shaken, leaving her feeling like Luke— alone and scared.

How many students had she helped through the years? Two-hundred kids, three-hundred? She'd lost track. She glanced at her watch. Ten minutes till her meeting with another student to talk about his recent life changes—his father going to jail for beating up his mother. She sighed, wishing she could take away all their pain and toss it into the ocean.

CHAPTER FIFTEEN

Sarah glanced at her watch. Georgia and Shirley were due to arrive and this thought caused her anxiety to climb the chart to a ten. After the incident at the doctor's office, she wondered if she and Georgia would ever be able to bond.

The doorbell rang. "They're here," she said to the baby and opened the door. "Come on in." Georgia and Shirley stepped inside and removed their coats. Sarah hung them up in the hallway closet as Shirley slid off her shoes, placing them next to the heap under the banister.

"You didn't have to take off your shoes."

Shirley grinned. "I do it at my house, so what's good for the goose is good for the gander."

"I appreciate that."

"Man! Dat girl done messed up my nails. Gonna call her tomorrow 'bout this messed up job, "Georgia said, changing the subject, and fanning her fingers.

Sarah's eyebrows scrunched. "Why is all that color running together?"

Shirley laughed. "I've done told that chile for years to stop letting just anyone touch her hair and nails, but Georgia's got a mind of her own."

Georgia rolled her eyes; put her hands on her hips. "Supposed to be a marbleized French manicure, but I think she done used the brush with acetone on it."

"Who did it?" Sarah asked.

Georgia exhaled a dramatic huff. "Some girl my sister knows. Said she knew what she was doin'. I think she needs to find a new profession or somethin'."

Sarah giggled. "Come on, Braxton's in here." She led them into the kitchen. "After he eats, I'll teach you his range of motion exercises, and if we have enough time, I'll teach you the apnea-monitor." She glanced at the clock on the stove and frowned. "Miss Bond should've been here by now." To Shirley she said, "I made a fresh pot of coffee. Would you like a cup?"

"I'd love a cup. Thank you." Shirley bent down and lifted Braxton into her arms. The shrill of the phone ringing caused the baby to jump and whimper. "It's okay, baby." Shirley whispered, patting his back.

Sarah reached into the cupboard and pulled out two apple-themed mugs and a glass. "Georgia? Would you mind answering it?"

Georgia rolled her eyes, but obeyed. After she hung up, she said, "That was Miss Bond. Said she'd be late. Had an emergency or somethin'. She's probably out breakin' up another family."

Sarah filled the two mugs with coffee, ignoring the comments Georgia made about the caseworker, "We'll use the free time to get acquainted, then."

Shirley rested her chin on the top of Braxton's head. "Umm, you smell good. You wash his hair in Kiwi shampoo?"

"I did." Sarah quickly glanced at the countertop. "You hungry? I have doughnuts and coffee cake."

"No thanks. I had my bran muffin and prunes this mornin', and Georgia had scrambled eggs and bacon."

Sarah warmed the baby's bottle. To Georgia she said, "You mind feeding him?"

"Me?" Her eyes widened.

"Why not?" Shirley asked, handing her the baby. "Do it like they taught you at the hospital. He's just like any other baby; you just got to take it slow."

"You can sit on the sofa and feed him. It's probably more comfortable."

In the living room, Georgia plunked down on the couch. Sarah poked the nipple between Braxton's lips, let the plastic bottle slide into Georgia's hand. She watched him smack and sigh. "Would you like tea of coffee "

"Soda pop." Georgia glared at Sarah as if she expected nothing less, then added, "Can you change the channel to cartoons?"

Sarah changed the channel, then feeling comfortable Georgia was feeding the baby the proper way, head elevated, she joined Shirley in the kitchen.

"I worry about my daughter," Shirley whispered. "She ain't been right since Jaron died. And now with Braxton being born with medical issues . . ."

"Don't worry. I'll do my best to help her." Sarah added creamer and sugar to her coffee.

"I really appreciate you opening your home to us." Shirley filled her mug, then joined Sarah at the table.

While they nursed their coffee, laughter drifted into the kitchen. Sarah set down her cup, went to the living room, and set the glass of soda on a chipped coaster. "What's so funny?"

"These cartoons crack me up!" Georgia proceeded to explain the names and story line of the shows she watched—*Rug Rats*, *Jimmy Neutron*, and *Dora the Explorer*—and my favorite is *Sponge Bob*. He has a friend that acts all stupid and moves in different shapes and thinks he can play the clarinet." She stopped laughing. "Where's my soda pop?"Sarah gestured toward the table.

"Can you burp him, Mama?"Georgia hollered.

Shirley entered the room, lips pressed tight as she extended her arms and took the baby.

"Ain't ya'll got any ice?"

"Georgia," Shirley said, leaning back into a stack of pillows. "You need to treat Sarah with respect."

Sarah went to the kitchen to get ice and overheard Shirley scolding her daughter.

"Sarah opened her home to help us learn how to care for Braxton. Now you need to act like you got some manners."

Sarah smiled as she pushed the glass against the fridge's ice dispenser. Five cubes splashed into the cup, reminding her of her childhood days when she had put a penny in the round glass jar and waited for the colorful candy to drop. Back in the living room, she handed the glass to Georgia.

"Thank ya," Georgia said, not bothering to make eye contact.

"Um . . . would you like to see pictures of Jordan while we wait for Miss Bond?"Sarah asked.

Shirley nodded. "That'd be nice."

Sarah went upstairs and pulled the pictures out of her

grandmother's trunk. When she returned, Shirley and Georgia parted, leaving Sarah a place to sit between them. She sat down, placed the scrapbook in her lap, and opened it to the first page.

Georgia gasped. "Wow! He looks like Braxton when he was in the preemie unit. He's a cutie. Isn't he, Mama?"

Shirley smiled. "Yes, he is."

Georgia glanced at each picture, pausing at times, as if she had some memories of her own to reflect upon. When Georgia paused at the pictures of Jordan in the incubator, Sarah remembered slipping her hand through the rubber opening on the side of the plastic bed and latching onto Jordan's hand, praying, *please live for Mommy*.

"When did Jordan die?" Georgia asked, interrupting her thoughts.

"In December." She wanted to say days before Christmas, but she lost her voice.

"Umm, girl . . .," Shirley said. "I know that must've been hard."

"We have a lot in common." Sarah placed her hand over Georgia's, surprised when she didn't pull away. "We've both had premature babies, and our children died. We can work through our grief together."

Georgia turned her gaze back to the scrapbook, and pointed to a picture with her messed up marbleized nail. "Is that a question mark on his head?"

"My Georgia has a way of saying things." Shirley snickered.

"That was Dr. Baker's trademark he left on every kid after a shunt revision." Sarah laughed.

"He could've cut a straight line," Georgia said.

"How did Jaron die? If you don't mind me asking?"

Georgia clasped her hands in her lap, then blew out a breath. "I don't want to talk about it."

"That's fine. I'm sorry you've had a lot to deal with." Sarah swallowed hard, contemplating her next question, almost afraid to ask, but she had to get it out. Finally she said, "Can I ask you another question?

"What?"

"Is Braxton's daddy violent toward you?" Sarah tried to keep her expression neutral.

"Nope," Georgia answered fast. "But I can't believe they're lettin' him out of prison early."

Sarah bit down on her lower lip. *Could Georgia care for Braxton with all of his needs? Would Children Services give a child to a father who was an abuser?*

Frustration, pity, and fear lumped in her throat.

Shirley massaged the baby's back. "How come you never told me he was gettin' out early?"

"'Cause you get upset every time I tell you somethin', Mama."

"You should've told me." Shirley shook her head.

Sarah changed the subject. "I'll show you how to work the apnea-monitor. If that's okay."

"Fine." Georgia scooted to the edge of the couch.

Sarah placed the scrapbook on the dining room table. When she returned, she sat on the floor and pulled the monitor into her lap. With the beeping lights facing outward, she pointed to the machine. "This green light indicates his respirations—how many breaths he takes in. This green light shows how many times his heart beats." She paused to look at Georgia and Shirley. They were listening intently. "So if the alarm sounds, first, assess him to see if he is breathing, then glance at the monitor to see if the red light is showing lack of heartbeats, or apnea, meaning, he's not taking in breaths. Does that make sense?"

"I can't learn all that medical stuff. By the time he comes home, he'll be off all that junk anyway." Georgia thrust herself backward into the couch.

"It's a lot of information, but we'll learn it together," Shirley said.

Sarah sensed Georgia's frustration. "How about we try range of motion?"

"I guess." Georgia sighed.

Sarah fanned a blanket on the floor. Shirley laid Braxton on it. Securing his right elbow with the palm of her right hand, Sarah moved his forearm toward his bicep. "See how I did that?"

Georgia offered no response.

"I see," Shirley said.

"And you have to massage his palms, so his fingers don't invert."

"Girl! I can't do this." Georgia placed her crossed arms against her chest.

Sarah felt like she was teaching a ten-year-old child. "You can't, or you won't try?"

"Humph!" Georgia's crossed arms heaved up, then down.

"Which is it?" Sarah asked.

Georgia leaned over and picked up Braxton. Pressing her back against the couch, she located the remote with her free hand and cranked up the volume to the television.

Sarah gave Shirley a reassuring smile. "Guess we'll try next time.

Let's finish drinking our coffee, while we wait for Miss Bond."

❦

"So," Shirley began, the steam from the coffee mug wreathing her face. "Do you have other children?"

"Yes. Luke is seventeen and very defiant. And Zack's fifteen."

"Luke's defiant like my Georgia?"

Sarah wanted to say "not exactly," but instead she said, "Sort of."

"Girl . . . Georgia's had an attitude since she was a little girl. When she was five, I was in the kitchen deep frying okra and called for her to come down the stairs. Of course she didn't answer, so I called to her again." Shirley paused to sip her coffee. "I went to the bottom of the steps to call her again and found her leaning against the wall. So I told her I'd appreciate it if she'd respond when I called her name. I'll have you to know that chile put her hands on her hips, looks me dead in the eye, and said, 'I heard you the first time.'"

Sarah laughed.

"Oooh. I was so mad. I wanted to twist her lips. I guess I just worry she'll say something to the caseworker to make her look bad."

"Oh I understand." Sarah could empathize with Shirley, because Luke seemed to be just like Georgia---defiant and oppositional. "Do you have other children?"

Shirley clasped her hands under her chin. "Nah. The good Lord blessed me with one chile. And Georgia was a handful, you know . . . my challenge. I never really wanted any more after I had her."

"Nothing wrong with that." Sarah picked up her cup to take another sip.

"Does Braxton have any of the doctors your boy had?"

Sarah set down her cup. "Yes, the gastro doctor. I'm afraid of how I'll respond when I see him."

"Well, I don't know the whole story, but I gather it isn't good. Just don't let those people bring you down. You seem like a nice lady who's had more than her share." Shirley finished her coffee.

Even though Sarah didn't know Shirley that well, she was beginning to like her a lot. "Can I get you another cup?"

Shirley pushed back her chair. "I'd like some water, but I'll get it."

The doorbell rang, and Sarah went to open the door.

"I'm sorry, I'm late," Miss Bond said. "I had an emergency with one of my other cases."

"I understand. Come on in." Sarah led the caseworker to join Shirley in the dining room.

Miss Bond's eyes scanned the room. "You have a lovely home." Her rose-colored blouse brought a glow to her chocolate eyes. She smiled at Shirley, then said, "Where's Georgia?"

Sarah gestured toward the living room.

Miss Bond went to the living room entrance. "Is she asleep?"

Georgia opened her left eye. "Nah."

"If you get sleepy, you need to lay the baby down, so he won't roll off your lap and get injured." Her voice was tight.

"Okay! Cut me some slack!" Georgia inched her way up the edge of the couch, steadying Braxton with her arms.

Miss Bond shook her head. Then to Sarah she said, "We need to talk."

"I'll be back, Georgia. Do you need anything?" Sarah asked.

"Yeah. A new set of nerves."

The way Georgia acted, Sarah guessed her psyche evaluation would show her at the age of maybe ten or eleven years old.

"Would you like some coffee, Miss Bond?" Sarah interrupted.

"I'd love some. How're things going?" She slid into a seat beside Shirley.

"It's been rough." Sarah handed Miss Bond the cup of coffee. "But we're adapting."

"Is this a good time to discuss the issues you said we'd talk about later?" Miss Bond dumped creamer into her cup.

"How much time do you have?" Sarah felt the knot at the pit of her gut tighten. *I wish she'd forgotten.*

"My next two visits were cancelled, and I don't have to be back to the agency until two."

"I'm going to give you all some privacy. I'll be out in the living room with my daughter and grandson."

After Shirley left, Sarah sighed. "It was the worst year of my life."

Miss Bond listened compassionately while Sarah shared the events of Jordan's death. She sipped her coffee over steamed glasses.

". . . and Dr. Aspen injured several kids, including the three who died."

Miss Bond offered a sad smile.

"Now it's up to the medical board to see if they want to discipline the doctors."

"Is that a scrapbook of him? Do you mind?" Miss Bond asked.

"No, help yourself."

Miss Bond flipped through the pages, then paused to stare at an eight-by-eleven picture of Jordan. He was lying on a quilted blanket, holding his red shovel. "Look at those pudgy cheeks. I bet you pinched them all the time."

Sarah grinned at the memories and wiped her wet cheeks.

"I'm sorry. I shouldn't have pressured you into telling me."

"I love reminiscing about him." Sarah blew her nose on a tissue. "So when the agency called to see if I'd foster Braxton, I couldn't resist taking him. I feel God sent him to me to help me with my grief, and I want to help Georgia." She lowered her voice. "But I worry about Braxton. Not that his mom would be mean to him; I just want, you know, whoever takes him to understand what is involved in caring for him."

Miss Bond tilted her head, her expression sympathetic. "You're doing a good job."

"I appreciate that."

Understanding Braxton's needs was important to Sarah. The baby was so similar to Jordan that she could tell you minute by minute the care required—endless appointments, therapy, including future appointments, possible developmental delays, and maybe even seizures, depending on the injury to the brain from the bleeds.

"Are you suing the doctor that you believe caused Jordan's death?"

Sarah steadied her trembling hands. "I placed his fate in the hands of the medical board."

"I'm sure they'll handle it."

"You know what else bothers me?"

"What?" Miss Bond tilted her head

"Some people think that the minute a child dies, parents should grieve for five minutes and get over it."

"I know life doesn't work that way." Miss Bond sighed. "I grieved myself to death when my dog died, so I can't imagine losing a child. Are you okay?"

Tears slipped down Sarah's cheeks and she wiped at them. "It was the most difficult thing I've ever had to endure, but I'm managing. It's just, sometimes, I still blame myself."

Concern flashed in Miss Bond's eyes. "Surely not. I mean, why?"

"Because my gut said transfer him to another hospital and I didn't listen." Sarah sighed. "If I could rewind the clock, I believe he'd still be here, but that minute's gone, and so is he."

"You really believe one minute would've made a difference?"

"I sure do."

"You didn't do anything wrong. You did your best for your son." Miss Bond patted Sarah's hand, causing her gold hoops to swing against her rose-colored cheeks.

"Tell that to my heart." Sarah placed her hand over her chest. "Now you know why I never shared my story with Children Services. Our family doesn't exactly fit a typical case file."

"I won't say a word." Miss Bond's tone was calm and reassuring.

"Can I ask you a question?"

"Sure."

"Why did Children Services take Braxton?"

"Is there someplace else we can talk?"

Sarah led her to the room she and Josh had turned into a home gym, and quietly closed the door. "I know she's been through a lot, but I'm worried."

"About?" Miss Bond looked over her gold-framed glasses.

"She said that Braxton's dad is getting out of prison early. That scares me."

Miss Bond folded her arms across her middle. "I was going to tell you today."

"Surely the judge won't give him custody."

Miss Bond sighed. "I've been doing this job for thirteen years and still haven't figured out the why and the how of it." She shrugged. "Did Georgia tell you why the agency took Braxton into care?"

"She said she needed financial help. But a woman I met in the graduate nursery said Georgia told the nurses she'd have a breakdown if she had to take him home with all of his problems, because her other baby died."

"True." Miss Bond shifted her weight.

"Is that the main reason Children Services took custody?"

"Not exactly," Miss Bond replied.

"There's more?"

"Do you know why her first son died?"

"No." Sarah looked at her with curiosity.

"She rolled over on him while she was asleep."

"But that doesn't make her a bad mother. It could've happened to anyone."

"No, it doesn't." Miss Bond frowned. "But until she can maintain housing, financial security, and obtain a psyche assessment to show she's able to care for him, then we can't send the baby home."

"What happened once she found out she'd rolled over on the baby?"

"She went downstairs and sat on the couch." Miss Bond paused when Sarah shook her head in disbelief. Then she continued, "She sat there for an hour before she told her mother."

"Maybe she was in shock." Sarah couldn't imagine any mother running away from her dead child, but she had. The night Jordan passed, she ran out of the hospital as fast as her legs would carry her.

"I would suspect so."

"Did anyone file charges?"

"The coroner ruled it as SIDS." Miss Bond forced a tight-lipped smile. "I just hope Shirley can arrange for a babysitter. so she can take him if Georgia is unable."

"Did Shirley say she might want him?"

"We have to look at all family members. If Shirley can juggle her schedule and obtain childcare while she's working, then the judge will send Braxton with her."

Sarah drew in a deep breath and exhaled. "Right now I'd say that Shirley is the best solution. And I know she loves him."

In the living room, they found Georgia filing her nails, watching *Sponge Bob*. "You can visit Braxton four hours a week. What days do you prefer?"

"Four hours?" Georgia's eyes widened.

"Yes, preferably in split sessions," Miss Bond replied.

Four hours a week? Sarah couldn't imagine only having four hours a week to visit her child.

"Me and Sarah will work this one out." Georgia stared hard at Miss Bond.

"Fine with me," Miss Bond shouldered her bag. "Sarah, I'll call you next week. Take care, Shirley."

When Miss Bond left, Georgia shot Sarah a look of disgust. "Man! That woman gets on my last nerve. She ain't gonna play me."

Sarah couldn't respond. She didn't feel like getting between Georgia and Children Services. She only wanted to be a fill-in mother for Braxton.

"Georgia, Miss Bond's only doing her job," Shirley said.

The firmness of Shirley's voice silenced Georgia's outburst. She placed the remote on the end of the couch and looked at her mom.

"You ready?"

"I can teach you everything you need to know about Braxton, if you'll let me," Sarah said, hoping Georgia would finally come to terms with the situation and want to learn her baby's care.

Georgia stood up, placed her hand on her hip. "Like it's gonna matter. Girl! I ain't the one dat needs help. It's them! They like breakin' up families. Humph!"

Sarah sighed. Even though she had doubts that Georgia could take care of Braxton, she wanted to help her get him back to where he belonged, in his mother's arms. *But would he be better off with Shirley?* "Do you really have to go so soon? I could get you another soda." She hoped Georgia would open up and tell her everything about the day her baby died, so she could get her own peace of mind.

"Yeah, I'll take another soda pop." Georgia followed Sarah into the dining room.

"Can I ask you a question?" Sarah felt like a detective asking so many questions, but she had to know. She handed Georgia another soda and slid into the opposite seat, waiting for Georgia to respond, but she didn't, just stared at Sarah with sad eyes. Sarah swallowed hard and almost lost her nerve, but then she said, "You heard me tell why Jordan died, so will you share Jaron's death with me? I mean, if we're going to have an open relationship, I'd like for you to feel like you can trust me."

Georgia popped the tab open on the can. "Did Bond say somethin'?"

Sarah hoped this would be the last question Georgia would ask because she couldn't lie, wouldn't lie. "We talked mostly about Braxton."

Georgia closed her eyes for a few minutes then opened them. "Okay," she said slowly, "I'll share, but I'm gonna need some tissues."

"Not a problem." Sarah handed the tissue box to Georgia and waited.

"Early that mornin', Jaron kept cryin' so I put him in bed with me. Girl, I was so tired, I dozed off." Georgia didn't look at Sarah when she spoke; instead, she stared through the patio door. "When I woke up, I leaned down to give him a kiss but . . . he felt . . . cold . . . not breathin'." Georgia paused to blow her nose. "I was in shock and think I lost my mind. So, when I finally told Mama what happened, she called the rescue and . . ."

Sarah nodded with tear-filled eyes.

Georgia sniffled. "Anyway, the rescue man showed up and they took Jaron to the hospital where they pronounced him dead. The coroner's report said it was sudden infant death, but I blame myself 'cause I shouldn't have put him in my bed."

"Were you lying on top of him when you woke up?"

She shook her head. "I still don't know what happened, but I blame myself." Tears spilled down her face and plopped on her jeans. "I didn't mean it."

"Shh . . . It's okay." Sarah began to rub her back. "You have to forgive yourself."

"I heard you say if you could get back dat minute, Jordan would still be here. I wish I had dat minute back, too."

"Did you tell the officials the whole story?" Sarah thought her heart would burst.

"I did. They didn't think I hurt him or anything like that."

"What about Children Services? Do they know the whole story?"

"I think Children Services is one nosy bunch." She blew her nose again. "They think since I lost Jaron, I can't take care of Fat Boy. I'm his mama," she cried.

"Could you take care of Braxton right now in the state you're in?" Sarah continued to rub her back. "Just think about it before you answer."

There were a few minutes of silence, and then she spoke. "Dunno."

Sarah reached for her hand. "You're doing the right thing. Give yourself time to heal and don't worry about Braxton. I'll take good care of him."

"But what if he ends up lovin' you more?" She looked at Sarah with pleading eyes.

Sarah's heart ached for her. At that moment, she wished she had a magic wand to wave to fix her problems, but there was no magic wand; however, there was something much more powerful than anything this world could offer. "Do you pray?"

"I used to all the time when I went to church with Mama."

"I missed a few months of church this past year myself, but I finally went back." Sarah smiled. "And you know what?"

"What?" Georgia sniffled.

"The Holy Spirit comforts me. Losing a child isn't easy, and I'll be the first one to testify to that. But right now I picture Jesus with a huge rocking chair. And you know what?"

"What?" Georgia almost smiled.

"I bet Jesus is rocking Jordan and Jaron. We already know he's the best babysitter, and we don't owe him a single red cent. But we owe him our heart by believing in him."

Georgia grinned so wide, her dimples blossomed. "Ain't no one ever explained somthin' like that to me before. You got it together, girl."

Sarah hoped this would be a new beginning for them, but she worried about the unanswered question. What if Braxton did love her more? Would Georgia resent her for it?

Georgia pushed back her chair and stood. "I best get movin'." She put on her coat and gave Braxton a kiss on the cheek. "See you later, Fat Boy."

Sarah glanced at Shirley who had tears pooling in her eyes. This moment bloomed full of beauty and possibilities. Shirley put on her coat and shoes, and at the door, she wrapped her arms around Sarah's neck and whispered, "Thanks for taking care of my grandson."

"My pleasure."

Sarah watched them walk hand-in-hand to the bus station, three houses down. *God, please mend Georgia's broken heart and teach her that love is plentiful.*

CHAPTER SIXTEEN

Luke shut the door and tossed his backpack on the steps. "Mama?"

"I'm in the kitchen."

He walked in and saw her swollen eyelids. He didn't need to ask what that was about. "Will you let me drive to conditioning tonight?"

"We'll see."

Luke plopped down on the barstool. "If you and Dad don't get it together soon my permit is gonna expire."

"Whose fault would that be?"

He shrugged, ignored her question. "I talked to Mrs. Frenchie today."

"What about?"

He stood again. The unhappiness he felt had settled and put him onto a new path, somewhere he didn't want to be. But it had never been this bad—a gut-bashing feeling that life would never be the same. The blackness overtook him and filled his mouth with a bitter taste. The words he never got a chance to say engulfed him—*goodbye, Jordan. I love you.* Since nothing satisfied him, he couldn't concentrate on even the simple things in life. His life was falling apart piece-by-piece.

"Did you see Mouse today?" Sarah interrupted his thoughts.

"For a minute."

"When you see him at ball tonight, just make sure you avoid him. Luke?"

He wanted to respond, but he felt clammy, dizzy. His mom wrapped her arms around his waist, eased him to the cold kitchen floor. Through a fog, he watched her race to the fridge, open it, and grab a carton. A glass shattered on the floor, and then he heard "Drink." She supported his head. "Did you eat lunch?"

He shook his head and sipped the juice.

"You have to eat."

Minutes passed. He still felt bleak, but his vision was clearing. He sat up, leaned against the cabinet, and drew his knees to his chest.

"I'll get you a piece of cheese. It has protein."

While she pulled the cheese from the fridge, he finished drinking the juice. She sat down beside him, took the plastic wrapper off the cheese, and handed it to him. He broke it apart and put it in his mouth. For what seemed an eternity, he collected himself. He reached into his jeans pocket, pulled out his wallet, opened it, and slid Jordan's picture from the vinyl sleeve. He understood how dark and frightening the world could be, but he had to know. "Tell me, Mama. I wanta know every detail about the night he died, so I can move on with my life."

⇛⇝

Sarah shivered at the memories, not wanting to rehash that night. All she ever wanted was to protect her boys from the vivid images that stalked her. She gently touched Luke's cheek. The sweet, innocent memories of his childhood cut through her like a knife. For a moment he was a four-year-old child again; only back then, he was full of laughter, just as he should be now.

"Please, Mama?"

She forced herself to look at him, saw the dull look in his eyes, the frown he wore. It saddened her the way life came at him with a force that stole away his innocence, his happiness. She realized he had to be told if it would save him from the unraveling hems of life. *Please God, let him understand.*

She took a deep breath, held if for a moment, then let it go. "Earlier that day, your dad and I went to a care conference. I told the doctors and nurses that if Jordan took his last breath, I didn't want anyone pounding on his chest to bring him back."

Luke gasped. "Mama! You didn't want them to bring him back? Why?"

"There were no choices. Doctor Baker said there was no more he could do. The brain herniation had taken a permanent toll. Jordan

110

barely responded when we tried to talk to him. So finally they ordered a test to see how many impulses were getting through to his brain." Sarah's gut tightened, but she continued anyway. "There was only one. After the conference, they transferred him to his old room, one floor below. I figured since he was out of ICU that meant he'd be okay." She paused to look at Luke. His jaw flinched, the vein in his neck throbbing.

"What else?" Luke asked, unblinking.

"The nurses caring for him worked overtime that day. Oh, Luke, I should've seen it coming. When I looked over at the nurse rocking him, I lost it when he gasped for air."

She didn't want to continue. In the past few months, she'd begun to heal, begun to push those negative images away and think only of the positive, but for Luke's sake she had to go on. "Jordan was dusky gray and limp. I screamed and ran to the elevator to find your dad, but when I was going down one, he was coming up the other. When I reentered the room, your dad was holding him."

She couldn't tell him that Jordan had died over twenty times and come back to life. And that initially she couldn't find the strength to go back into his room. "When I held him, the nurse turned the monitor away from us. I knew what Jordan wanted to hear." She rubbed her stomach, trying to ease the nausea. This wasn't the way she pictured sharing his death, but for Luke's sake, she composed herself. "I told Jordan that he would always be my hero, and that someday I would take in kids with special needs just like him. Then I said, Jesus is waiting, Jordan. Go to him. I wish . . ."

She couldn't finish. She felt a rush of pure, blinding anger, and lowered her head.

"Mama?"

"I couldn't even cry when he passed, Luke. Instead, I sat in the windowsill and looked to the sky, hoping I could catch a glimpse of him being carried away by the angels." When she lifted her head, Luke's fists were clenched tight.

"Did he suffer?"

"Why would you want to know?"

Luke's teeth clenched. "Did. He. Suffer?"

She turned her head, stared at the empty highchair. "Yeah," she cleared her throat. "He fought for his last breath."

Luke stood up and zipped his jacket.

"Luke! I'm sorry, but nothing we can do will bring him back," she cried. She chased him down the hall. "Luke!" He ran faster, almost colliding with Zack. He slammed the door shut before she could even say "please."

She hustled through the house as fast as her tired legs would carry her, grabbed her keys and purse. "Zack! Help me get Braxton ready."

Inside the SUV, they buckled up the baby and sped out of the drive. They circled the street to Mike's house, but Luke was nowhere in sight. "I planned on letting him drive to conditioning tonight." Sarah's voice was shaky. "I shouldn't have told him about Jordan's death. I knew he'd be upset, but what choice did I have?"

"You told him about Jordan?"

"He collapsed on me. I was only trying to help."

"Mom! Calm down and go the speed limit."

Sarah felt the gentleness of Zack's pat on her back. Whipping the SUV to the side of the road, she laid her head against the steering wheel and wept. There was never a time in her life, barely even a minute, when she didn't remember what she'd lost. She knew exactly how Luke felt.

"Don't worry, Mom."

She thrust herself toward Zack. "Tell me Luke will be okay."

He continued to pat her back. "He will. God always has a plan. Now let's go. Dad will be home soon, he'll know what to do."

She gazed into Zack's reassuring eyes, then nodded and said, "Okay."

When they returned, Sarah changed the baby's diaper, while Zack preheated the oven. He opened the fridge and removed the thawed chicken. He rinsed off each piece and placed them into a shake-n-bake bag, then shook it. He put each piece in a pan and slid it into the oven.

Sarah slid the dirty diaper into a plastic Ziploc bag and threw it into the trashcan. "I'm sorry you and Luke had to fend for yourselves when Jordan was in the hospital."

Zack rinsed his hands and wiped them on his jeans. "You have nothing to feel guilty about." He pulled a knife from the butcher block.

"Hello?" Josh's voice echoed, causing Sarah to jump. He walked into the kitchen and hung his work coat on the barstool. "Why is Zack holding a knife?"

"Because I'm gonna poke holes in the potatoes."

"Honey, you look like you played a role in Rocky."

Zack leaned against the counter. "Got bad news. After Mom told

Luke about Jordan's death, he took off. We went looking for him, but no such luck."

"What?" Josh's face reddened.

"He was falling apart." Sarah didn't appreciate the look he had given her. She realized he was only trying to protect their boys as she had been, but he wasn't there when Luke almost collapsed, didn't see the pleading way he'd looked into her eyes when he said he had to know.

"So you have no idea where he is?"

"Dunno," Zack said.

Sarah's stomach churned. "I'm going to find him. If he checks in, call me on my cell."

∾◦⤚

Rain drummed down hard on Luke when he rounded the corner onto Hole Creek Road.

"Luke!" Mike hollered.

Luke crossed the street and cursed the rain that pounded his forehead. "Hey, bro's," he said to Mike and Dustin.

Mike grinned. "Thought you were grounded?"

Luke didn't respond. He knew if he said a word, the floodgates would open.

"Wanta go hang out? Section Eight is gonna be kickin' it tonight and laying a few tracks," Dustin said, his spiked, fiery-dyed hair took the beat of the rain but stayed in place from the cement he'd rubbed in it.

"Yeah, I'll go." Luke admired Dustin, and he knew that someday Section Eight would climb to the top of the charts with their new hit "Brains." And there was more to Dustin that Luke admired besides his talent for music. He liked his "eat me alive" tattoo and his body piercings, but most of all he loved his carefree attitude.

"I thought you had conditioning tonight?" Mike ducked his head under the half-raised garage door.

Luke glanced around, ignoring Mike's question, and chuckled at the makeshift band room. A neon Budweiser sign hung crooked on the wall. Blue and white stripped lounge chairs lined the far right wall. An electronic dartboard hung on the left wall.

He chuckled when Cyclone started singing "To the left, to the left."

113

Luke knew he was totally goofing off. *No way would Cyclone waste his talent on a song like that.* He'd sing his bashing song titled "Brains." He plunked down next to Mike on a backseat they'd ripped out of Dustin's dad's Chevy, then shifted his gaze to Dustin's girl, Tiffany. She ran her black-painted nails through her spiked hair as she strutted toward Luke. Bending from the waist, her chest met his face. "Want some?"

Luke knew she'd meant a swig of Captain Morgan. "Yeah." He snatched the bottle from her, took a long drink before he handed it back. Drinking didn't make him happy, didn't take away his troubles, but it did take the edge off of his emotions. And tonight, he needed to feel numb.

Tiffany took off her pink leather jacket, tossed it on the lounge chair and strutted back to Dustin.

Mike's eyes bulged. "Mmm."

"Get a grip," Luke teased, "she's already taken."

Mike hung his head and pretended to pout. "Will I ever find a girl like that?"

Luke chuckled. "In your dreams."

Mike pulled a bottle from under his XXX Titan jersey and grinned. He tilted the bottle and took a drink. When he lowered it, he grinned. "I couldn't resist. Saw old Jacko sitting in my old man's closet."

Luke loved this moment, the loudness, and the musky scent of the garage. He grabbed hold of the bottle's neck and tilted it, taking in a satisfying drink. Jacko burned his throat and exploded in his stomach. For the next half-hour, they listened to Section Eight and passed the bottle back and forth. *Why didn't Mama try to save Jordan? Will she give up on me, too?* The more he dwelled on it, the angrier he became. He was too sober. And that was the problem. He took the bottle and guzzled it, not caring how much it burned. He needed the booze to keep the thoughts away this time. Every time.

Thirty-seven minutes later Mike said, "Whatdaya say we split, man? We can go back to my house and get my car."

Luke grinned. "Sounds like a plan."

"You okay?"

"Couldn't be better." Luke slurred his words. When he stood up, he stumbled as he put his thumb up to Cyclone and Dustin.

"Be cool, dude," Cyclone said into the microphone.

They walked to Mike's house through the hard spitting rain, and Luke loved it. He didn't have a care in the world. When they came to the front porch of Mike's house, Luke said, "Where's your aunt?"

"Passed out on the couch. She worked thirteen hours." Then Mike disappeared into the house.

Luke waited outside on the cracked concrete porch. Finally Mike reappeared, jostling the keys in front of his face, grinning. "Ready to go squeal some tires?"

A smile lit Luke's face. "Ready."

They drove through town listening to Dustin's prerecorded tracks, the song "Messed Up" screaming through tired speakers.

Messed up, all right. Life or me? Luke thought.

Mike whipped the Sunbird into the overcrowded parking lot at the Shoe Barn—the store that not only carried the latest styles of shoes at a discounted price, but also carried their favorite rap CD's, jewelry, and other items. Old Jacko had flushed away Luke's anger. No useless tears tonight. The only emotion embracing him now was excitement—how to get the shoes he'd been wanting without getting caught.

He paused to stare in the store's tall glass window at the shelf sporting the baby blue and white leather shoes—the ones he'd wanted a month ago. The shoes his mama refused to buy. *I bought you two new pairs five months ago.* Five months ago, he whispered under his breath mocking his mama.

"Ready?" Mike said.

"Yeahhh."

Mike headed to the CD isle, and Luke went to the shoe aisle. He found the box of shoes he wanted. Lifting the lid, he grinned. *Man these shoes are tight!* Just when he thought it, his mama's words came flooding back, and he felt the first hint of remorse, but he wanted them *now*. He didn't want to wait until he got his first job and spend his cash, hard earned mopping floors or washing dishes, or whatever job he could find.

He sat down on the padded bench and exchanged his old shoes for the new. Then he glanced up and down the aisle, placed the box on top of a pair of Nike sandals, and headed to the CD aisle where he found Mike sorting through a stack. Mike shot him a quick sly smile, ripped the plastic wrap off the CD he wanted, and shoved it in his oversized jacket.

For the next ten minutes, they appeared to be serious shoppers—placing cans of pop into a cart, CD's of various rappers, and a pair of black clogs.

"What ya think, dude?" Luke shifted his gaze to his feet.

Mike's grin assured Luke the shoes were way cool.

"You ready, bro?"

Mike grinned again. "How you gonna get out of here without getting busted?"

A smile itched Luke's face. "Remember Joe?"

Mike looked at him confused.

"From Carlisle?"

"Yeah."

"We came in here about six months ago. Trust me, dude. They won't even know I did it." Luke ditched the cart and strutted past Mike with his self-induced cocky attitude. Then, very calmly, Luke walked past the checkout counter toward the door. He turned his head and saw the cashier ringing up other customers. "Let's split."

Inside the car, Luke's heart rate slowed. "Woo-hoo! Mountain Dew!"

Mike started the ignition. "I can't believe you pulled it off, dude."

"Hey, bro, don't be takin' no lessons from me." Luke placed his left shoe on the dashboard, admiring it.

"Don't worry, I won't," Mike said, placing his stolen CD into the disk changer. Whipping the worn-out Sunbird onto the street, he cranked up the volume, drove up two streets, and turned into Community and killed the ignition. The rusted car sputtered and died. "Tell me what's eatin' at you man."

Luke shot a look at him. "What?"

"What?"

"I was on cloud nine."

"Well excuse me for interfering." Mike stared out the window.

Luke bit down on his lip to keep it from trembling. For the next few minutes, the only sound was the soft rain tapping the windshield. Finally he said, "Mama told me how Jordan died."

Mike attempted to put his arm around Luke, but he pushed it away. "Sorry, dude. You're not my type." Then he added, "It was her fault."

Mike didn't respond. Instead, he ejected the CD and placed it into the plastic holder.

"Did ya hear me?"

"Yeah, I heard, but it wasn't your mama's fault. I heard the story."

"You knew?"

"Yeah. My mama took your mama out for supper one night so they could talk. Right after Jordan died. Remember?"

"She didn't even try to save him."

"She had no choice. He was suffering. Your mama couldn't have prevented his death."

Luke felt the anger starting to erupt. "Thought you were my friend."

"I am, but I can't let her take the blame for somethin' she didn't cause."

Even though Luke's anger was beyond boiling, he felt proud that his friend could love his mama enough to come to her defense. But he didn't understand her reasoning. "She could've let them try to save him."

"Are you trying to find a reason to blame her?"

"No, dude, it's the truth."

Mike shook his head. "You're wrong. Your mama fought for him and would've traded places with him if she could've."

Luke couldn't argue that. He'd seen her fall to the ground that day, begging God to take her instead. Finally he said, "You're right, man."

"Yeah, I'm right. You ready to go? I bet your mama's worried. I know I can be a pain, but let me tell you somethin' that I hope I never have to repeat. Love your mama with all your heart and soul 'because when she's gone—you think your world is upside down now, you ain't seen nothin' yet."

The only light came from the tennis court and cast distorted shadows into the car, but Luke could see the tears leaking down Mike's face. This time he wrapped his arms around him. "It's okay, dude. I know you miss your mama."

"I'd lay down and die to get her back," Mike cried.

CHAPTER SEVENTEEN

Sarah laid her coat on the chestnut bench in the hallway. She found Josh and Zack in the living room playing *Kerplunk*. Every time the marbles made their way down the plastic spiral tube, Braxton squirmed.

Josh looked up. "Did you find him?"

She sighed. "No. I drove over to Mike`s. The lights were out at his house. No one at the pool hall or bowling alley has seen him either."

"I won, Dad. Wanta play again?"

"Nah. I'm going to talk to your mother."

Zack slid the long colorful sticks and the marbles back into their package.

"What's our plan when he comes home?"

Sarah folded her arms. "I don't know."

The phone rang. Josh raced to answer it. "Hello." He scratched his head. "Yes, he should've called. Hopefully he'll be there tomorrow." He put the phone back into its base. "That was Coach Spears wondering where Luke was tonight."

Aren't we all? Sarah walked to the window and gazed out into the night sky. Braxton began to cry and Josh picked him up.

"He's probably still hungry. I would be if someone only gave me milk and a little cereal," Zack complained.

"We have to go slow to make sure his body can tolerate it," Josh said.

While Josh and Zack talked, Sarah worried about Luke. *Please don't let him turn to alcohol tonight. Remind him how much we love him, just as you do, Father.*

"Honey, try not to worry. I know it's hard, but . . ."

She turned away from the window. "I'm going upstairs."

"Take as much time as you need, honey."

She made her way up the steps to Luke's room. It warmed her to see all the trophies that cluttered his shelves and, dresser, and the ribbons he'd pinned to the wall with blue and yellow tacks. She eased herself down onto his bed, took hold of the stuffed monkey, lifted it to her nostrils and drew in a deep breath, trying to get a hint of Swiss Army, Luke's favorite cologne, and Jordan's innocent smell—Johnson's Baby Lotion.

How many tears had she cried? She'd lost track. Watching Luke drown in a sea of self-pity was something she hoped no other mother would have to endure; although, she knew they would. Somewhere across the country, this minute, mothers were crying over sick babies, the death of a child, the burdens of teenagers suffering through peer pressure or other unnecessary baggage they hadn't claimed, but somehow managed to stumble on.

She laid the monkey on Luke's pillow, then walked to his dresser and picked up his toddler picture. Gazing into his brown eyes she whispered, "Where did you go, Luke?" She traced her fingers across the glass of the picture, remembering those toddler years—thunder thighs and chubby cheeks. She felt a smile beginning to emerge when she remembered the "park days," set aside twice a week to go play. She could still hear his little voice when he turned his head to say, 'Mommy, watch this.' Then off he'd go, barreling down the slide, headfirst. She placed the picture back on his dresser, lifted his junior high school picture, and brought it into focus. *Where's Luke? The teen that knew how to laugh and wouldn't miss a conditioning practice?* She wiped at the tears that splattered the glass. *I know you're scared and confused, and that your arms ache to hold your baby brother. I'm sorry.* She placed the picture back on the dresser and wiped the dust off his CD player with her shirttail. She jumped when the front door slammed. She slipped out of his room and seated herself at the top of the step. She heard Luke say, "Dad! Lay off! I was at Dustin's listening to them record."

"But you're grounded."

"Mama should've never told me about Jordan."

"But you begged," Josh defended.

Sarah made her way down the steps and went to the dining room.

"Where'd you get those shoes?" Zack asked.

"Huh?" Luke stumbled, grabbed hold of a chair.

"Josh!" Sarah screamed. "Help him!"

"Sit," Josh said, helping Luke into the chair. "You're drunk."

"Am not, just feeling good."

"Why?" Sarah wiped her wet face with the pads of her fingers.

"Honey, sit down," Josh demanded.

She sat down and placed her folded arms on the table, lowered her head and sobbed. "God, please help us."

"How much did you drink?" Josh asked.

Luke rubbed his temples, shrugged. "Not sure."

"You can't remember?" Sarah raised her head. She wanted to pull him into her lap, tell him she was sorry that his brother died, sorry he couldn't find his way back to stable ground, and sorry she had told him about Jordan's death, even though he'd insisted so he could move on with his life. *But move where to? The next bottle of booze?*

Josh crossed his arms across his chest. "Where did you get the shoes?"

"I've had them for about . . . two weeks."

"That's a lie," Zack hollered from the living room.

"Zack," Josh warned. "Since you want to help out, come get your brother a cup of coffee."

Sarah dreaded to ask the question that she knew would shake up her world and send her into another whirlwind of emotions, but she had to. "Did you shoplift?"

Luke nodded.

She sighed. "I told you I'd buy you a pair of shoes when we got caught up on the bills."

Silence.

"You're taking the shoes back," Josh said.

Luke slammed the table with the backside of his hand. "They'll put me in jail until I'm old enough to vote!"

"Maybe jail time would do you good." Zack set the cup in front of Luke.

"Zack!" Josh's voice was firm.

"Okay."

"How can we help? You're falling apart," Sarah pulled a napkin out of the holder and blew her nose.

Josh cleared his throat. "It's obvious being grounded isn't working."

"What you gonna do? Give me another father lecture?"

Sarah saw the sadness in Josh's eyes and it broke her heart.

Josh sighed. "I've been putting off doing this for awhile. But it's time." He walked into the living room, picked up the cordless phone, and punched in some numbers. "Hey, Mock?" Then he slipped out the front door. When he returned, he laid the phone on the dining room table and said, "Next Thursday we're going to an AA meeting."

Luke barked out a laugh. "I'm not going."

Josh kept his composure. "I said next Thursday night we're going to an AA meeting and that's final." For a moment the silence gained weight. Finally, Josh said, "I have something to confess."

"Can't imagine Mr. Spit-and-Polish doing anything wrong," Luke said sarcastically.

"I was a teenager many moons ago, too."

Luke snatched his cup from the table and took a drink.

"When I was eighteen," Josh said, "I went out one night with a bunch of buddies. I literally drank nine shots of Jack and Coke, then drove home in my worn out Beetle."

Luke chuckled. "I can hardly believe you drank."

Josh shuddered at the memory. "The alcohol made me feel like I was indispensable. I turned a corner going fifty miles an hour, ran a red light, smashed a Men Working sign, and almost hit a police cruiser."

"I bet Grandpa Kiser was ticked at you," Luke said, taking another drink of coffee.

"He let me spend the night in jail and . . ." Josh's eyes widened as if remembering that night in full detail.

Sarah patted his arm. "You okay?"

He nodded. "The next day, at court, they suspended my license. I was allowed to drive only to and from work, and I had to take classes on driving safely and do community service."

"That's all?" Luke asked.

Sarah sighed. "Not exactly. We paid for it for years."

Luke's eyebrows raised. "Huh?"

"Our insurance rates, even after I married your dad, were outrageous, not to mention he could've killed himself."

"Or someone else," Luke said and finished off his coffee.

"I almost did. That morning when my dad drove me home, he said that the officer driving the car I almost hit was his friend. Todd and Dad used to run fire and rescue together until Todd decided he wanted to be an officer."

Luke's eyes widened a fraction bigger as if he was shocked his dad had a past.

Josh continued, "He had a wife and three kids, soon to include a newborn. I could've killed my dad's best friend, left his wife without a husband, and his kids without a dad. How do you think that made me feel?"

"Like junk," Luke replied.

"After that I swore I'd never drink again. So, I've decided that until you turn eighteen, or prove to me and your mother you can be responsible, you're not allowed to get your license."

Luke smacked his hand on the table. "That's not fair. Just because you were irresponsible don't mean I'll be."

Josh's eyes narrowed. "I think you've already crossed the line."

Luke pushed back his chair and stood up.

"Sit back down. I'm not done yet," Josh demanded.

"I don't want to sit. You think just because you almost killed your dad's friend that I should pay for what you did."

"I made a mistake, but with all due respect, I'm not the one who needs help. I'm going to make sure my son doesn't make the same mistakes I made. And you're taking back the shoes you stole and apologizing to the storeowner. I'll be back down in a minute."

Zack joined them at the table and shook his head.

"Just because I stole a pair of shoes, it ain't gonna send me to hell," Luke said.

The word "stole" ripped through Sarah like a razor. The more she thought about it, the angrier she became. "And you're supposed to set the example for your brother to follow. Maybe you need to follow after him."

Luke narrowed his eyes at Zack. "That would be a negative." He got up slowly and walked to the front door.

Josh returned and placed a kiss on her cheek. "We'll be back."

Sarah went to the window and watched them back out of the driveway. All she felt was dread, and a vague form of panic. She knew those old feelings creeping up all too well—the shakiness, the constriction in her throat, and the rubbery legs. She sat down at the computer and watched the screensaver flip between pictures. A smile lit her face when a picture of Zack burying Luke in the sand appeared. She wished the not-so-good issues of her life could be placed on the sand, so that the water could come and smooth away the roughness. *Surely, there's a way for Luke to find stable ground without bars.*

Luke turned on his dad's stereo. "What a friend we have in Jesus" filtered through the speakers. He slid down in his seat and rested his elbow on the center console. *Just pretend. Act as if life is just hunky-dory. Go in that store and apologize, show up for conditioning, get good grades, and then maybe I'll be able to convince them I'm gonna make it.*

Josh whipped the SUV into an empty parking slot and cut the engine. The lights in the store were still on, but the neon light outside was not. They climbed out and walked to the front of the store. Josh tried to open the door, but it was locked. He saw the man at the register counting money and he knocked.

The man waved his hand and mouthed, "Sorry we're closed."

Josh mouthed, "We need to return shoes."

The man ignored them, kept counting money. Josh knocked again.

"We're closed," the man mouthed again.

Josh held one shoe to the door, pointed to it, and mouthed, "Stolen."

The man walked to the door, opened it. "What?"

"Sir, I don't mean to bother you but my son owes you an apology. He stole these shoes." Josh held them for the man to see.

The man's eyebrows scrunched as he looked at Luke. "I needed to be home an hour ago, but come on in." He locked the door behind them, then led them down a long aisle to a gray metal door, and held it open. "Have a seat."

Luke eyes scanned the cluttered room. Shoe boxes, cases of CDs, and his favorite candy M&M's sat in a glass jar on the desk. The man entered and stood by a stack of boxes.

Josh extended his hand. "I'm Josh Kiser."

The man grinned. "Call me Fred."

"I'm sorry we had to bother you, but my son is going to make a wrong, right."

"I appreciate that. As for you young man, have you read our sign that says 'Anyone caught shoplifting will be prosecuted'?"

Luke drew in a deep breath. "No."

"Since you are returning them, I won't press charges, so consider yourself lucky. And be grateful you have a dad who cares. Now what do you have to say?"

Luke immediately shifted his thoughts to Jordan because any

thoughts of him would cause the tears to erupt. "I'm sorry."

"I know we all can make mistakes, but we learn from them, right? If this ever happens again, I will press charges and my store will be off limits. Is that clear?"

Luke swiped at his tears with the backside of his hand. "Yes."

"Did you trample through mud?" Josh asked, glancing down at Luke's feet.

"Oops."

"Show me where you put your other shoes?" Fred said.

When they returned, Josh pulled his wallet out of his jeans pocket, while Luke put his old shoes back on. "How much do I owe you?"

"Seventy-two dollars."

"How much?" Josh looked puzzled.

"You have to excuse my dad. My Mom buys him everything, including his underwear."

Fred looked surprised. "Oh?"

"The last time I bought a pair of shoes, they only cost me twelve bucks."

"That was like twenty years ago," Luke mumbled. He watched his dad dig through his wallet, and he felt remorse. He knew his dad worked a lot of overtime to pay for Jordan's medical bills.

"Do you take credit?"

"That'll be fine."

Luke felt his guts stir. Now he really felt like a loser. "Sorry, Dad."

Josh didn't make eye contact; instead, he signed the slip Fred had handed to him and said, "This won't happen again."

Fred nodded. "I'll walk you back to the front."

Inside the car, the silence started to press Luke. "I said I'm sorry."

"Apology accepted."

Silence.

"I'll pay you back when I get a job."

"Fine." Josh adjusted his rearview mirror.

"Why are you so quiet? I know it hurt to pay for the shoes, but I tried to make a wrong a right."

"Because I forced your hand."

Probably. "Normally, you'd be lecturing me till the cows come home."

Josh pulled the vehicle to the side of the road. "I'm very disappointed. You think because your brother died it gives you the right to pawn your feelings off on other people."

"I'm not pawning anything off."

"Could've fooled me. You can't see what you're doing to yourself. If you don't get it together soon, I'm afraid you're going to be my next inmate. That will be something to be proud of."

"I thought you were proud of me? You said you were."

"I'm not happy with the poor decisions you make."

"Dad! My mind tells me to pretend everything is just fine. Put on a happy face. Be a golden child like Zack. Well I can't pretend I'm happy, when I'm not."

"You could be, but you won't listen. You won't go to therapy. You don't like going to church. And anytime someone tries to give you good sound advice, you don't want to hear it."

"Don't you work a lot of overtime to try and block your pain?"

"I work to pay the bills. The Bible even makes reference that a man should support his family. And I manage to put a little bit back into savings so when I retire, me and your mother can live comfortably."

Luke felt the weight and truth of what his dad said. He wished he could be more like him. "What do I need to do?"

Josh twisted in his seat. "Take one day at a time and lean on God. He doesn't want you to suffer."

"He doesn't hear me when I pray," Luke said, "and I don't know what it's gonna take for me to get it through my head that there's nothing I can do to get Jordan back. I miss him so much, I just wanta die, Dad." He opened the car door and sped out into the oncoming traffic.

"Luke!" Josh got out of the vehicle and chased after him. "Stop! You're gonna get hit by a car."

Through tear-filled eyes, Luke made his way across the street and fell down in a ditch. "Give Jordan back!" He beat the ground with his fist until he felt his dad's gentle hand touch his shoulders. "It's okay. Let it out, Son."

For several minutes, Luke beat the ground until his fist oozed with blood.

Josh offered him his hand. "Come on."

A man pulled his trailblazer to the side of the road. "Is everything okay?"

"Yes. Thanks for asking." Josh helped Luke up the muddy-grassy area to the curb and across the street to the vehicle. He pulled a thick blanket out of the trunk and wrapped it around Luke's shoulders. Then they climbed inside and started for home.

Luke shivered. "Dad, I'll keep trying."

"I love you, Son. We'll get through this," he said and turned the heat to high.

Luke shivered, letting the blast of warm air from the vents envelop him. He watched the moon play hide-and-seek with the housetops. "Dad?"

"Yeah, bud?"

"Why did you drink?" He tightened the blanket around his shoulders and kept his injured hand tucked in the other.

"I thought it was cool when I hung out with my buddies, but I was wrong."

Luke didn't have to ask himself why he drank. He knew why—to silence the anger within. It started three months after Jordan died. One stolen six-pack from a painter's truck led to a shot of Jack, then to a half-a-bottle of Crown. Three months ago, when he and Mike had finished off a bottle of Crown and half-a-bottle of Jack, he had choked on his own vomit and almost died. He could hear his mother's words spoken at his bedside as if she had said them yesterday, "We lost Jordan and now this". *So, why wasn't she upset when she found the bottle in my room?* he wondered.

She was. You were so wrapped up in yourself, you couldn't see the truth, the little voice inside him said.

❧

Sarah put the folded dishcloths in the drawer. For the past twenty minutes, she'd channeled her worry into work. Zack stood at the refrigerator, door wide open.

"Mama?" He put two cheese sticks on a plate and popped them into the microwave. "Do you think Luke's gonna be okay?"

She leaned against the counter and folded her arms across her chest. "I believe that in time, he'll be fine. God can make something good come out of a bad situation."

"Do you still think about Jordan?" Zack pulled the melted cheese sticks out of the microwave and poured pizza sauce onto the plate.

"There's not a day that goes by that I don't think about him, but I'm learning to lean on God. Does that make sense?"

Zack tilted back his head, allowing the cheese to glide into his mouth. "It makes sense to me."

Sarah heard the front door open and close. Josh entered the kitchen and placed his keys on the counter. When Luke walked in, cuddling his right fist, she ran to him. "What happened?"

"It's nothing."

"You're bloody."

"Honey, let me clean him up, and then I'll tell you what happened." To Luke he said, "Go into the bathroom." Then he paused to stare at Sarah. She saw the reassurance in his eyes. In the bathroom, Luke stuck his injured hand under the water faucet, while Josh pulled a bottle of rubbing alcohol and other supplies from the medicine cabinet. He set them on top of the sink. "This might burn," Josh said, pouring the alcohol over his cuts, "but it'll clean out the germs."

"Ya ouch." Luke cringed.

Josh patted the wound with a cotton ball, then he spread a thin layer of Neosporin on Luke's hand and knuckles. Next, he placed two nonstick bandages to the wounds and wrapped his hand with gauze.

"Are you sure he doesn't need stitches?" Sarah asked.

"Mama, I'll be fine."

When Josh secured the gauze with tape, the scene before her eyes made her think of the parable Jesus used when a man had fallen among thieves. After they stripped him of his raiment, and wounded him, they departed, leaving him half-dead. A priest and a Levite came by and just stared, not bothering to help him, but a Samaritan came to where he was and bound up his wounds. *Lord, Josh can clean Luke's physical wounds, but Luke needs you to heal his sin sick soul. Please continue to be longsuffering.*

"That should do it," Josh finally said.

"How did it go?" Sarah asked.

"I got lucky."

Thank you, God, Sarah thought.

The phone rang, and Zack ran to answer it. "It's Miss Bond." Zack handed the phone to Sarah.

Her heart rate skipped a beat. *Please, no more stress tonight.* "Hello."

"Sorry for the late call but unfortunately I had to bring work home with me tonight. Can you come to the agency tomorrow at two o'clock?"

"Is there a problem?"

"Braxton's dad wants to be included in a case plan. Evidently, they gave him an extensive probation. I'm sorry, Sarah."

Sarah hung up the phone and sat down, cupping her cheeks with her hands. She felt defeated. *God please . . . If Braxton doesn't go home with his mom or grandma, please find a way for me to keep him.*

"What did Miss Bond want this late?" Josh asked, interrupting her thoughts.

"Braxton's dad wants to work a case plan. I have to go to a care conference tomorrow at two." She sighed heavily. "Why do they let inmates out of prison so early?"

"Our prisons are overcrowded and the state's financial budget is in the red zone, so they let out the less serious offenders."

Sarah sighed again. "Busting someone up is not serious?"

"I didn't say that."

"I know you didn't, sorry, I'm just stressed."

"Don't you have an appointment tomorrow with your therapist?"

"Yes."

"I have a vacation day I could take if you need me to watch Braxton," he said and rubbed her stiff shoulders.

"Take it. I don't want to drag him in and out of the cold. So . . . are you going to tell me what happened tonight?"

"Boys. Head on up to bed," Josh said. After the boys went up the steps, Josh explained the events of the evening to Sarah.

She wanted to cry, but she felt like the well had dried up. In fact, she felt a tinge of relief that Luke had found a way to let out some of his bottled up feelings; although, beating his fist onto the ground wasn't healthy.

"I told him he could've been my next inmate."

CHAPTER EIGHTEEN

Luke couldn't sleep. Instead he lay down on his bed, backside up, and touched his pen to the paper to write.

Dear Jordan,

I was mad 'cause mama didn't try to save your life, but Mike set me straight. And she's fostering a baby. I'm afraid when he goes home, it's gonna break her heart. I think Dad worries I'll be his next inmate. I wish Mama could take her sewing machine she uses for all that craft junk and sew my heart back together. The only relief I get is when I drink, but lately drinking does nothing but get me in trouble. Tell God—

He couldn't finish the letter. His tears fell on the paper, saturating it. He rested his head on his hands and fell asleep.

❧❦

Sarah lay quietly in her bed after watching the family who'd witnessed their home burn to the ground leave safely; all five of them packed in their car like a bunch of sardines. Through the window, she saw Mr. Moon. Tonight his eye slits shifted downward, his lips drawn just as hers had been earlier this evening. Maybe he'd stared through too many windows this night, causing him to mirror the image of everyone's pain.

She took her therapist's advice, drew in ten slow breaths, and imagined herself on a beach. She could feel the warmth of the sun embracing her, feel her toes dig into the sand, and in the distance, she heard children running happily through the water.

Sleep . . .

Mommy, come play with me.

Jordan? She tried to wake up. She walked down a corridor of a hospital until she came to a blue and yellow-striped curtain. She pulled it back, went to the bed and lowered the rail. Picking him up, she cradled him into her arms. *I missed you bunches.*

Help me, Mama!

Luke? She held Jordan tight. *Where are you?*

Over here, Mama. She placed Jordan back into the bed and lifted the rail. Glancing around, she saw two other curtains. *Back here, Mama.*

Mom! Help me!

Zack! She ripped back the next curtain. Something terrible had happened. She screamed, *Zack!*

"Sarah, wake up."

Her body felt heavy and cold, almost chilled.

"It's only a bad dream." Josh's voice sounded like a distant wind. She opened her eyes slowly as Josh brushed her cheeks. "It's okay."

The tears flowed down her cheeks and on her red satin pillowcase.

"Are you okay?"

"I got to hold Jordan, Josh, but then . . ." She sat up. "Something happened to Zack."

"It was just a bad dream." Josh helped her lie down.

"Remember four years ago when I had a dream about Luke?"

"The one where he was lying on the ground, his head oozing blood?"

"And it came to pass. That kid hit Luke with his skateboard and busted his head open. So why would I dream about Zack?"

"Honey, right now your life is chaotic, and it's probably just manifesting itself through your dreams."

"Jordan was so beautiful, Josh."

"I know. Try and get some rest." He placed his head on her pillow. She felt the warmth of his breath against her cheek.

"Do you think Zack is going to be okay?"

"He gets his yearly checkup—he's fine."

"But Luke kept calling for me to help him."

Josh placed his hand on her shoulder and massaged it until she relaxed. She felt his hand slowly ease off her shoulder, drop on the bed. She slipped out of the bed and went to Luke's room. She started to turn off his light when a paper caught her eye. She lifted the pad and read the letter. After she finished, she purposely left the paper right where Luke had it, turned off his light, and closed the door behind her.

She stopped down the hall to check on Braxton. He slept on his left side, thankfully not tangled in the wires.

Downstairs, she sat in front of the fire and folded her hands. *God, please keep Zack safe. I remember a preacher said that if I keep praying for Luke, it would be like I was stacking bricks in hopes that, eventually, the load would be too heavy for him to carry, and he'd fall to his knees and cry out to you. So . . . put another brick on that pile.*

❧❧

The next morning during phys-ed class, Luke sat on the wood floor, stretching his calf muscles. He lifted his head and saw Mouse approaching.

"Loser." Mouse snickered.

Crack-head idiot. Leave me alone. Luke didn't feel like getting suspended again, so he sucked up Mouse's verbal spars.

Mouse tucked his hands under his armpits and, flapped his arms like wings. "Chicken! *Bawk! Bawk! Bawk!*"

"Hey, Mouse," Jonathan said. "Let's get out of here. Coach is headed this way."

Mouse glared at Luke, then trotted away, snickering.

Coach Spears put five basketballs in the wooden trunk next to the bleachers. "Coming to conditioning tonight?"

"Yep." Luke stretched his right hamstring.

"Everything okay?"

"Couldn't be better."

The last thing Luke wanted was to tell the Coach how Mouse was treating him; he didn't want to feel the repercussions when Coach put Mouse in his place.

Coach Spears blew his whistle and pointed toward the locker room. The guys took off running. "Get going," he said to Jonathan, who was hanging with one hand from the basketball rim. "Wrap it up, Luke."

Luke went to the locker room and grabbed his backpack from his locker. He tried to shut the door, but it wouldn't close. Mouse had his hand on top, blocking it.

"Can't run from me now." Mouse thrust his chest at Luke, attempting to scare him. "What's your little brother's name? Isn't it Zack?" Mouse covered his mouth, pretending to laugh.

Luke knew he should tell Mrs. Frenchie about Mouse's harassment, but what then? Get made fun of by the other students? He couldn't chance it. He'd find a way to avoid Mouse, so he'd stop getting suspended. "Don't even think about putting one hand on my brother."

"Or what? You'll run to the teacher and tell?"

Jonathan sidled up next to Mouse. "Come on, dude. He ain't worth your time."

Mouse slammed the locker shut, but Luke didn't move. If Mouse made one move, he'd waylay him again. *Some people have to learn the hard way.*

"Loser." Mouse pressed his body toward Luke, laughing and, almost knocking Jonathan over. "Let's split, man."

Luke watched them turn the corner, then sat down on the concrete bench. *If that jerk lays one hand on Zack, I'll beat him so bad, his mama won't recognize him.*

Coach Spears rounded the corner. "You okay, Luke?"

"Yeah." He stood and walked past the coach. "See ya tonight."

In study hall, Luke pulled his trigonometry book out of his backpack. Glancing over, he saw Mouse whispering to Jonathan.

Brain-warped idiot. He didn't know for sure if Mouse smoked crack, but rumor had it that he did. Luke pulled out his calculator and punched the pads, trying to figure out the ratio between the sides of right triangles with reference to its acute angle. *Man, this junk is hard. I used to be able to figure this stuff out.* But the more he tried, the more he erased, the end result was a blank piece of paper ripped with holes.

∾∾

Luke sat down in the counselor's office and, tucked his backpack between his feet.

Mrs. Frenchie smiled. "I'm proud of you, Luke. The makeup work you turned in has helped your grades. You're carrying a *C* average in all your classes."

"Thanks."

"Have you given any thought to the packet I gave you?"

Luke smothered a grin. "Me? Armed forces?"

"You're very smart and have a lot of potential. And they'll give you an enlistment bonus that you can use for college."

"To be honest, I'm thinkin' that's what I'm gonna do."

"Oh, Luke. I think you'll be a fine soldier." She tucked a strand of hair behind her ear. "Do you want to talk about Jordan?"

Luke shifted in his chair. He knew what she was anticipating, but he didn't feel like answering twenty questions. Keeping himself restrained from knocking Mouse's lights out was tiring. "What's to talk about? He's gone."

Her eyes were tender. "Sometimes we need to take the time to talk about our loved ones. Do you have good memories of him?"

Luke hesitated for a sec, then said, "Yeah. He had this monkey that we played with all the time. And . . ." He blew out a sigh of frustration.

"Take your time. I know how hard this must be for you. But when we share good memories of our loved ones, it can ease our mind and help in the healing process."

"I'd make a monkey sound till he laughed so hard the tears spilled down his face."

Mrs. Frenchie smiled. "That's sweet."

Luke breathed in deeply, then slowly blew it out. "And one time he thought I left the room, so I scared him when I said "BOO," but he didn't even cry. He just giggled."

"Sounds like you two had fun. I want you to understand that a loved one's death doesn't fit into the picture of life as we know it. Survivors often feel pain that can't be explained. But the good news is that someday you'll be back to functioning normally."

Luke swallowed the lump in this throat, steadied his voice. "I don't know about that."

Mrs. Frenchie leaned back in her chair. "Most times, though, a day barely passes that you won't think about him. But if there is, don't feel guilty. It's a part of the healing. For now, I want you to focus on the joy Jordan brought to your life."

He nodded.

"Stay strong." She smiled.

Luke stood. "Thanks. I better go."

In trigonometry class, he couldn't concentrate. Mrs. Frenchie was right. He did need to focus on the good times he'd had with Jordan. *But how?* He grabbed the book out of his backpack—the book Mrs. Frenchie had lent to him—and read the last two pages. He learned that the woman who had lost her husband could never have survived his death if she hadn't leaned on God to help her.

Luke sighed. He had heard about God all of his life, but hadn't experienced the joy others talked about by actually knowing him one on one. Sure, at one point he had faith there was a God, had faith in many things, but all that changed in a second. Frustrated, he thumbed through the last few pages of the book until he found the author's picture and bio. A scribbled note at the bottom of the page caught his eye.

Dear Annie,

Losing Abbey and Rick has to be devastating. I'll keep you in my prayers.

Love Marsha.

Annie? The end-of-period bell rang, startling Luke; he'd missed the teacher's lesson.

CHAPTER NINETEEN

Through her car window, Sarah watched the RTA bus, sooty and exhaling black smoke, trundle to a stop. A few disgruntled-looking people made their way down the sidewalk to the visitation department at Children Services.

She glanced at her watch. In twenty minutes, she'd meet Braxton's daddy. Tapping on her plastic coffee cup with the only unbitten fingernail on her right hand, she breathed deeply, trying to steady her shaky nerves. She rummaged in her purse for her cell phone then called home.

Josh answered on the third ring. "Where are you?"

"Waiting for Braxton's family."

"How'd it go with your therapist?"

"She's worried that if Braxton goes home, I'll fall apart." She laughed. "My therapist is worried about me."

"Well honey, don't worry. Get through this day and come home."

Sarah flipped the lid down on her cell phone and put it in her purse. She glanced at her watch. In five minutes, the others would arrive. *Then what? Will Braxton's daddy give me a hard time because his son is in the system?*

Georgia pecked on her window, causing Sarah to jump. She held the button until the glass disappeared into the doorframe.

"Mmm...girl...I'm nervous." Georgia's dimples were as deep as Braxton's. She fidgeted with the snaps on her leather jacket.

"That makes two of us." Sarah held the button until the window went back up, then tossed her keys in her purse. She climbed out of the SUV, then clipped the door shut behind her.

"Oh, girl, there he is." Georgia drew in a long breath.

A man, a little over six-feet, wearing jeans, a black sweatshirt, and a blue bandana tied at the back of his head, walked down the hill toward them.

Miss Bond approached them. "I'll see you at the conference. Sign in at the front desk and get a nametag. Someone will escort you up."

"Ah, snaps. Here we go," Georgia said.

Before Sarah could take her first deep, calming breath, he was at the front of her SUV.

Georgia put her hands on her hips. "Don't be lookin' all nuts at me."

"Girl, shut up." His face scrunched when he spoke. He turned to Sarah and pulled her right hand to his mouth, kissed the top of it. Instead of letting go, he lifted his head and said, "I'm Jamaal, and I'm grateful you're taking good care of my boy."

Sarah inhaled a big gulp of air and pulled her hand to her side. "Thank you."

Jamaal turned to face Georgia. "This is some nonsense makin' me come up here for a visit just 'cause you went and gave up our son. Some mother you are!"

Georgia jabbed her finger one inch from his face. "Don't be comin' up here in my face tellin' me nuttin. I done ask for help. Where were you? Huh? Yeah! Sittin' up in some jail, shootin' it with a bunch of bunkies, and then wanta blame me for somethin'. Humph!"

"Shut up, woman!" Jamaal swatted Georgia's hand to her side.

"I'm gonna turn around and leave now, Sarah, before the police come and put me in some cuffs." Georgia walked toward the brown brick building. Jamaal trailed after her.

Sarah made her way down the sidewalk, pausing to stare at the statue—a man sitting in a rocker, holding a happy child. At the entrance, cigarette butts overflowed a gray metal ashtray. A man stood next to it, hot-boxing a cigarette.

She opened the door and went inside. Glancing at the multicolored seating arrangement in the middle of the room, she saw Georgia studying the paintings of the African-American children, then walked to the desk, signed in, and put the nametag on her shirt.

"Over here, Mama." Georgia yelled.

Sarah turned to see Shirley entering. Her makeup made her look ten years younger. She waved at Georgia, then said, "Good morning,

Sarah."

Shirley nodded at Jamaal. Sarah didn't think she had a mean bone in her body. *No. Shirley definitely didn't have any bad traits at all. She's a woman full of grace.*

"Ya'll 'bout ready?" Georgia asked, coming to stand beside Shirley.

The receptionist handed Shirley a nametag. "Here's Missy now. She's going to take you up."

Missy led the way to the elevator. "I wish we'd get another huge snow so I could take my kiddos sledding one more time."

In the elevator, Georgia stayed close to Shirley and watched the green numbers on the elevator window.

"Here we are," Missy said when the elevator came to a halt. "The conference room on your right. Miss Bond will be with you shortly."

Sarah walked into the room and seated herself. A stack of papers rested on the table to her left. Jamaal sat down beside her. Georgia and Shirley sat opposite.

"How was prison?" Georgia asked, sarcastically.

"You better shut up, girl. I didn't come up in here to fight, just to get my son back."

"We'll see 'bout that." Georgia sneered.

Shirley placed her hand on Georgia's. "Calm down."

Miss Bond entered and sat down at the head of the table. Sarah inched her chair closer to Miss Bond, bumping her shin on the leg of the table.

"Bet that hurt," Jamaal said.

Sarah grimaced, then forced herself to think about something else beside the stressful environment. Miss Bond wrote something on her yellow pad and sifted through some papers. She wore a pink pendant on her gold chain.

"That's a pretty necklace," Sarah said.

"Thank you. I wear it in memory of my aunt. It represents breast cancer awareness."

Sarah could relate. She put her hand to her neck and felt for her blue and black butterfly pendant—the one she'd bought after Jordan passed. She only took the necklace off when she showered.

Miss Bond pulled a stack of papers from a manila folder and said, "I arranged this meeting so we could discuss long-term goals for Braxton, and to relay information in regard to individual case plans. This week my supervisor and I will discuss potential family members as caretakers, and what each case plan should contain. I will notify each of you to discuss these issues."

Jamaal interrupted. "What ya mean 'bout each case plan?"

"Any family member wishing to care for Braxton will have to complete a case plan before we will consider placing the child with them."

Jamaal cleared his throat. "Such as?"

"We will conduct a home study and a background check which includes personal information and financial stability. The caretaker must be willing to attend all of his medical appointments." Miss Bond glanced down for a minute, then added, "And last week the judge signed the order for the county to have temporary custody."

Georgia sighed aloud. Jamaal tapped his fingers on the tabletop.

"Now," Miss Bond said, "if Georgia passes her psyche evaluation and completes her case plan, we'll return Braxton to her."

"There ain't nuttin wrong with me," Georgia interrupted.

Jamaal shook his head. "There ain't? You gave our boy to Children Services. Somethin' done wrong with your head."

Georgia pushed back her chair and stood. Sarah felt her heart gallop. She wasn't sure if she should flee the scene or stay and help Miss Bond. She was beginning to fear for Braxton's safety. She wished Josh were here, or someone in security who could intervene should something happen.

"You!" Georgia pointed at Jamaal. "You shouldn't even get a chance to get Braxton, not someone who's been up in prison for bustin' up someone."

Jaamal pointed his finger at Georgia. "Don't be runnin' your mouth to me."

Miss Bond stood up. "I want both of you to sit down now! Any more outbursts and I will call for security. Is that clear?"

"Yes, ma'am," Shirley said, helping Georgia back to her seat.

Jaamal returned to his seat, still glaring at Georgia.

"Now, Georgia. What would you like to say?" Miss Bond asked.

"I want my boy back, but if I can't get him, I don't want him goin' with his daddy." She played with the buttons on her checked blouse. "I want my mama to raise him."

"My supervisor and I will discuss who we think will be suitable to work a case plan. Meanwhile, Braxton will remain in Sarah's care. Do you plan to visit him at the Kiser's home for four hours each week?"

"Yup." Georgia didn't look up.

Miss Bond glanced at Jamaal. "You can visit the baby at our

visitation department. Will Fridays work for you, Sarah?"

"That's fine. I schedule his medical appointments on Mondays and Wednesdays."

"I'll sit in on the first few visits." Miss Bond shuffled some papers. "Does he have any upcoming doctor appointments?"

"He'll be seeing the gastro-doctor, soon. I'll let you know when they schedule the appointment." Sarah's stomach felt queasy.

"Any questions?" Miss Bond's eyes scanned the room.

"No," Sarah answered.

Miss Bond winked at Sarah before she rose, indicating the meeting was over.

Georgia and Shirley walked to the door, hand in hand.

Jamaal lingered. "You comin', Sarah?"

"No. I need to talk to Miss Bond." After Jamaal left, she helped Miss Bond push in the chairs. "That was tense."

"Happens all the time."

"Sounds like you have a very stressful job."

"I do."

"I best get going. Have a good day." Sarah shouldered her purse.

"You, too. Thanks for coming in."

Sarah made her way to the elevator. She didn't trust Jamaal, didn't know whether Georgia would meet the requirements to care for Braxton, and wondered if Shirley's job would allow her to take him. A smile quirked her lips at the thought that maybe she and Josh would get to raise Braxton as their own. Then her thoughts shifted to Dr. Porfor, and she worried how she would respond when they came face to face again.

❧❦

Sarah found Josh and Zack at the dining room table, playing a game of *Chess*, and Luke was hovered over his trigonometry book. "Where's Brax?"

Josh didn't take his eyes off the game board. "Napping."

Zack moved his queen. "Checkmate."

Josh winked at Sarah, and she knew that meant he'd let Zack win. She went into the living room and kicked off her shoes.

Josh snuck up behind her and, spun her around. "How'd it go?"

She rolled her eyes.

"That bad, huh?"

"It wasn't awful, but it wasn't great."

He wove his fingers into hers. "It'll get better."

"So you say." She smiled, but her mind was still on the day's events. Was it possible they had a chance of keeping Braxton?

He followed her into the kitchen.

"Josh, you make the best coffee," she said, smiling.

Zack snickered and put the lid back on the game box. "Mom says that when she's too tired to make it herself."

"I get the hint."

"Care if I go watch *Batman* since I got my studies done?"

Josh tousled Zack's hair. "What? No preaching today?"

"Mom?" Zack pointed to his hair. "Will you cut this mess tonight?"

"Don't worry, I'll cut it."

He hugged her, then sped off to watch TV.

Sarah plopped down on a barstool and watched Josh carefully measure one-half decaf to one-half regular coffee. The doctor had warned her to lay off the caffeine, or it would cause more anxiety.

She yawned.

Luke got up, closed his trigonometry book, then went to the fridge to grab and apple. He closed the door with his elbow. "Dad, don't forget I got conditioning at six o'clock."

"I won't. Hey, I got good news." Josh pulled two mugs out of the cupboard.

"Good news in this house is a rarity," Luke said and bit into his apple.

Josh filled two mugs with coffee, stirred in cream and sugar, then handed a mug off to Sarah.

She blew at the stem, then took a sip. "What?"

"The secretary at the medical board called to tell us they disciplined Dr. Aspen. He's no longer allowed to practice in our state."

Sarah choked on her coffee, burning her nostrils. She grabbed a napkin out of the holder and blew her nose. "You're kidding."

"There's more. Dr. Porfor got a write-up for not coming to Jordan's rescue when he knew the shunt had malfunctioned. Isn't that good news?"

Sarah couldn't respond. She'd prayed for this day to come. She wanted justice for Jordan, and she'd hoped Dr. Aspen would never have the opportunity to touch another child in their state again, or any state for that matter. *Thank you, God.* "He'll just go to another state to practice."

"Honey, you can't call every state and protect every kid."

She couldn't help but laugh. Josh was right, but she could email all the medical boards and warn them about the doctor.

"Why can't she?" Luke took another bite of his apple.

"Exactly." Sarah saw the sheen of tears in Luke's eyes.

"If she doesn't that jerk will go state hopping and kill other kids."

"It's not fair, but we don't have any control over that." Josh refilled his coffee mug.

Luke sighed. "He was only in our state for what, a year and a half?"

"A year." Sarah knew how he felt. When Josh took Luke to conditioning, she planned to email the medical boards and warn them about Dr. Aspen.

"Doesn't anyone care if a doctor state hops?" Luke asked.

Sarah stood and stretched her arms toward the ceiling. "Honey, I don't know how it works, but I intend to find out."

Josh intervened, "Don't. At least our state disciplined him, and now we should just leave it alone."

"But, Dad, if you were a parent in another state, wouldn't you want to know? I mean what if it was your kid?"

"It was my kid," Josh replied.

"Exactly," Luke said.

Josh leaned against the kitchen counter. "I'm pretty sure other medical boards will check his past work record."

Sarah hoped that after tonight every state would be on the lookout for Dr. Aspen. "I saw Toni today, and she's worried about you, Luke." He didn't respond, so she continued. "Are you finding it easier having Braxton here, I mean, with us?"

"I don't even know the kid. But since you brought it up, I need to know if you're planning on takin' him to my ball games?"

Sarah knew exactly where this conversation was headed. "I assume you're talking about how Mouse will respond when I show up with Braxton at your games?"

"Well it doesn't take a rocket scientist to figure it out."

"Don't get smart with your mother," Josh scolded.

"I'm not getting smart. But the minute mama shows up with that kid, you know Mouse is gonna run his mouth. I don't feel like getting thrown off the team or getting into any more fights. I only got three more months, and my school days will be history."

Sarah felt a tiny headache beginning to form behind her eyes. "I can't hide out with Braxton worrying what others will say."

"But this ain't about you, Mama."

She massaged her temples. "No. I'm not the one with the issue."

"I'm just saying that Braxton will be an excuse for Mouse to attack me."

"Then we'll stay home."

"But you promised you wouldn't do that. Now you're going back on what you said?" Luke's face turned red.

"What do you want? It's not my fault you go to school with a kid that's a racist. And furthermore, I think Mouse is going to use anything against you whether Braxton is black or not because he's jealous."

"Just come then."

It hurt Sarah to see Luke upset, but what other option did she have? "I'll tell Mouse that he's a foster child, or I'll talk to his father."

"Don't you dare. Then he'll really go out of his way to come after me."

Josh rinsed out his mug and placed it in the drainer. "Luke's right. Don't interfere."

"Today he was already making threats about me having a brother named Zack. If he lays one hand on Zack, I'll beat the tar out of him," Luke said.

Josh frowned. "If he bothers you again, tell Mrs. Frenchie."

"Easy for you to say, Dad."

Sarah saw the worry in Josh's eyes. "Honey, I agree with your dad."

Josh interrupted. "I went to school with this guy named Marshall who had a problem with me because I was the starting pitcher for the baseball team. When I got picked for the select team and he didn't, his threats turned severe."

Luke's eyebrows rose. "Really?"

"Yep. And one day he threw me against my locker and broke my nose."

Sarah shivered at the thought. "See, honey. That's why you have to talk to someone if this becomes a problem. I don't want you to get hurt."

"Did that kid get suspended for breaking your nose?"

"He got more than that. Grandpa Kiser pressed charges. That's why I wanted to get into the field of corrections. So I could help inmates who were bullies or victims of it."

Sarah smiled. "Ah. I didn't know that."

Luke sighed. "School's a lot different now. Kids will shoot you."

"We need to pray that the remainder of your senior year will be less of a hardship," Sarah suggested.

"Mama, I don't think God cares if someone beats me up. You act like he'll intervene and pass me a nunchaku from heaven."

Sarah laughed. "A what?"

"A nunchaku is a fighting stick used in martial arts. Mike taught me that."

"No. I don't believe God will send you whatever you called it, but he does care about you."

Luke changed the subject. "I'm starving. What's for supper?"

"We can order a pizza," Zack's voice piped in from the living room.

"So you can eat one by yourself?" Luke asked.

Zack walked to the dining room hutch and shuffled through the pizza coupons. "Pizza Parlor has a sale. Buy a large pizza, get the second one half off, and a two-liter coke."

"Order it," Josh said.

"When did Braxton eat?" Sarah filled the sink with water, drizzled in some Dawn dish soap, and lowered his dirty bottles into the water.

"He should be getting up any minute," Josh replied.

As if on cue, Braxton's cries filtered into the kitchen. "I'll get him," Zack said, "after I order the pizza."

"I'm gonna go finish my homework." Luke left the room.

"Try not to worry, Sarah," Josh said, "but I know you will. The thing I adore about you the most is that when you love someone, it is body and soul, whole-heartedly, forever. That's what makes you special and why I'm so thankful I married you."

"Thanks, Josh." She took the bottlebrush from the dish drainer, shoved it into a dirty bottle, and swished it around. "I need to talk."

"Go ahead." His voice was unrushed and gentle.

"I know that Jordan's life counted for something," she said, rinsing out the bottle and placing it upside down to drip dry on a clean dishcloth.

"Where did that come from? Of course it did."

"I know he taught us to love unconditionally, even if the end result is more pain. And taking him in was a sure way for us to share our love." She picked up another bottle and pushed the brush into it.

"So what's bothering you?"

"I have a confession to make." She swirled the brush around inside the bottle like she was scrubbing the inside hole of a toilet, then rinsed it out and placed it on the dishcloth.

"Okay." Josh's voice remained even.

"When I prayed to get another baby like Jordan, I wanted one who could fill the void. I'm not saying that Luke and Zack aren't special, but medically fragile kids are . . ." She searched for the right word. "Unique."

"Honey, I knew that."

"But there's more." Sarah wiped her hands on the back of her jeans.

"You love Braxton, and if we have to give him back, you'll have a hard time." Josh confirmed.

She swallowed hard. "Yes."

"We can take only one day at a time. God will see you through this if he does go home."

If he goes? She laughed. Of course he would probably go—blood and family took precedence over strangers. Even Miss Bond had warned her that most of the children eventually go home.

She stood on her tiptoes and wrapped her arms around his shoulders. "Sometimes, I just need to vent."

"You're stronger than you give yourself credit for."

Zack came into the kitchen. "He's hungry." Braxton was sucking on Zack's left forearm.

"Come here, Brax." Sarah freed him from Zack's arms just as the doorbell rang.

"Hey, Luke?" Josh hollered up the steps. "The pizza's here." Then to Sarah he said, "I meant to tell you earlier Dr. Porfor's office called. Braxton's appointment is Monday at 9 a.m."

Sarah's heart thumped while she waited for the baby's bottle to warm. She lifted it out of the warmer, moved to the living room, and sat feeding Braxton, while Josh and the boys ate pizza.

"Zack! Save a few pieces for mom," Luke said.

Then, while Josh and the boys talked about Luke's upcoming baseball games and fishing, Sarah was painfully aware, every now and then, in the midst of the laughter drifting into the living room from her family, that someone was definitely missing. *Jordan, I wish you were still here.*

Braxton finished his bottle. Sarah wiped his milk-splashed lips with a cloth diaper, then traced the creases of his chubby wrist with her fingers. He stared at her through his dark eyes and grinned, kicking his little legs. Then he opened his mouth as if he was going to babble; instead, he spit up. The warm juices ran down the sides of his mouth and dripped on her jeans. She wiped his lips, his neck, and then she lifted him to her shoulder and patted his back. His legs stiffened as he let out a big belch, then he laid his head on her shoulder and exhaled a warm breath against her neck.

"I wuv you. Maybe, just maybe, you can stay with me forever."

CHAPTER TWENTY

Sarah flipped on the light in Luke's room. She lifted his box springs and smiled when she found no alcohol. Next she checked his footlocker, drawers, and closet. Satisfied, she went to turn off the light when a flower-patterned book poking out of Luke's backpack caught her eye. She pulled it out, and a paper fluttered to the ground. She stooped to pick it up, then sat on Luke's bed to read it.

Dear Jordan,

I finished a book my counselor lent me about a woman who lost her husband to cancer. She finally asked God to help her with her pain and said he brought joy back into her life. I guess some people got saved after her husband died 'cause of the way he lived his life. I still ain't sure what being saved means, and I ain't gonna tell Mama 'cause she'll drag me over to the preacher's house. I felt bad that I stole a pair of shoes the other night and could've gone to jail. I'm sure God already told you the story. He probably thinks I'm a loser, too.

Tears scalded Sarah's eyes. *Please God,* she prayed, closing her eyes for just a moment.

Please continue to be longsuffering with Luke.

She flipped through the pages of the book and settled on one with a picture of a Fear-Face-Cycle clock. As she studied it, she understood the author's intent just by looking at the phases of fear that could cause you to stay stuck in grief forever. But she hadn't. She'd stepped on old roads and opened her heart to Braxton. Even if he was to return home with his family, she no longer could allow the "what ifs" to take priority any longer, but rather she'd have to take each day as it came and place her cares into God's hands, just as she'd done before.

She traced her finger around the clock and found the phase of grief that currently held Luke victim—the phase of doubt, negativity, and terror. The stage of morbidity and even isolation. *God please, don't let him have suicidal thoughts.*

She leafed further and found a post-it-note on which Luke had written only one word. *Memorize.* She carefully lifted the note and read the passage aloud. "You will never be alone on the Isle of Faith. You'll be safe because I will always be at your side. Many people never find this Isle because of unbelief."

Sarah closed her eyes. *Thank you, God. I hope Luke's starting to get it.*

Downstairs, she found Josh in the living room.

He lowered the volume on the TV with the remote. "Something wrong, honey?"

"Do you ever feel weak and feeble?"

"I think we all do. Why?"

"Do you ever have fear?"

He slung his arm around her shoulder. "I came to realize that I am what I am by the grace of God, and that summed up my fear."

"But how do you deal with stress?"

"Honey, when things in life are stressful, I hide behind His shield. I'm not talking about earthly issues, I mean spiritual ones. God knows what we need before we even ask. For example, I don't ask God to plow our driveway when it's snow covered, but he might lay it on a neighbor's heart to do it for me."

Sarah couldn't keep from laughing.

"What's so funny?"

"I don't see God shoveling our driveway either. So when you're at wit's end, you basically ask God if He can help you out with something."

"Honey, you know as well as I do that the storms in life that we face are spiritual ones. The rest are merely earthly issues. I try and not dwell on the earthly junk because they bog me down. I learned a long time ago that worrying makes me sick to my stomach, so why worry when I can pray?"

"You're right. I'm guilty of taking my troubles to God and then taking them back."

"That's just your nature, honey."

"You're right." She stretched out on the couch, and propping her legs on Josh's thigh, watched the program with him. Detectives Benson and Stabler were frustrated by the justice system because their prime suspect was able to buy his way out of a conviction with his high-priced lawyer and manipulations. Sarah frowned. *Would the justice system be fair and make sure Braxton is given to a family member who will take good care of him?* she wondered.

⊱ ⊰

The next morning Sarah awoke and rubbed her stiff neck and achy hip. She had fallen asleep on the couch and Josh hadn't bothered to wake her. It had been weeks since she had gotten a good night's sleep, since Braxton woke up wailing every three or four hours needing to be fed. In the kitchen, she popped an Osteobiflex into her mouth, chased it down with a sip of water, then dug down into the washer and pulled out the baby's T-shirts, sleepers, and blankets, and tossed them into the dryer along with a cling-free sheet. She had washed them the night prior between sending letters to the medical boards and snooping through Luke's room.

"Mornin'." Luke brushed past her and, grabbed a bottle of water out of the fridge.

"Hey. How was practice?"

"Same ole." He chose an apple and took a bite. "Will you take me driving tonight?"

"Shouldn't be a problem." Sarah filled Josh's travel mug with coffee. "You want a bowl of cereal or oats?"

He shook his head. "Not hungry."

"Eat lunch today, so your blood sugar doesn't drop."

Josh entered the kitchen, smiling. "Yes, Dr. Kiser."

"You ready, Dad?" Zack stumbled, trying to put on his left shoe. "We're gonna be late."

"Zack! You're the only kid I know who worries about getting to school twenty minutes before the bell rings. Chill. And sit down and put your shoes on before you fall," Luke demanded.

Josh cupped Sarah around the waist with his arm. "Have a good day."

She rubbed her neck. "Thanks for letting me sleep."

He chuckled. "You were sawing logs. That's why I didn't bother you. Plus I know today's gonna be stressful, when you see the "quack" as you call him." He grabbed his mug, grinning.

Luke slung his free arm around her neck. "Have a good day, Mama."

"You, too." Then she hugged Zack.

After they left Sarah locked the door and sat at the table with her first cup of coffee. Soon Braxton would wake up, and she'd feed and dress him, and then it would be time to go see the doctor. For once, she wasn't nervous. She knew exactly what she was going to say.

∾∾

On the drive home from the hospital, Sarah's knuckles turned white from gripping the steering wheel. She turned on the radio. "I'm Already There," played softly— the song she'd adopted after Jordan passed. How many nights she'd gazed out the window and felt goose bumps travel up and down her spine while she sang "I'm the moonlight shining down."

She drew in a deep breath, trying to calm her twisted nerves. Dr. Porfor knew Jordan's brain had been under pressure. *I trusted him*. Stuck at a red light, she sighed. *Why did he retreat to silence? Was he afraid he'd get reprimanded by the good-ole-boys club?*

The light changed to green, and she turned on to her street, replaying in her mind what the doctor had said. "I refuse to be Braxton's doctor. He's a liability risk to our hospital."

Sarah wanted to spit nails. *This dispute wasn't about Braxton. He's retaliating because of the write up.* She'd feared she'd eventually unload on this doctor, if given the opportunity, and that's exactly what she'd done. "You didn't bother to say a word about Jordan's brain herniating. Then you walk in here and say you won't see Braxton because he's a "liability risk" to your practice. You're afraid of me because I'm a mother who knows her stuff, and if you make another mistake, I'll be on your trail," Sarah said, satisfied that her words caused the doctor's face to turn as red as a cherry tomato.

And then Miss Lewis, the social worker, just had to put in her two-cents. "Mrs. Kiser, your comments are totally unnecessary."

"So was Jordan's death." When Sarah said it, the hot tears came, but she hadn't held back. "I didn't want to bring Braxton here to begin with. To be honest, I wouldn't want to bring a dead rat here." Sarah's heart rate quickened, and her body shook like a leaf tumbling in the wind. She felt an impending panic attack.

"I will contact Children Services and let them know," Miss Lewis said.

"Tell them what?" Sarah wiped her tears with her palm. "That I'm an extremist when it comes to advocating for children?"

"This conversation is over," Dr. Porfor said and left the room.

Sarah took Braxton's carrier inside the house and set it by the TV. She rubbed her bicep as she picked up the phone to call Miss Bond. *Now they'll probably take Braxton.* While she waited for Miss Bond to answer, she chased down her anxiety pill with a sip of cold coffee still on the table from earlier that morning.

The phone rang once, twice. Miss Bond answered on the third ring.

"It's Sarah."

"I already heard. Are you okay?"

"Shaky, but thanks for asking."

"I figured this would happen after you told me what happened to Jordan. I should've told you to take him to another hospital."

Sarah exhaled a sigh of relief. "Whew! I thought you'd be upset."

"How could I be? I'm grateful I have a foster mom who cares about her kids. Did the others come to his appointment?"

Sarah laughed. The way she said "the others" made them sound like aliens. "Yes, they were there."

"Okay. I'll call you later in the week and let you know how Georgia's psyche evaluation turns out."

Sarah hung up and dialed Dr. Bleu's office. She'd promised Georgia that before the clock struck midnight, she'd find a doctor for Braxton. Dr. Bleu impressed Sarah. He took time to talk with her during office hours and understood her concerns.

"Don't worry, I'll manage his reflux, and it's fine to feed him cereal. I'll call in a script for Zantac. Follow up with me in three weeks," Dr. Bleu had said.

Braxton had fallen asleep in his car seat while she was on the phone. She unbuckled him, took off his coat, and put him in his bed. Downstairs, she grabbed the liniment—a Chinese herbal mixture her preacher had given to her for aches and pains—and massaged it into her hip. On cold days, her hip moaned. The injury happened a year ago, when she and Josh had taken the boys sledding. Without warning, Josh pushed her down the hill. The sled plunked into a huge hole, came out flying in the air like a saucer, and then spat Sarah onto the cold, hard ground. Her doctor couldn't repair the cracked hip because the tumors they'd found in her pelvis took priority. She still hadn't bothered to fix it. She didn't have the time with caring for a family and an infant. And it didn't bother her, really, because her family always came first.

She sat on the couch, leaned on a stack of pillows, and trailed the English Ivy she'd stenciled along the top of the living room wall until she drifted off to sleep.

Mommy? Jordan stood on a white sandy beach. There were no braces supporting his legs, no tubes pumping food into his stomach, and his sandy colored hair looked soft as silk.

Jordan?

Sarah smiled when he stretched his arms toward her. They were about to embrace when she heard a voice in the distance call her. "Mama? Wake up!"

She sat up and rubbed her eyes. "What time is it?"

"It's 1:45. School dismissed early. Teacher conference." Luke sat on the floor next to the warm fire, a opened can of Pepsi in his hand.

"How was school? Any problems with Mouse?"

He shook his head. "How did the doctor visit go?"

She changed the subject. "When I went to school, we didn't have pop machines. No wonder kids are so hyped."

He grinned. "Times have changed, Mama."

Wasn't that the truth? Times had changed. She couldn't believe that in the past year and a half she'd lost her four-year-old son, watched her oldest son drown in his own tears, and added a new baby to her family.

Luke took a swig of his Pepsi. "So— how did the appointment go?"

Sarah sat beside him, hoping the fire would warm her stressed bones and calm her achy hip. "Dr. Porfor said Braxton is a liability risk and refused to be his doctor."

Luke chuckled. "Sounds to me like he's afraid if he does somethin' wrong, you'll go after him again."

"Most likely."

Luke took another swig of his pop. "What'ya gonna do?"

"I took care of it. Dr. Bleu said he'd monitor Braxton's reflux."

For a while neither spoke. The only sound came from the auger, delivering pellets into the stove. Sarah wished he would share how he felt about Sunday's service, but was afraid she'd ruin their moment together if she brought it up. "Did you eat lunch?"

"Yep."

She stood and straightened her spine. "I best go start supper and check on Braxton."

While she folded the blanket, Luke turned on the TV to watch the prerecorded episode of *House*.

"'House' again, huh?"

He flopped on the couch. "Yep. He's in a mental institution, actually the patient this time." He glanced up. "Did I tell you he's addicted to Vicodin?"

Sarah glanced at the TV. "Really?'

"Uh-huh, but he's still a good doc. I think stress drove him to addiction."

When Luke turned back to the TV, Sarah went to the baby's room. Braxton had rolled from his side to his back and was batting at the tiger on his crib gym.

"Good afternoon, Pumpkin," she said, startling him. "I'm sorry. Mommy didn't mean to scare you." She placed the gym on the floor and changed his diaper. Then, picking him up, she whispered in the top of his curly black hair, "Let's go see Luke."

She put Braxton in his baby swing, secured blankets around him, and wound the handle. She stooped to pick up his rattle, and then placed it in his hand. When she turned, Luke's gaze was fixed on Jordan's picture on top of the DVD cabinet, tears blurring his eyes. "You're done watching your show already?" He didn't respond, so she said, "What are you thinking about?"

Luke clicked off the television, giving her an I-don't-feel-so-good look and rubbing his stomach.

"What's the matter?"

He sat on the floor by the fire again. "I need to talk about somethin'."

She sat down on the sofa, waiting for him to speak.

"Sunday, Truman said that faith comes by hearing, and then somethin' about believing. But how do you know when you really get him, I mean, Jesus?"

She realized this might be her last chance to offer Luke the wisdom the Lord had given her. "Honey, he makes his presence known. And when he comes into your heart, trust me, you'll know."

Luke wrapped his arms around his knees. "But how?"

"It's like the wind. You can't see it, but you know it's there. Why? Was he calling to you?"

Luke shifted uneasily. "I think."

She scooted to the sofa's edge. "Can I share my experience with you?"

He nodded.

"When I was your age, I went to a revival. Every word the preacher said penetrated my heart. When they gave the altar call, the Holy Spirit was giving me the invitation to come and accept Christ, but I didn't go forward; instead, I went home and worried that if the world came to an end, I'd go to be with the devil." Sarah squeezed her eyes shut for a brief moment. *God, please help me get this out.*

She opened them to see Luke wipe at his tears with the front of his hands. "Honey, when God speaks to our heart, and by the eye of faith, we can see what Jesus did for us at the cross. Then we can choose to accept it or not."

"So, on Sunday, should I have prayed?"

"Only you know the answer to that."

He frowned. "I felt bad."

"And now?"

"I'll be fine." He stood up. "I gotta go study."

When Luke left, Sarah started tidying the room.

"Mama!" The panic in Luke's voice caused her to jump and drop the coaster.

"The kid. Braxton." Luke scurried down the steps and ran to the living room before Sarah could respond. He threw the blankets in the floor, unfastened the lap belt, and lifted Braxton into his arms. "Help him, Mama!" The look in Luke's eyes chilled her.

Braxton's extremities were extended and rigid. Only the white of his eyes showed. Sarah felt a flush of panic, but the nurse in her responded. "Give him here." She laid the baby on the floor, on his right side, and glancing at the wall clock, made a mental note of the time—*3:20 PM.*

"Call 911!" Luke pleaded, dropping to his knees beside her.

"Honey, calm down. He's having a seizure."

She knew the symptoms, having seen Jordan seize over a hundred times in one day. She had cried when the doctor diagnosed him with infantile spasm—a rare seizure disorder.

"His lips are blue," Luke shouted.

Sarah placed her hand on Braxton's chest to feel it rise and fall. She'd forgotten about the apnea monitor until it alarmed. The red light indicated apnea. Glancing at the clock, she mentally documented the time—*3:21 PM.* "I'll give him one more minute to recover. If he doesn't, I'm calling 911." She breathed in a sigh of relief when Braxton's extremities relaxed. He slowly opened his eyes, but he appeared dazed.

"You scared us." She lifted him into her arms. Slowly, his lips returned to their natural color. Now that the tense moment had passed, she lost it and sobbed.

"It's okay, Mama." Luke rubbed her back.

"I know." She cried. "It's just . . ."

"The seizure hit him hard like they did Jordan," Luke affirmed.

She nodded. "I need your help, Luke. Go start the SUV, and after I leave, call your dad and tell him I took Braxton to the ER."

When Luke left the room, Sarah held tight to the baby. *This can't be happening.*

"Mama?" Luke set Braxton's coat, her purse, and the keys on the end of the couch. "You need me to go with you?"

"I'll be fine, but thanks for the offer, and for noting Braxton's seizure."

Luke frowned. "No prob."

Sarah put Braxton's coat on him, and before leaving, she looked at Luke. "I love you. Tell your dad I'll call him later with an update."

CHAPTER TWENTY-ONE

Sarah peeked at Braxton in the rearview mirror. "Hey, Brax." He turned his head to the sound of her voice. "We're almost there, baby."

Suddenly, the bittersweet memories of yesterday were alive. Sweet, in the sense that when she looked at Braxton, she glimpsed Jordan—the way he curled his lips when he pouted, his magical smile that could brighten up any room—bitter, because they were born premature and had acquired equal amounts of physical ailments.

Her thought of Luke and how he'd responded to the seizure. She'd seen the tears that glittered in his eyes, the concern on his face when he offered to come with her. *God, please comfort him.*

She pulled the SUV into the ER parking lot and took Braxton inside. Since she'd been here last, they'd roped off a section where parents would have to stand in line and wait to be seen by the triage nurse.

"Miss?" A woman behind the desk called to her. "Before you get in line, I need to see your insurance card."

Sarah handed it to her. "He had a bad seizure."

"Aw—poor thing. Hey, Amanda, come here."

A tall thin blonde walked over. "What ya got?"

The woman glanced at the name on the card. "Braxton had a bad seizure. Want to take him on back?" Sarah breathed a sigh of relief. She'd avoid the long line and crowded waiting room.

She heard a man say, "She just got here." Sarah knew exactly how he felt. How many nights had she waited for them to call Jordan's name?

❧◦❧

Luke's dad answered on the second ring. "Capt. Kiser."

"Dad!"

"What's wrong, Luke?"

"Braxton had a bad seizure. Mama took him to the ER."

"Is he okay?"

"I think."

"You don't sound too good. I'll come home soon as I get these two inmates settled."

Luke hung up the phone and, dashed upstairs to his room. He threw himself on his bed, burying his face in his pillow. *Why did I agree to take Braxton? To make mama happy,* he reminded himself. He contemplated calling Mike. Twenty-seven more days of being grounded was more than he could bear. It'd been at least two weeks since he'd touched a drop of alcohol, and if there was ever a time he needed to flush away his grief, it was now. He stood up, and was going to do just that—call Mike—when he spied the book his counselor had loaned him, poking out of his backpack, beckoning him to pick it up. So he did, and reread a passage on page 255.

You have been shipwrecked in the icy waters, but Jesus wants to save you. He is our life raft. All you have to do is believe.

Luke laid the book on his desk.

"Hey. Whatya doing?" Zack suddenly appeared in the doorframe.

Luke raised his head. "When did you get home?"

"I've been here awhile. I didn't see the SUV and thought Mom took you driving."

Zack picked up the book. "What's this about?"

"Some lady lost her husband and was afraid she'd never be happy again or somethin'."

"Mind if I see?"

Don't know why you'd want to. You got the precious word, Mr. Perfect. "Sure."

Zack opened the book and read for a brief moment, then asked, "What's the Isle of Faith?"

"Don't pretend you don't know what it means."

A deep frown creased Zack's forehead. "I guess this lady just, well, gave a different way to think about it. Hmm . . . I like how she put it, come to think of it." He narrowed his eyes. "But you ain't got to act all mean about it. Did you and Mouse get in a fight?"

Luke couldn't tell him that Mouse had brought up Zack's name three times last week as a scare tactic. Zack would worry himself into an asthma attack. "No. Braxton had a seizure."

"What?" Zack held his hand over his chest and gasped. "When?"

"About an hour ago. Take a breath, he's fine."

"Does Dad know?" Zack laid the book back on the desk.

"I called him. He'll come home soon as he settles down some inmates."

"How's Mom?"

"Upset."

"But you don't think she should be?"

Luke sat on the edge of his bed. "Quit putting words in my mouth, but I hope she doesn't stay there all night. She was supposed to take me—"

"Driving. I bet she feels bad," Zack interrupted.

"I just wish—"

"That Mom wouldn't have taken Braxton?" Zack interrupted again, scratching his head.

"You did it again." Luke's said, a hint of frustration coloring his voice.

Zack rubbed his forehead. "Sorry."

Silence slipped between them. Luke, rubbing his hands together, finally broke the silence. "I wish I could understand how to get to the Isle of Faith."

"The woman's husband died, and she found joy because she found this Isle of faith?"

"Yep."

"So she's a Christian." Zack asked..

"Does it matter? Why does everything have to be about whether you're a Christian?" Luke couldn't keep from being irritated. He wanted the booze so bad, his mouth watered. "How did you know when you got Jesus?"

Zack folded his hands behind his head. "I just knew."

"But how?"

"I can't explain it, Luke. It's better felt, than told."

Luke rubbed the stubbles on his chin. "Mama's rooted like a short-leaf pine on that Isle."

Zack chuckled. "Quit makin' fun of her 'cause she's short."

"I'm not. It's really a tree. And there's a tree called the tree of heaven, too, but it has a long name even Truman couldn't pronounce."

For a moment, the silence gained weight. Luke finally spoke. "So, once you decide to accept Jesus, do all your problems go away?"

Zack shifted his weight. "Just 'cause you trust in God doesn't mean you'll never have pain. It just means that instead of turning to bad things for comfort, God will comfort you. Truman could probably explain it better."

Luke considered that. "So instead of me turning to alcohol to solve my problems, I'd just say, God, it's me again with another crisis, help me out here, buddy."

Zack grinned. "Somethin' like that, but not exactly."

"Is that what you do?"

"I try and not worry when bad things happen. I mean, look at Mom. She prayed for God to send her a child like Jordan, and he answered her prayer. Since Braxton's having problems, she could easily give him back, but she won't because he makes her happy."

Luke closed his eyes. It felt good to talk to Zack this way, as true brothers, who had something more than a sad past that left a bitter taste in their mouth. Memories came at him like a kaleidoscope. "I really miss Jordan."

"I know."

"I'm that obvious?"

"You've been the center of attention since he died."

Luke chuckled. "That bad, huh?"

"We all make mistakes," Zack said, walking to Luke's dresser to study the trophies he'd earned last year during ACME baseball.

"Maybe Dad will take me driving."

"And out to eat." Zack rubbed his stomach. Then he picked up a trophy from Luke's dresser. "Mom and Dad are so proud of you."

Luke shook his head. "They shouldn't be proud of me for nothin'."

Zack set the trophy down and placed his hands on his hips. "Why would you say that?"

"Because I'm not like you."

Zack folded his arms across his chest. "What's that supposed to mean?"

"Well, let's see. You never do anything wrong. You read your Bible all the time, and—"

"You could, too. It's a choice."

Luke rolled his eyes. "So you're basically saying I'm a piece of dirt?"

"I didn't say that. Stop putting words in my mouth."

Luke could feel his blood begin to boil again. "But that's what you meant."

"No," Zack insisted. "But you do treat your family like dirt sometimes, especially me." Zack reached for another trophy.

"Stop nosing through my stuff!"

"I'm not. And see what I mean? You treat me like . . ." Zack didn't finish; instead, he turned to walk out of the room.

"You think you're perfect?"

Zack stopped and turned. "I don't think that."

"You act like it. And you're eyes are always glued to your Bible."

"Hey, say it, don't spray it." Zack laughed.

Luke stared at him for a second, and then he laughed. Deep down, he had to admit he yearned to be like Zack. "I'm sorry. I shouldn't have acted that way."

Zack put his hand up to silence Luke. "Don't apologize."

"I already feel like crap, okay, so don't tell me I can't."

"I didn't say you couldn't. I just wish you wouldn't."

Luke inched back on his bed, bent his knees, and put his head on his folded arms. "What do I gotta do?"

Zack sat down on the edge of the bed. "You're asking me for advice?"

"Yeah. I'm askin'."

"For starters you need to accept Jordan's death. And I'm not saying it's gonna be easy, because it ain't. But once you do that, you won't need alcohol to help you cope. And . . ."

"Don't stop now."

"You'll learn what unconditional love means."

"I already know what it means."

Zack stared at Luke.

"It means," Luke said, "to be loved without doing something to deserve it." He swallowed the lump beginning to rise in his throat.

"Do you think you're worthy of that kind of love?"

"I hope so," Luke said softly.

"Well, you are."

Luke didn't move. It felt like concrete blocks had him anchored to the bed. He wanted to get up and wrap his arms around his brother; instead, he said, "I guess."

"I'll say this again, and then I gotta go study. When you're willing to take the risk and accept Jordan's death, then you'll start healing."

Luke sat up straight. "How did you get so much knowledge at fifteen? See what I mean? You're gonna be a preacher someday, mark my word."

"Like I said before, I think God wants me to graduate and go to college."

Josh appeared in the doorway. "What's going on?"

"We were just having a brotherly chat," Zack said.

Josh grinned. "Is Braxton okay? Did your mom call?"

"No. She hasn't called," Zack said. "You wanta take us out to dinner? And take Luke driving?"

"Yeah. That sounds like a good idea. Let me get changed and grab the cell phone, in case your mom tries to call."

CHAPTER TWENTY-TWO

Sarah had waited patiently for over an hour for the doctor to come into the room; the stillness grated on her nerves. Finally, a woman entered. "Sorry for the wait, I'm Doctor Turner."

Sarah tried to smile, but failed.

"I ordered a CT scan for this little guy, and an EEG. Has the tech been in yet?"

Sarah shook her head. "Did the receptionist contact Children Services?"

Dr. Turner paused to look at Braxton's chart. "This says we have permission to treat. So, his seizure lasted two minutes?"

"Yes, ma'am." Sarah rubbed her fingers through Braxton's springy curls.

Georgia's voice carried though the door. "Thank ya." She burst in the room; her eyes were red and swollen. "Is he okay?"

"He is now," Sarah said.

"Girl . . . What happened?"

"He had a bad seizure. How did you find out?"

"Miss Bond called."

"Sorry to interrupt, but I plan to admit Braxton to ICU tonight for observation," Dr. Turner said.

Sarah swallowed hard, still unable to digest what had happened. "Okay."

Georgia leaned over the bed, straightened Braxton's blanket. "You don't look so hot."

"It's been a day," Sarah replied.

Georgia ran her fingers through her not-so-freshly weaved hair. "I know that's right."

Sarah stepped back. "I'm going to step out for a breath of fresh air."

"Go on. I got Fat Boy."

In the hallway, Sarah watched a father pull a child in a red wagon while pushing the IV pole. A mother sat rocking her screaming baby. *God, please help these little kids get better, and please let us receive good news.*

A technician stood at the entrance. "I'm here to take Braxton down for his CT scan."

"Can you wait till foster mom gets back?" Georgia asked.

Sarah eased past the tech. "I'm here."

"We'll take him down in this bed since he's hooked up to a monitor," the tech said.

Sarah was glad the tech made that decision. The day's stress had left her drained. They walked alongside the tech and came to a metal door. Georgia pointed to the sign that read: ONLY ONE PARENT PERMITTED. Sarah turned toward the undersized waiting room.

"Girl, go on."

Sarah paused. "Are you sure? I don't mind staying out?"

"Nah. Go."

The technician instructed Sarah to lay Braxton on the bed. She helped him secure blankets on opposite sides. "He's ready," the tech called out to the nurse.

The nurse entered and injected medicine into Braxton's IV port. "This machine can be loud, and he has to lie still, so the medicine will make him drowsy. Is there anything I can get for you?"

Sarah recalled the times Jordan had been in this same room for numerous CT scans, and how the music from the portable CD player soothed him. "Do you have any music?"

"I do." The nurse retrieved a portable player from the long gray metal table and handed it to Sarah. "You'll have to wear one of those blue vests if you plan to stay in here during the scan."

Sarah lifted the weighted vest, slipped it on, and went to stand beside Braxton. The nurse placed three straps across his body, then joined the technician in the small booth.

"You'll hear a whirring sound," the tech said over an intercom.

Sarah didn't need to be reminded. Slowly the narrow bed made its way into the doughnut hole. She was surprised Braxton hadn't moved despite all the noise.

Once he was inside the machine, he stirred. Sarah turned on the CD player. "Somewhere over the rainbow" began to play. She held the player at the machine's entrance and turned up the volume. Braxton drifted back to sleep.

After the noise ceased, the bed slowly emerged. Through a small window, Sarah watched the nurse and tech talking inside the booth; a computer screen radiated the room in green and yellow colors. They took turns pointing to the screen. *Please God, don't let them find anything.*

"Okay. I'll take you back," the tech said, entering the room.

Suddenly, the old territory became more familiar. It seemed every hall they walked, every turn they made, reminded Sarah of Jordan. She turned her head so the tech wouldn't see her moist eyes.

"Here we go." The tech eased the bed into the room. "The doctor should be in soon."

Georgia sat down and opened the *Cat in the Hat* book. She flipped through the pages, then glanced up. "You mind if I spend the night?"

"Of course not. I think I'll go home and check on my family."

Georgia held tight to the book. "Nuh—uh. You ain't leavin' me here all by myself."

I won't stay with Braxton if he's admitted to the hospital. He has his own mom to do that. Sarah had meant to keep her promise to Luke. She had told him she'd take him driving. *Would he understand?* For a moment, she debated whether to stay or not, but the minute she glanced over at Georgia and Braxton, she saw two kids with different needs. "I'll stay, but I need to call home."

❧

Inside Braxton's ICU room, Sarah stared at the huddled crew at the nurses' station. Braxton had had his EEG earlier, and she wondered about the results. *Why don't they come in here and say something?* Georgia had fallen asleep with her head on the mattress beside her baby's head.

Finally, someone knocked at the door. "Mrs. Kiser?"

Sarah turned to the familiar voice. "Dr. Krymer?"

"Nice to see you again." Sarah loved Dr. Krymer's Poland accent.

"Are you Braxton's doctor?"

Doctor Krymer tucked a brown strand of hair behind her ear. "Yes."

They exchanged sad smiles.

"Why did you choose to foster a sick baby, if you don't mind me asking?"

Sarah turned to the window. The clouds shifted, obliterating the moon and causing the world to look bleak, matching her mood. She turned back to the doctor. "Before Jordan died, Josh and I got our foster care license and planned to take in a couple of kids to increase our family. But when Jordan fell ill, we put them on hold. I prayed for months for God to send me a child like Jordan."

"Are you sure you can handle the stress? Braxton will be a fulltime job. I'm quite surprised by your decision."

Sarah couldn't lend her thoughts to worry. At a time like this, she didn't want to fall back into the "what if" phase and let the monster scare her into forbidden worry. But how could she not worry? Braxton had had a bad seizure. "I'm taking one day at a time, and helping others is how I work through tough times."

Doctor Krymer tilted her head, her expression sympathetic.

"How bad are his results?"

"The CT scan was fine, but . . ."

Georgia's eyes popped open. "The EEG ain't no good?"

Dr. Krymer walked to Braxton's bedside, offering her petite hand. "I'm Dr. Krymer. You must be Braxton's mom."

Georgia extended her hand. "I'm Georgia. So what ya know?"

"I'd like to start your son on Phenobarbital. His EEG showed abnormal discharges in the brain."

Georgia collapsed back into the chair. "I can't believe this."

Sarah let the words sink in. This wasn't the time for fear. This day definitely called for hope, and she was going to believe there would be a happy ending.

"I believe the medicine will help," Dr. Krymer concluded.

Sarah walked over to Georgia and placed her arm on Georgia's shoulders. "She's a good doctor."

"I trust your opinion, but why do bad things keep happenin'?" Georgia swiped at her tears with the backside of her hand.

"I can't answer that." Sarah felt Georgia's pain. She'd lost track of the times a doctor came to the bedside to deliver bad news about Jordan. Swallowing hard, she fought to keep her voice stable. "When the brain has been injured at birth due to intraventricular hemorrhage, seizure disorder can follow."

Dr. Krymer added, "That's why I ordered the medicine. It should take care of the seizures."

"What other choice we got? Give it." Georgia reached over the bedrail, found Braxton's hand, and curled her fingers around it.

"The nurse will be in soon." Dr. Krymer removed her stethoscope from her neck and placed the round piece on Braxton's chest. "His lungs are clear." She looked at his oxygen sats. "Is he having many apnea events?"

"No," Sarah answered. "What kind of seizure disorder does he have?"

"Generalized seizure disorder."

"Can he outgrow it?" Georgia asked, wiping her eyes.

"Only time will tell." Dr. Krymer patted the baby's right thigh. Sarah choked back the tears. How many times had she patted Jordan's thigh?

"If either of you have any questions, feel free to call me at the office. I'll see him for follow-up about a week after discharge. Have a good evening and try not to worry. He should do fine."

After Dr. Krymer exited, Sarah sat down and closed her eyes. A faint glimmer of hope flashed in her mind. *Of course Braxton would be fine. He has the best doctor on staff caring for him.*

❧◆❧

An hour later, Sarah reentered the ICU and slipped around the curtain.

Georgia placed the *Curious George* book on the bedside table. "Hey. What did Josh say?"

"He's glad I'm spending the night." *Thank God, Luke understood.* "How're you?" Sarah draped her coat over the back of the rocker.

"Okay. Fat Boy done fell off to sleep. I think that medicine made him groggy."

Their eyes met, a sad understanding passed between them.

Sarah took a deep breath. "I know you're scared, but fear doesn't have a voice until you give it one."

"I know that's right. Girl, my fears all got minds of their own."

Sarah knew exactly how Georgia felt. She'd stayed in the "fear factor" state after Jordan passed until she fell victim to "panic mode." She became afraid to answer the phone for fear it was bad news. She feared Luke would be swallowed up by his own grief, feared Josh would have an accident on his way home from work, and feared that Zack would blame himself for one bad thought—I want my mommy back. Her fears consumed her until she felt smothered. And one day, out of the clear blue, a severe panic attack hit without warning, causing her to believe that death was surely pending.

"Did you see that?" Georgia pointed to Braxton. His eyes popped open and his gaze shifted from Georgia to Sarah.

"There's our boy." Sarah leaned over the metal rail and patted his arm. "You gave us a scare." She tickled his right armpit and he wiggled in response. "Do you want to change his diaper and feed him?"

"Nah. You got him." Georgia adjusted the lighting, making the room a shade darker.

Sarah peeled back the covers and checked Braxton's diaper. After she changed him, she pulled him into her arms, then glanced over at Georgia. "Do you want to hold him?"

Georgia grinned. "Give me Fat Boy."

"I'm going to go make him a bottle. Do you need anything?"

"Nah."

Sarah added three scoops of powdered formula to six ounces of water and shook the bottle. Back in the room, she paused behind the curtain when she heard Georgia say, "No matter what, I will always wuv you."

Sarah skirted around the curtain. "Here you go. There's six ounces in it, so I'd burp him after four."

Georgia put the bottle to Braxton's mouth and he latched on to the nipple. In less than five minutes, he'd downed four ounces, then he belched.

"Boy, you're ready to eat some fried chicken," Georgia said, wiping his lips.

Sarah sat down in the rocker and stared at the pocked ceiling. *No matter what, I will always wuv you. What did she mean by no matter what? Was she afraid she'd lose Braxton to Jamaal, or me?*

"I'm gonna lay Fat Boy down. I'm hungry, and he's going back to sleep."

Sarah held the monitor wires while Georgia put him in the bed. She was happy to see that Georgia was taking charge and appeared to be enthusiastic about his care. She could teach her things that she'd only dared to ask when Jordan was alive. Maybe this was a new beginning for them.

Sarah pulled the blanket up to cover Braxton's shoulder. He immediately opened his eyes. "You go to sleep, little guy. I'm going to find something to eat with your mommy." She gently brushed her fingertips down his cheek, until he closed his eyes.

"You ready?" Georgia asked.

Sarah nodded and turned on the radio. "Have You Forgotten" filtered softly over the speakers, causing Braxton to grin even with his eyes shut.

Sarah walked alongside Georgia to the cafeteria.

"Why you teachin' my boy to like country music?"

"I was just . . ."

Georgia slung her arm around Sarah's shoulder, almost knocking her off balance. "Don't be gettin' yer feather's in a ruffle, I was only clownin' around."

Sarah laughed. "You're funny."

They came to the cafeteria. It had closed an hour ago.

"What they think, parents ain't hungry at this hour?" Georgia complained.

"They have vending machines on the second floor," Sarah suggested.

Georgia exhaled a huff. "I guess."

They exited the second floor and went to a small room that held three vending machines. Georgia dropped quarters into the slot to purchase a ham and cheese sandwich. "Snaps. This thing done stole my quarter." She hit the machine with the palm of her hand.

Sarah rummaged through the bottom of her purse. "Here you go. I have a spare quarter."

After Georgia heated her sandwich in the microwave and retrieved a soda pop from the machine, she sat down on the sofa beside Sarah. "I know they ain't gonna give me Fat Boy."

"Don't be so sure."

"Girl, I think they just wanta find somethin' wrong, but I got somethin' for them." Georgia rubbed her stomach and grinned.

"What?"

Georgia tucked her chin and smiled. "You don't know?"

"Know what?"

Georgia set her can of Pepsi on the wooden table. "You got to promise not to say a word."

Sarah hesitated. If Georgia told her that Jamaal had done something, like assaulted her, she'd be forced to tell Children Services. Finally she said. "I won't say a word."

"I'm prego," she whispered.

"As in pregnant?" Sarah's stomach flip-flopped. "Why?"

Georgia's eyes glowered at Sarah. "Whatcha mean, why?"

"Children Services will find out. Georgia! Listen to me. They took Braxton from you until you could get more stable. You think for one minute they'll let you keep that baby? And it's too soon. Chances are you might have another preemie. Did you think this through?"

Georgia's voice turned sharp. "Don't go soundin' off at me. I ain't done nuttin wrong. You got my son. What you got to be so worried 'bout?"

Sarah felt her face flush. "Maybe I care about you."

Georgia looked surprised. "I wouldn't know why."

"Because you happen to be the mother of the baby I'm fostering."

Georgia threw her sandwich on the table and scrunched up her face. "Then you listen to me. I buried Jaron! The system done took Fat Boy. All I wanted was help. I ain't gonna stand a chance next to ya'll tryin' to fight for him." The tears trickled down her face.

But what if he loves you more? Sarah let the words sink in. "Is this about us? Are you afraid Braxton will love me more?"

Georgia turned to stare at the pop machine.

The silence answered her question. "So that's it." Sarah leaned forward and rested her elbows on her knees, massaged her temples. "So what do I tell him when he grows up?"

Silence.

"You want me to tell him his mama just gave up and threw in the towel? Is that what you want?" Sarah rocked herself back and forth.

Georgia turned abruptly to Sarah, tears slipping down her cheeks. "At least I didn't go and put Fat Boy in a garbage can, or shoot up drugs. I only ask for help."

"And I'm proud of you for not doing those things, but Children Services is trying to help. Everything is a process, but if you'll give it time, things will work out. You can't give up. Promise me for Braxton's sake, you won't give up."

"But he'll love—"

Sarah stood and, put her hand up. "DON'T. Braxton will know you're his mommy, and he'll love you. I wish I could find the words to say to make you believe. This isn't going to be easy because nothing ever is, but if you'll just trust me on this one thing then . . ." Sarah couldn't finish. She wanted to be strong for Georgia, but this was too overwhelming.

"But you're his mama. I only gave Fat Boy birth. He done knows your smell and your smile. Girl, you saw the way he looks at you when you talk. His eyes light up and he grins when he hears yer voice.

Yer voice! Not mine."

"But he's a baby," Sarah reasoned, "and someday he'll understand."

Georgia sniffled. "No he won't. I done seen the movie *Losing Isaiah*. In the end, that boy loved his white foster mama so much he 'bout done grieved himself to death when the judge gave him back to his black mama. Trust me on this one, Sarah. They know who's takin' good care of 'em."

Sarah put her hands on her hips. "I'm asking you not to give up."

Georgia finished her soda, set the can down on the table. "I'll visit my boy this week, but after that . . . Whatever happens, Jamaal can't get custody 'cause he's a psycho. I ain't sayin' I'm a saint, but he'll hurt Braxton. Jamaal's got anger issues. He told me yesterday that Miss Bond gonna let him work a case plan. Now that's messed up. Humph!"

"So, after Friday, you're probably not going to see Braxton?"

"If they see me carryin' a baby, the minute I give it birth, they'll be all up in my business. I'm gonna have me a baby ain't no one can take. This baby gonna love me!" The tears leaked down her cheeks.

Sarah lifted Georgia's chin and looked into her eyes. "If Children Services takes permanent custody of Braxton, and I get to keep him, I'll let you see him as often as you like."

"I appreciate that, but we'll see. Don't get me wrong, Sarah. I'd lay down and die for him, just as you would've Jordan, but this is too much." Georgia wiped her eyes. "Tell Fat Boy I do love him. I'm gonna go home now. I don't feel good."

Sarah patted her back. "Braxton will always love you."

"Maybe I'm too emotional right now."

Sarah helped her to her feet. "Probably so."

At the front entrance of the hospital, Sarah slung her arms around Georgia's neck. "Take care of yourself. And don't make any hasty decisions."

CHAPTER TWENTY-THREE

Luke walked toward the counselor's office, worrying how to respond to the questions Mrs. Frenchie might ask about the book. He couldn't be like the author because he hadn't found the Isle of Faith. Before he had a chance to knock at her door, a teacher he'd seen around the school, but didn't know, pushed by him and poked his head in the counselor's room. "Hey, Annie, I'll pick you up at six. And you have a student waiting to see you."

Annie? The author had scribbled a note at the back of the book. Is Mrs. Frenchie, Annie?

Mrs. Frenchie joined them in the hall. "Hey, Luke. Go on in. I'll be with you in a sec."

Luke took his seat and instantly fixated on the picture that sat on the desk. *It has to be her. She lost her baby, Abbey, and her husband, Rick.* Pity lumped in his throat.

"Okay. See you later," Mrs. Frenchie closed the door and sat down. "How're you doing, Luke?"

"I'm fine." He pulled the book out of his backpack, handed it to her.

She waved her hand. "No, no. That's yours to keep."

"Thanks. Can I ask you a personal question?"

She sat up straighter and smiled. "Absolutely."

"Well . . . at the back of this book you gave me I found a note addressed to Annie from the author. And well . . . sharing her condolences about Annie losing Abbey and Rick. So I was wondering if you're Annie?" He pointed to the picture frame on her desk. "And if that is Abbey and Rick?"

Mrs. Frenchie smiled wider this time. "It's okay, Luke. Actually, I met Marsha who authored the book at a conference. After the accident, she mailed me the book she'd written."

Luke swallowed hard. "What happened to them?"

It took her a minute to answer. "They were killed by a drunk driver. I was away at a writing conference for the week when Rick's mom called to give me the news."

"So you were going to be a writer?"

She hesitated. "I was, but my life changed that day."

"Well how did you like, you know, get over it?"

"Initially I became a hermit. I'd sit for hours and stare at the empty highchair or the place where I'd set Rick's plate for dinner. Then one day my mom told me I had the right to be confused, angry, and sad, and that God understands."

Luke shifted uneasily. "Is that why you're here? To help kids like me?"

"Yes. Had I not taken this position, I don't know where I'd be."

"I'm sorry for your loss."

"Thanks, Luke. I appreciate that." She rested her elbows on the desk and tucked her folded hands under her chin. "Do you feel like talking about Jordan?"

"I need to talk about something else, I mean, if that's okay?"

She nodded.

He leaned forward and clasped his hands between his knees. "We got this foster baby named Braxton. And the other night when he started seizing, my mom took him to the ER, but she looked like she was scared."

Mrs. Frenchie's eyes showed concern. "So what's your question?"

"I thought once you got Jesus, that . . . you just prayed and dumped your garbage in his lap, so you didn't have to worry anymore."

"Sometimes people think that Christians should look victorious all of the time. But the Bible says it rains on both the just and the unjust."

Luke considered that. "I take it you're a Christian?"

"I am."

"I have another question, if that's okay?"

She nodded. "Yes."

"Can only a Christian reach this Isle I read about?"

"Marsha used the term "Isle of Faith" just to make a point of how safe we are once we accept Jesus as our savior."

Luke raised an eyebrow. "Explain it again."

"In order to get Jesus in here," she pointed to her heart, "you have to have faith that he died for your sins. Faith is our purchasing power. And he's our life raft. The Isle of Faith is simply a spiritual place that all born again believers are a part of once they accept him. I suppose another term for the Isle of Faith would be the Household of Faith. Does that make sense?"

Luke nodded. "Yep. A lot."

"When Abbey and Rick passed, I had the same questions you have now. I went to church with my folks and wondered what those other people had that I didn't. They'd testify about how they loss their dad to cancer, their mom to stroke, their aunt to breast cancer, and some had lost even their own children. Of course, they cried because they're human, but they seemed to be coping better than one could imagine. Later I learned how. They had God, something I didn't have at the time."

"So Christians basically go ape nuts when something bad happens, but then say I got the Lord and everything's just gonna be hunky dory?"

"Not exactly. Being a Christian doesn't exempt me from pain, but I don't turn to other means to help me cope; although, Christians falter, too. We're only sinners, saved by Grace."

Luke lowered his head.

"If I can help you with anything, I will."

He looked up. "Thanks. I better get goin'."

"Take care. And don't worry, you'll find your way."

Luke took the long way home, avoiding Community. *Why rescue me, God? I'm a loser.*

He came to the front door of his house and entered slowly. In the kitchen, he spotted his mama and Georgia sitting at the dining room table, sharing a pitcher of tea.

"And God cares when we're hurting," his mama said to Georgia.

"I know that's right. My mama says it all the time. Hey, Luke. You done grew a few feet, I mean inches," Georgia said.

Luke grinned and grabbed a handful of homemade chocolate chip cookies.

"Everything cool?" she asked.

Luke wiped at the crumbs that had tumbled to his shirt. "Cool whip."

"Would you like another glass of tea?" Sarah asked.

"Yeah." Georgia didn't take her eyes off Luke. "You 'bout ready to graduate?"

"Can't wait."

"I know that's right. I quit in the eleventh grade." She shook her head. "Wished I'd a finished, but it's too late now."

Sarah refilled her glass, set it back down. "It's never too late."

"Mama, I'm gonna go watch the tube," Luke said, licking his fingers. From the living room, he heard Georgia and his mama's voices. Georgia was saying, "Hand me that picture." For a moment there was silence, then he heard, "Umm, you must've been blessed with a green thumb. And what's up with the word SHMILY?"

Luke hit pause on the remote to silence the TV. His parents had said it to each other in times past, but when he had asked what it meant, his mama said, "When I die, you'll see it on my tombstone." He strained to listen now, but his mama's voice could not be heard.

Georgia laughed. "That's cool. I can't grow nuttin'. And what kind of flower is this?"

"That's actually a butterfly bush. When Josh and I planted the garden in memory of Jordan, we chose every plant for a reason. The butterfly bush simply meant he was free to fly. This yellow flower is a coreopsis, and it reminds us of his sunshine smile."

"That's tight. Can I ask you a question?"

"Sure."

"Did ya ever go to church and feel like your heart was gonna explode or somethin'?"

"I did when Jesus was knocking at my heart. All I had to do was open the door and let him in."

"Did you sweat like a pig?" Georgia asked.

"I felt nervous. I think it's related to the earthquake going on in your soul," Sarah replied.

"I know that's right. I feel like mine's about to erupt like a volcano."

"Keep praying," Sarah said.

"We'll, I'm 'bout to raise up on outta here." Georgia walked into the living room and gave Braxton a kiss. "Hey, Luke? Stay cool whip."

"See ya," Luke replied, then clicked off the TV and went into the kitchen. "What'd she want?"

"Her weekly visit with Braxton."

Luke took the orange juice carton out of the fridge and took a swig.

"She's a lot fatter than when I saw her the last time."

"Uh, um. You can finish that carton and throw it away."

He belched, then guzzled the rest of the juice.

"How was school?"

"Same ol.'"

Sarah lifted the cooked chicken out of the pan and placed it on a platter, thankful Luke didn't mention Georgia's weight issue again.

"You makin' dumplings?"

"Yes."

Luke rubbed his stomach. "Yummy, my fav."

"How're your grades?"

"Okay. I'm gonna go study. Call me when supper's ready."

In his room, he sat down on his bed and lowered his head. *It can't be that simple. God? I'm gettin' the hang of trigonometry, so what's the formula to this? I think I must be under contraption, oops, I mean conviction. You gotta help me sort this out.*

"Hey." Zack trudged in, interrupting his thoughts.

"Dude? What the heck happened to you?"

"Shh . . ." Zack closed the door. "How was your day?"

Luke's eyebrows knitted together. "Someone beat you to a pulp, and you're worried about me?"

Zack rubbed his swollen eye.

"Has Mama seen you?"

"Not yet."

"Did you fall?"

Zack shook his head. His lower lip quivered.

"What?"

"Tommy." Zack wiped at his tears.

Luke hopped off his bed and punched his dresser. "Ya-ouch! I should've known. I swear I'm gonna beat the tar out of Mouse."

"No! It'll get worse."

"I should've known that jerk was up to no good. When?"

"After school, when I was walking home. Tommy and Jason were waiting by the bushes when I crossed over Lacombe."

Luke opened his dresser drawer and grabbed a shirt. "I'm goin' over to Tommy's."

"No! Luke! God doesn't want us to get revenge."

Luke yanked the shirt over his head. "Mrs. Frenchie said He cares about us. So, I'm pretty sure He wouldn't want you gettin' your block knocked off. What did Tommy say?"

"Called me a black-lover but used that "N" word."

"Nah, Zack, I'm sorry. You gotta tell Mama. Mouse's been asking me if I had a brother named Zack."

Zack looked at Luke through one eye. "You should've told me."

"I told him he better not lay a hand on you."

"You can't tell Mom or Dad!"

"But it'll get worse. And I'm picking you up after school from now on. This won't happen again!"

"I'm not tellin' Mom or Dad the truth."

"You're gonna lie? God will get mad at you."

"Nuh—un— I won't be lying. I just won't tell them everything. So, butt out!" Zack left the room.

❧

Luke found his dad downstairs, pulling off his work boots. He lowered his voice and said, "Tommy hit Zack and gave him a shiner. Zack's scared and doesn't want you and Mama to know."

"Where is he?"

"Upstairs." Luke trailed his dad into the kitchen.

"Where's your mom?" Josh asked, as the French doors opened, and Sarah stepped inside, setting her muddy shoes on the rug.

"Hey, honey. Could you hand me a wet towel?"

"Couldn't wait, could you?" Josh asked, grinning.

"I only went outside to turn over the soil in Jordan's garden while I was waiting to finish supper. Zack!"

Zack hopped up on a barstool, didn't respond.

Sarah washed her muddy hands in sanitizing detergent, then peeled Zack's fingers from his face. "Let me see." Zack's eye was already bruised purple and swollen. "What happened?" Sarah grabbed a dishtowel from the drawer, a bag of frozen peas from the freezer, then securing them in the towel, she covered Zack's eye with the icepack.

"Might as well tell the truth. I already told Dad," Luke advised.

"Since when did you start tellin' the truth?"

"Knock it off," Josh reprimanded.

"Tommy hit him 'cause of Braxton," Luke blurted out.

Sarah put her arms around Zack. "Don't worry, honey. I'm calling the principal"

"I'll go over there," Josh interrupted.

Zack sobbed. "You can't. It'll get worse. The principal can't do nuttin'. They'll just say it takes two people to fight or say he'll talk to Tommy."

"I told Zack I'm pickin' him up after school from now on. Let them try it again, and I'll knock their heads together," Luke said with gritted his teeth.

"Where you goin', Josh?" Sarah asked.

"I'm going to call the police and make a report instead. They can go over there and talk to Tommy's dad."

"Dad! You can't," Luke said. "Tellin' the principal is one thing, but if you call the cops, Mouse will never let me live it down."

"I agree with your dad."

"But, Mama," Luke persisted.

"Luke. This has got to stop before someone gets hurt."

Before the police left, they handed Josh their business card and told him to call again if there were any more problems. Luke slid off the bottom step and walked to the living room. He sat down on the couch beside Zack. "Feelin' better?"

When Zack didn't respond, Luke looked at his mom. She was exercising the baby's legs, just like she used to do with Jordan. *When you're willing to take that risk,* Zack had said. Luke forced the thought away and tickled Zack's big toe. "I'm sorry."

Zack pulled his knees toward his chest. "Tomorrow, I'll probably have two black eyes, thanks to you."

Luke couldn't contest that statement. No matter what happened at Mouse's tonight—whether his dad got mad at Tommy for hitting Zack, or flat out didn't care—he would feel the repercussions of telling on Tommy.

Josh sat in front of the fire. "Listen, boys. The officer told me he has been over to Mouse and Tommy's house on numerous occasions, so I suspect there will be retaliation. If either says one word, tell the principal."

"Doesn't his dad care?" Luke asked.

"Rumor has it he's at the Topsy Turvy every night gettin' drunk," Zack said.

"What about their mom?" Josh asked.

Zack repositioned himself on the couch, stretched out his legs. "Tommy's mom left two years ago, took off with some guy."

Josh sighed.

Luke's anger stirred. "I don't care. That doesn't give them the right to beat up people."

Zack patted his eye. "We're lucky we have parents who care."

"Look at that kid on TV," Luke shouted.

"Tone it down," Josh scolded.

"Don't that remind you of Zack when he was five years old?"

"Yes it does." Josh laughed.

The boy on the mac-n-cheese commercial wiped at his pudgy cheeks with his spoon, his glasses smudged with food.

"Remember that time when you brought Zack's plate to the supper table, and he looked at you wide eyed and said, "We're havin' meatloaf, mashed tators, and grass?" Luke chuckled. "I can't believe he thought the green beans were grass."

Zack inched his way up the couch and frowned. "If you're trying to cheer me up, you're seriously failing."

Luke patted Zack on the left thigh. "Don't worry, bud. I'll have your back."

"I won't have yours. I'm not gettin' tromped on again."

Luke stood. "I'm gonna go get ready for ball practice."

"We'll eat when we get home," Josh said.

"But I'm hungry now," Zack complained.

Luke paused. "Want me to get you a plate of dumplings?"

"No, I'll get my own food."

The phone rang and Luke answered it.

"This is Shirley. May I speak with Sarah?"

⧷◈⧷

Sarah hung up the phone. The news she'd received from Shirley was not what she had wanted to hear. She hoped the judge wouldn't give Jamaal custody, and she worried about Georgia. The test results showed that her mentality level was equal to a twelve-year-old. Shirley ended by saying, "Tomorrow I'll come for a visit. We'll figure it out."

Sarah couldn't help but worry. She'd told Shirley she hadn't heard from Georgia since she'd been out to visit. And she wondered if Georgia told her mom about the unborn baby. To calm her nerves, she picked up the long lighter from the hutch, lit a tea light candle, and slid it under the warming plate. Within minutes, the scent of cinnamon swirl filled the air.

"I figured he'd run his mouth." Luke's words hit Sarah before he walked into the dining room.

"That was fast."

"Coach had an appointment, but we got our uniforms."

"Did Mouse say anything?" Sarah set a steaming bowl of dumplings on the table.

Luke sighed. "He didn't say a word, but I suspect he's just biding his time."

"Was his dad at the ball field?"

"I didn't see him," Josh sat at the table. After saying the blessing, he ladled a spoonful of mashed potatoes onto his plate.

Josh," Sarah said, "next year, I think I'll home school Zack."

"Really?" Zack patted his eye with a cool cloth.

"Now she gets the bright idea." Luke stuffed a spoonful of dumplings in his mouth.

"I'm sorry, Luke, but you didn't have these issues when you were younger."

"No big deal. I only got three more months and I'm home free."

"Ewe, gross. Tell Luke to cover his mouth! That's disgusting!" Zack complained.

"Yes, Luke. Please swallow your food before you speak," Josh said, picking up his napkin to dab at his lips.

"I was also thinking that we probably shouldn't make plans to go to Florida this year," Sarah continued.

The room fell quiet and everyone stared at her.

"I know we haven't stayed home for a holiday since Jordan died, but Luke's graduating and will be off to college, and I can't leave Braxton with strangers."

Josh reached for her hand. "Are you sure? I planned on calling the resort next week."

"I'm sure. I'll bake cookies, fudge, and triple-layered brownies. And we can get the lights from the attic, and Frosty, and . . ."

"We can go to Orchard's Farm and cut down a big Christmas tree," Zack chimed in.

"As long as Mama ain't tryin' to put the thing up in October like she did before," Luke said.

"Yeah, Mom. The house could burn down," Zack said.

"That was an artificial tree," Sarah defended.

"Think Thomas will be a starting pitcher this year?" Josh asked, grabbing a biscuit from the bowl.

Luke shrugged. "See what Coach says."

While Josh and the boys chatted about upcoming baseball games, Sarah saw the laughter in Luke's eyes, the smile on his face. *God please let these outward signs of happiness eventually reach his soul.*

CHAPTER TWENTY-FOUR

Sarah poured two steaming cups of coffee and joined Shirley at the table. "What's on your mind this afternoon?"

Shirley set down her cup, her gold hoop earrings dangling against her neck. "I don't want Jamaal getting custody of Braxton. It's got me all tore to pieces."

Sarah raised an eyebrow. "So what are you thinking?"

Shirley looked Sarah dead in the eye. "I want you to know that whatever I decide, you'll always be a part of Braxton's life. Now Sarah, this decision has not come easy, but in the event that the courts are leaning toward giving Braxton to Jamaal, then I've decided that I will take action. Meaning, I plan to take custody of him. But I need someone I can call upon in the event he'd get sick, or if I have a question. And I need you to teach me all of his care. Would you do that?"

Sarah smiled. "Of course."

"And I won't have anyone to watch him while I'm at work. So—

"Of course I would watch him," Sarah said, not giving Shirley a chance to finish.

Shirley patted Sarah's right arm. "We'll work out a payment plan."

Sarah waved her hand. "No way. Babysitting would be my pleasure."

"And if you'd agree to it, I'd like for us to take turns on the holidays and weekends."

Sarah grinned. "You got yourself a deal."

Shirley latched hold of her coffee mug. "Now this is only if Georgia can't get custody."

Zack stomped down the stairs and came into the dining room. "I need something for pain."

"Whatever happened to you?" Shirley asked.

"A kid hit him," Sarah said, handing him a Tylenol.

Shirley squinted. "I hope the other boy looks worse than you," she teased.

Zack chased down his pill with water and went back upstairs.

Shirley shook her head. "These kids now days. Whatever possessed that boy to do such a thing?"

Sarah wasn't sure how to bring it up, so she said, "It was a cultural issue."

"What?"

Sarah frowned. "This boy named Tommy goes to school with Zack, and his brother Mouse goes to school with Luke. They're racist. So when they found out we had Braxton, he hit Zack."

"Mmm . . . The ignorance of some people. It won't ever stop, Sarah, until some people can see the soul of a man instead of his color."

Sarah nodded. "I agree."

"Well . . . I better run along. When Braxton wakes up, give him a kiss. By the way, since I'm off every Tuesday, is that a good time for you to teach me?"

"That'll work."

Shirley gently squeezed Sarah's arm. "I thank the good Lord everyday that Braxton came to your home."

"And I'm thankful that Braxton has a granny who cares."

After Shirley left, the phone rang. Sarah pinned it between her ear and shoulder, listening to Miss Bond while she added Downy to the rinse cycle on the washing machine. She had just hung up when Luke came into the kitchen.

"Hey, Mama. Where's Dad?"

"He took Zack to get a new bike seat and tire. Can I ask you something?" She opened the dryer door.

Luke looked at her, puzzled.

"I know." She smiled. "A parent asking advice."

Luke grinned. "What?"

"Do you think the judge will send Braxton home with Jamaal?" She reached into the dryer. Luke's face turned red when she untwisted a bra from the socks and hung it over her shoulder.

He cleared his throat. "What about his mom?"

Sarah couldn't answer that question. She hoped Georgia would call and give her an update. And Jamaal called to cancel Friday's visit at the agency, Miss Bond had said. "Georgia's not going to work a case plan."

"Why?"

She wouldn't betray Georgia and mention the unborn baby. "Not sure."

Luke grabbed the cookie bag from under the sink. "Won't his grandma take him?"

"She wants to, but the caseworker said that if Jamaal comes to all of Braxton's doctor appointments, and his visitations, then he'd most likely get custody."

"I don't mean to change the subject, but can we shop for a car soon, since I got my license?"

"You'll need a job to pay for your insurance and gas."

"It cost me twenty-two dollars. I'll add that to your account." Josh entered the kitchen, grinning at Zack.

Zack reached above the dryer and grabbed his baseball glove. "Wanta play some pitch and catch?"

"Let me get my glove," Luke said.

Josh rubbed his forehead. "We have the AA meeting Thursday."

Braxton wailed. "What's the matter, little guy?" Sarah closed the dryer drawer with her elbow, then lifted him out of his swing and handed him to Josh.

Josh placed him on his shoulder and rubbed the bald spot on the back of the baby's head. "Have you talked to Dr. Bleu regarding early intervention?"

"I'll probably hold off for awhile, since I've already started his therapies. You have to remember that even though he's four months old, we have to correct his age, meaning, this month, he's really only a month old or otherwise he'd appear to be behind on his milestones." She handed the warmed bottle to Josh. "And for a one month old, you're doing GR-EAT." She tickled Braxton's toes.

Josh offered the baby his bottle and sat down. "Shouldn't he be sitting up by now, though?"

"Honey, even babies born on time don't sit up until they're about six months or older. Not every child is the same."

Josh nodded. "I keep forgetting. You'll be alright, little buddy, especially since you got Mommy working with you."

Sarah couldn't take all the credit for Braxton's achievements;

although, she was a firm believer that the earlier you started working with your premature newborn, the better the outcome, in most circumstances. She'd been told it might take him longer to walk, talk, and do things other babies his age could achieve on time, but Braxton was a trooper. He'd already rolled from his belly to his back, gained head and neck control, and was grasping objects. She knew the early morning therapies of teaching him to crawl and sit up would pay off eventually, and then she'd tackle teaching him how to walk around furniture. She'd learned with Jordan, it was a slow process.

Josh carried Braxton into the living room, sat down on the couch, and turned on the TV.

"Want me to finish feeding him?" Sarah copped a squat on the floor beside his feet.

"I got it."

The boys burst through the front door and came into the living room. Zack bent his knees and inhaled deeply.

"Here." Luke tossed him the inhaler. "Take a puff, wheezy. I'm gonna go change."

"You, okay, Zack?" Sarah asked, coming to stand beside him, and patting his back.

He took a puff and put the inhaler in his pocket. "Yeah." He sat down. "Can we rent a movie tonight or play a board game or something?"

Josh snickered. "No movie, but we could play *Clue* if your mom wants to."

"That sounds like fun."

"I wanta play *Sorry* too." Zack laughed.

Luke fled down the steps into the living room, and snatched the remote from his dad's hands, and turned the channel to the local news. His face pale and sweaty.

Sarah's heart sped up. She hopped up off the couch just when the phone rang.

"Zack can you get the phone?" Josh bounced the baby up and down on his knee to keep him from crying.

Luke pointed to the TV. "The woman," he said, just as Zack handed her the phone

"It's Miss Bond."

Sarah couldn't imagine why Miss Bond was calling. She'd already talked with her earlier. She took the phone from Zack and put it to her ear. She heard the TV newscaster's voice blaring. "A woman was hit by an automobile earlier this afternoon. The full story when we return." She walked to the edge of the living room and, covered her right ear with her hand so she could hear. "Miss Bond?"

Miss Bond's voice choked. "Sarah?"

Sarah took her hand off her ear and looked around the room. Her family had their eyes glued to the television set.

"I wanted to tell you before you saw it on the evening news." Miss Bond sniffled. "There's no easy way to say this, but . . . Georgia was hit by a . . . car."

"Is she okay? I mean what hospital is she at? Hold on a minute." Sarah set the hand held phone back into the receiver because it was getting harder to hear. She picked up the desk phone. "Miss Bond?"

"I'm here."

"Sorry. The battery must be getting low on my other phone."

"What happened?" Sarah glanced around the room. Luke sat on the edge of the couch, his face cupped in his hands. Josh's eyes filled with tears, and Zack held Braxton as they listened to whatever was happening on the news. Whatever it was, it had upset her whole family.

"Sarah, Georgia's . . . dead."

Sarah quickly sat down in the chair. Every muscle in her body tightened. She twirled the coiled black cord with her trembling fingers. "Did I hear you right?"

Josh came to her side, patted her back.

"How? When? Why?" She cried. Through tear-filled eyes, she watched Zack pass Braxton to Luke.

"I don't know all the details. Jamaal called the agency about an hour ago, and they paged me. He said it's all over the news."

Sarah turned her head toward the television. Police cars circled the site of the accident. She shivered and squeezed her eyes shut. *This can't be happening.* "No, God!" The phone fell to the desk in a clatter.

Josh came to her side. "Sarah, listen to me. Take a deep breath. There's nothing we can do right now. Zack, get your mom a glass of juice. Her skin feels clammy. And bring me her purse."

Sarah tried to take a deep breath, tried to relax, but this had caught her off guard. She tried desperately to form the words "Georgia's dead" to tell Josh, but the look in his eyes told her he already knew.

Josh picked up the phone and told Miss Bond he'd call her back. When he hung up, he pulled Sarah into his strong arms. "I'm sorry."

She wanted to scream, but she felt as if someone had stuffed a golf ball in her throat. *How will I tell Braxton someday that his mommy died? Will I even be able to keep him safe, considering Georgia's warning about Jamaal?*

"Here, Dad." Zack handed Josh the glass of juice.

"I need you to swallow your pill." Josh held the glass for Sarah.

Sarah opened her mouth while Josh placed the anxiety pill on her tongue. The concern on his face made her think of something beside her own pain.

"I know, honey." Josh tilted the glass. "Just drink."

"Wa . . ." Braxton cried.

"It's okay, little buddy." Luke said. "Shh . . ."

"Come on, Sarah. You need to lie down. I'll help you up the steps," Josh said.

She didn't want to lie down. "No!" she cried.

"But you'll feel better," Josh insisted.

She wanted to hit something really hard to make the pain in her heart subside—hit something for Luke to make his pain dim, hit something for Braxton for life being unfair, but the minute she glanced at Luke, her fears slid back into the recesses of her mind, and her breathing pattern evened.

The scene before her eyes—Luke had Braxton snuggled against his chest, just as he'd held Jordan. Braxton didn't seem to mind the tears that plopped onto his face; instead, he gazed at Luke and flapped his little legs. "Ba . . . baa . . ."

Luke lowered his head and planted a kiss on his tiny chin. "I wuv you, Brax."

Sarah latched on to Josh's hand. They stared in amazement at the beautiful scene before their eyes.

"Will he—will he ever know how mu—much his mommy loved him?" Sarah asked through sobs.

Josh gave her hand a comforting squeeze. "I'm sure he will."

CHAPTER TWENTY-FIVE

"Hush little baby, don't say a word. Mama's gonna buy you a mockingbird." Sarah held Braxton close while she hummed the song and gently rocked him. She gazed around the room, Jordan's room, thinking how, when everything was turned upside down, Braxton had come into their lives, giving them a new direction. The room was no longer a shrine, but rather a place where gumball colored toys flowed out of toy boxes, baby bibs and diapers sat stacked evenly under the changing table, and even the linens had been changed to Tigger and Pooh—the room now painted butter cream with a strip of mint green separating the upper and bottom walls. Bees cut out of fabric were glued to the wall beside the tree Sarah had painted.

She inhaled a deep breath. Everyone in her family had given Braxton the unconditional love they'd given Jordan. And even though Luke had been slow to respond to the baby, tonight something had changed. He'd held Braxton just as he'd held Jordan. And that thought alone thrilled Sarah.

She gazed down and caught Braxton eyeing her carefully. She pulled his tiny fingers to her mouth and kissed them before his eyelids drooped. She tucked him in his crib, turned on his nightlight.

She wiped at tears with the backside of her hand and tiptoed out of the room.

In the dining room, Josh and Zack sat at the table discussing the Leviticus Priesthood.

"And Jesus is the High Priest," Zack said.

"That's right, buddy. You're getting it." Josh smiled and closed his Bible.

"Are you going to the funeral, Mama?"

She hadn't even thought of going to the funeral until Zack mentioned it. Of course, she'd go. For Shirley. And she was taking care of Georgia's baby. *I'm gonna have me a baby ain't no one can take.* Sarah's head began to spin. "Oh, no!" she cried, holding onto the counter.

Josh guided her to a chair. "Honey, I know it's hard, but we'll get through this."

Sarah had promised Georgia she wouldn't tell anyone about the baby, but things were different now—there was no baby, no Mommy to care for it. "Josh, you don't understand."

"I do understand, honey," he said, patting her back, "I am feeling . . ."

When Josh didn't finish, Sarah twisted in her chair and latched hold of his hand.

"Josh, Georgia was going to have a . . . baby. Two lives were lost."

Josh gasped, shaking his head. Finally, he spoke. "I'm—I'm sorry."

"This just doesn't seem fair. I mean, her first baby died, then she loses Braxton to the system, and now Georgia and her unborn baby are dead. Why do some people go through so much?" Sarah brought a trembling hand to her forehead.

"You mean she was pregnant?" Zack asked.

"Yes." Josh lowered his head and sniffled. "Lord, help her family."

"Well, everything happens for a reason," Zack advised. "And sometimes we don't even know the reasons why bad things happen, but God does. Not that he caused it, it's just . . ." Zack burst into tears.

Josh wrapped his arms around Zack's neck and kissed the top of his head. "Sometimes things just happen, buddy. A mindless accident."

The room fell silent as if everyone felt the weight of Georgia's death.

"I'm going to take Luke some supper." Sarah said.

In the kitchen, she placed two pieces of pizza in the microwave and poured a glass of juice. While she waited for the microwave to *zing*, she thought of Luke. *I'll be a mortician. I'll be the all-star pitcher in the major leagues. I only got three more months of school. Then what? What will he do? Could this tragedy be a new beginning for Luke?*

Hands loaded, she made her way up the stairs and tapped the door with her toes. Slowly, it opened. She flipped on the light, and then set his supper on his desk. Luke held tight to Mr. Monkey in his bed.

"Want some company?"

His cheeks were wet. He inched up in his bed and leaned against the headboard. "It isn't fair. Braxton's just a baby. He's been through enough, and now he has to lose his Mama."

Sarah wanted to take Luke's pain away, add it to her own heap. "I know, sweetie," she said, patting his hand and sitting down on the edge of his bed.

"Our life is turning into a serious 911 comic strip."

She couldn't argue that. "Oh, Luke, it's unfair, there's no doubt about it, but . . ." Sarah pulled him into her arms. "We'll get through this, sweetie."

"Why does life have to be so tough?"

She patted his back. "You've been through so much, Luke. I know you wanted to be a mortician, and maybe that would be a good thing for you. You could really comfort other families."

Luke shivered against her chest. "No, Mama. I've had enough of death."

"Have you considered being a psychologist or a nurse? You have a lot of love to give to others."

He chuckled. "Maybe even a preacher."

Sarah forced a smile. "Perhaps."

"Did Georgia believe in God?"

Sarah patted his back. "I would suspect. She talked about him just the other day."

"Just when I thought life couldn't shock me anymore, I got slammed again. I wish these hailstones would find another place to land."

Sarah could only imagine how he felt. He hadn't yet dealt with the issues of losing Jordan, and now had to hear the news of Braxton losing his mother. They'd dared to step on old roads again that brought more pain, but the pain would eventually dull and they'd move on as they'd done in the past.

"Will Jamaal get custody of Braxton?" Luke asked.

She didn't want to think that far ahead. She planned to go to the viewing, and she'd see him there. Would he see her as the enemy? The words Georgia had said came flooding back, *Jamaal will hurt Braxton*. "I don't know what's going to happen, Luke. Let's just pray Braxton stays with us, or goes home with his grandma."

❧❧

Sarah thought about Shirley's words from the night before, that Georgia said she was a fighter. Sarah sighed and whispered into the dark. "No, Shirley, you're the fighter." And she was. Shirley had spoken to her supervisor at work and had planned a two-week vacation in order to learn Braxton's care—to keep him out of Jamaal's hands.

She splashed cool water on her face, trying to dismiss what she'd witnessed last night at Georgia's viewing. Nothing prepared people to face death, and that was exactly what she had encountered. Again.

Tears scalded her eyes when she thought about the champagne roses that cascaded over the top of Georgia's casket. Angels knelt in all four corners of the casket. Pictures of her children, Braxton and Jaron, had been tucked inside the white satin lining of the casket. Georgia's hair was smooth and touched the tip of her shoulders. Her clasped hands rested above a Bible. Her newly manicured nails were marbleized pink and white. And then there was Jamaal. At least he didn't treat her like the enemy; instead, he introduced her to his brother, Ray, before she stepped out into the dark, Josh holding tight to her hand.

She rummaged through her bottom drawer and chose a brown-suede jogging suit, put it on, and briefly ran her fingers through her hair. Shirley was due to arrive any minute. Downstairs, the house was too quiet. Josh and Luke went to the AA meeting, Zack was down the street playing with Chad, and Braxton was napping.

The doorbell rang. Sarah opened it and looked into Shirley's sad eyes. "Come on in."

"It's been a day," Shirley said, shrugging out of her coat, then putting it on the hallway bench.

Sarah wanted to say are you okay; instead, she said, "I'm so sorry."

Shirley set her spiked heels beside the door. Then she hugged Sarah. "I'm doing as well as expected."

When Sarah let go, she gazed into Shirley's watery eyes. Sarah returned a sad smile, took hold of Shirley's hand, and walked her down the hallway to the kitchen. Even though Shirley was sad, she looked stunning in her two-piece black satin suit. Her hair was neatly pinned at the base of her neck, and her bronze jewelry complemented her white blouse.

"How's my boy?"

Sarah sniffled, wanting to say he's fine, but I'm falling apart. Instead, she said, "He's napping. But I can get him up. Would you like a cup of tea or coffee?"

"A cup of tea, please. And let our boy sleep."

Sarah filled the copper pot with water and placed it on the stove.

"What exactly happened to Georgia?" Sarah asked, joining Shirley at the table with two steaming cups.

"The coroner said it was an accident. One of the witnesses said she was talkin' on her cell phone, and cryin' at the same time. Evidently, when she stepped out onto the road, she didn't see the car. It threw her a couple of feet, and then a truck came barreling down the road, and . . ." Shirley burst into tears. "It happened so fast. One minute I'm at your house, and the next, I'm finding out my daughter died."

"I'm so sorry."

Shirley patted Sarah's hand. "I know, but you got to go on and be strong for that grandson of mine till I can get custody."

Sarah fought the tears. "I will."

"You know Georgia wanted you to have Braxton if she couldn't. She came to love you. Talked 'bout you all the time."

Sarah raised a skeptical eyebrow.

"I know. Took that chile a long time to get used to you. She was afraid Braxton would love you more, but I told her that love is what makes this journey more bearable." Shirley cut her eye at Sarah. "I don't want Jamaal chewing up our baby boy like he did Georgia. We're gonna get him, Sarah."

Our boy? Sarah thought, and the words broke her heart.

"I figure if I show up at all of his appointments and learn his care, I might stand a better chance of getting him than Jamaal. So, whatever you can teach me, I have two free weeks to learn."

Shirley opened her purse, pulled out a packet of seeds, and handed them to Sarah. "Last time I was with Georgia she bought these for you. When I was gettin' ready to leave, I saw them in the windowsill."

Sarah glanced at the packet in her hand. *You must've been blessed with a green thumb or somethin'.* She smiled at the memory, then said, "I know how tough it can be losing a child, and when I thought I couldn't get through another day, I prayed."

"If I didn't have the good Lord, I would've thrown in the towel after Georgia's daddy died."

Sarah sniffled. "You're a good woman, Shirley."

Shirley cut her eye at Sarah. "Georgia did tell you?"

"What?"

"You don't know, do you?" Shirley's gold tooth glinted when she smiled.

Sarah shook her head.

"Georgia done had an experience—a wonderful one. I'll see my daughter again, thanks to the good Lord. She was sassy like your Luke. Georgia told me all about him. Said he was defiant, like she had room to talk." Shirley smiled faintly. "After she got saved at the revival the night before the accident, she said, 'Got to go call Sarah and tell her.' Then she rambled on and on about you having a green thumb. The only way she felt she could express her thanks was by giving you a packet of seeds to plant in your garden. She hoped you would do it in memory of Jaron, just like your Jordan."

Shirley then pulled a large green bag out of her purse and handed it to Sarah. "Just watch the thorns. Thing done looks like it's dead, but it'll come back to life." Shirley paused, as if reflecting, then said, "I used to look through the window and stare at my barren garden. I'd think without the mulch and the flowers it looked naked. Didn't take me long to learn that things grow that the gardener didn't even sow. And I'm kinda like you in a way, Sarah. When I was able to garden, I'd lose myself for hours, marveling at how pretty the flowers were. This got me to thinkin' about the roses that will never fade. I'm talkin' 'bout the good ole saints."

Sarah placed the green bag on the floor. "Thank you."

Shirley folded her hands under her chin. "So when you see the roses bloom, I know you'll think on spiritual things."

Sarah pulled a tissue out of her pocket and blew her nose. "You have no idea how much I've been blessed."

Shirley stood. "Now let's get down to business."

For the next hour, Sarah demonstrated how to do Braxton's meds and therapies, practicing on a stuffed teddy bear since he was still napping.

Shirley glanced at her watch. "I have to go, now. I have an appointment with my attorney at four o'clock to see if he can help me get custody of my grandson. But I'm so thankful that God sent us an angel."

Sarah bent down, gathered up the forgotten toys they had used for play therapy the night before—the Lollipop Drum Mallet, two musical hand bells, a Peek-A-Boo Bag A-Z, and the sensory tactile ball, and placed them in the toy bin.

Shirley slid on her coat. "Sarah?"

"Yes?"

"That angel I'm talkin' about isn't Braxton."

Sarah gave her a confused look.

Shirley grinned, looking tired. "It's you. Georgia told me that you were her angel because you helped her find the road home."

Tears spilled down Sarah's cheeks. She blew her nose again. "Thanks for sharing."

Shirley walked to the front door and put her shoes on. "Now don't you worry, I have enough faith this is going to work out."

"Braxton has a wonderful granny."

Shirley turned to smile one more time before making her way outside. "I better hurry. My neighbor was gracious enough to pick me up."

Sarah closed the door, hoping that Shirley would get to keep Braxton. Glancing at her watch, she realized she had another two hours before Josh and the boys would be home. In the kitchen, she couldn't keep from thinking about what her mama had taught her. *Sarah, be strong and always trust in the Lord, Never give up on what you believe in, even if in the end, the result is more pain.* The same words of wisdom she'd given to her boys. She smiled, pulling her Paula Deen bake ware from under the stove. Tonight she was going to cook a feast for her family.

⁂

Sarah and Braxton sat at the wooden picnic table Josh had built three years ago when she heard the SUV door slam.

"Honey?" Josh called through the patio door.

"Out here," she hollered, and put Braxton in his swing.

Josh slid the screen door open and poked his head outside. "Wow. What's the occasion?"

She laughed. "Me, you, Braxton, Luke, and Zack."

She lifted the lids off the dishes and set them to the side. Next, she lit the hurricane lamps, setting one on each end, and unwrapped the silverware.

Josh stepped off the deck. "Need some help?"

"Would you mind starting a fire in the pit? It feels a little nippy."

Josh stacked three logs in the pit. "Zack's out front testing out his bike. I told him to hurry, that you probably had dinner cooked."

"I'm surprised he came home early. How did it go at the meeting?"

"It gave Luke a lot to think about. He was quiet on the way home." Josh snapped a few twigs and placed them on top of the logs. He lit the fire, and within minutes, black smoke snaked into the air.

Sarah prayed that Luke could connect with one person at the AA meeting—hoped that one sad story shared would be enough to change his mind about drinking.

"Hey, Dad, Mom." Zack stepped into the yard. "Want me to get Luke?"

"Yes, please." Josh answered, and then laughed. "You cooked enough food for an army, Sarah."

The table was spread with marinated grilled chicken, homemade potato salad, buttery ears of corn, homemade salsa and chips, and twice-baked potatoes. "Doesn't pay to cook when you're starving." Sarah giggled, rubbing her stomach.

Luke and Zack joined them at the table. "Hey, Dad, wanta play some checkers when we're done eating?" Zack asked.

Josh took a swig of root beer, chasing down his chips. "Sure."

Sarah had stenciled a checkerboard on the picnic table in colors of navy-blue and red. They had spent summer evenings playing hillbilly golf, corn hole, and checkers.

"So . . ." Josh began. "We didn't have much time to talk earlier. How did it go with Shirley?"

"She's a fast learner, and she's coming back tomorrow. I don't think she'll have a problem getting custody of Braxton, if Jamaal can't."

While Sarah talked, she couldn't help but notice how quiet Luke had been since he had come home. Normally he had to be silenced by Josh because of verbal spars toward Zack, or told to swallow his food before he talked. Tonight, he chewed his food rather slowly and stared off into space.

"Cat got your tongue tonight, Luke?" Josh asked, putting a potato on his plate.

Luke leaned over and rooted through the cooler. He pulled out a Mountain Dew and opened it with his teeth.

"Luke, please. I've told you before, you're going to break a tooth," Sarah said.

Luke didn't respond.

"How was school today, Zack?" Josh smothered his potato in butter.

Zack bit into his ear of corn. "No problem. I saw Tommy."

"Did he offer any negative remarks?" Sarah questioned.

"Nope."

Luke continued to stare into the distance. This time his attention was on Sarah's garden. She thought she saw him swipe at a tear.

"Are you okay, Luke?" she asked, waiting for him to respond.

He wadded up the napkin, threw it on his still food-covered plate. "No."

"Did Michigan reject your application?" Zack asked.

Luke didn't smile, didn't come back with his own verbal spars. "Nope. I ain't going to college."

Sarah was surprised by his answer; although, they hadn't discussed college much since Jordan had passed. "What will you do?"

"Mama! You gotta graduate before you can go anywhere."

"And you will," she said.

Luke put his elbows on the table and clasped his hands together under his chin. "Not if I don't get my grade up in English."

"I didn't know there was a problem with English." Sarah dipped a chip in the salsa and took a bite.

"Yeah. You haven't said anything to us. As a matter of a fact, we haven't even seen your interims," Josh said.

Luke pulled his wadded report from this pocket, tossed it on the table.

Josh wiped his hands and picked it up. "Say what?" He handed the paper to Sarah.

She glanced over the report. "Luke? How did you manage to get two *D*'s and an *F* in English?"

"Since I've spent all my time trying to figure out trigonometry, I didn't study English like I should've."

Sarah's stomach clamped. She hadn't expected this so close to graduation. "Have you spoken with Mrs. Frenchie regarding a tutor? Have you asked your teacher if there are any extra credit assignments you can do?"

"Mama! I covered all my bases."

"What about ball?" she asked.

"No ball. I'm off the team until I get my grade up. Coach is upset because I'm not the only one not qualified to play. They lost one of their backup pitchers, too."

"Mouse?" Josh asked.

"Yep. Our team doesn't have a prayer this year. The only starting pitcher left is Thomas, and he ain't very good at pitching. I told Coach he should've trained Jace, but he wouldn't listen to me."

"I don't care who the starting pitchers are, Luke. You will get your grade up—or else." Josh's tone showed a trickle of disappointment.

"I'm struggling to keep my trigonometry from falling to an F. There's no way. It ain't gonna happen!"

Sarah put her plate into the plastic liner. "I'll make an appointment with Mrs. Frenchie."

"No, Mama. You can't fix this!"

"I'm sure your dad could help you study," she suggested.

"After we help Mom clean up, go get your book," Josh said.

Zack chugged his Mountain Dew, then said, "I can't believe you're flunking our native language."

"Keep quiet, Zack," Josh said.

"I can help him, Dad. I'm really good at English."

Sarah picked up Braxton and went inside to change his diaper.

"I'm sorry I keep letting you down, Mama. But if I don't graduate, the moon ain't gonna fall out of the sky. No one is gonna suffer but me," Luke said, trailing her.

She lay Braxton in his crib, then fanned a blanket on the floor. "Sit down, Luke."

She squatted beside him. "Honey, I want you to graduate. In this day and age, without a diploma, you won't be able to go to college, and it will be very hard finding a decent paying job."

"I wish I could be a hero like Jordan."

"Jordan couldn't run around the block, but you can pitch in baseball. He didn't have the opportunity to even start kindergarten, but you have the potential to graduate and go on to college."

Luke sighed. "So you're saying I'm a failure?"

"No, that's not what I'm saying. But we don't give up because something presents a challenge; we learn from our mistakes and move forward." Sarah kept her tears at bay with every struggling breath.

Luke cleared his throat. "Tonight at the meeting, I . . ."

Sarah curled her fingers around his left hand. "What?"

"This guy named Matt was there. After they said the serenity prayers and talked about the twelve steps and stuff like that, Matt told us his story. Said he'd been coming to the meetings for about three months, and this is the first time he felt he could say something."

Sarah listened passionately.

". . . but then he said, 'I'm an alcoholic. I used to have dreams of going to college and playing football, but I threw it all away for my next shot of booze and drugs.' Needle marks that looked like train tracks covered the inside of his left arm. I felt sorry for him."

"What else did he say?"

"He got choked up and couldn't finish, so his dad, Keith, took over. Keith said Matt started drinking his senior year after his mom got killed in an automobile accident. Then Keith said that he himself was a recovering alcoholic, but he turned back to the bottle after his wife died. He blamed himself for Matt's failure. But tonight, he could proudly say that Matt received his GED two days ago and was leaving for boot camp in a month."

"How did that make you feel?"

"I could relate. I haven't had a drink since the stolen shoe incident; although, I've been tempted. What he said made me take a look at my own life and . . ." Luke couldn't finish.

Sarah patted his back. "You're not a loser. You saw a bit of yourself in Matt tonight."

She waited for him to respond.

"Yeah, I did. I found comfort in knowing I wasn't the only guy in the world soothing my emotions with booze."

"Oh, sweetie, I'm glad you could relate. That's a beginning."

Luke stared into her eyes. "Mama? Please don't give up on me."

"I'll never do that."

"Matt seemed like a really nice guy. He must've been about twenty-two or so, but it's never too late, is it?"

"No, Luke." She patted his thigh. "Nothing is ever lost."

He drew in a breath and exhaled.

She took him by the hand. "Come on. Let's go sit in the backyard with your dad and brother. I'll make you a smore, and then you two can study."

CHAPTER TWENTY-SIX

In the weeks that followed, Sarah wondered if Luke would graduate. Against his wishes, she called Mrs. Frenchie and learned that Luke could take an online English course if he didn't make the grade. The bad news was that by the time he would receive the online credit; his class would've already had their graduation ceremony. The counselor said, "Tell him not to get discouraged, they have another ceremony in August."

Sarah sat on the couch now, shivering at the thought of taking the baby to the agency for an afternoon visit. In the past two weeks, Braxton had been back for two follow up visits with his doctors. Shirley and Jamaal had attended. Shirley was worried that Jamaal was making progress toward completing his case plan and worried she wouldn't be able to get custody of Braxton. Her attorney told her that if Jamaal cooperated and proved to the court he could care for the child, then the judge had to send the baby home with his father.

Two good things had come out of the appointments—Braxton's seizures were under control, and the apnea monitor had been discontinued.

Later that afternoon, Sarah carried Braxton up the concrete path to Children Services. She spotted Jamaal standing by the door.

"Hello, Sarah." He held the door open.

Sarah greeted him and smiled as she signed in at the desk.

"You can go into room 23," the receptionist said.

Sarah walked into the room and placed Braxton on her lap. He gave her a toothless grin.

Jamaal held out his hands. "Can I hold my boy?"

Sarah lifted Braxton to him, then she took a seat beside him.

He stared into the baby's eyes. "How's my son?"

"A . . . waa . . ." Braxton turned his head to Sarah.

"It's okay," Sarah said, patting his right hand.

"A . . . waa . . ." Braxton wailed.

Jamaal's face scrunched. "Hush, boy. Knock that whining off."

Sarah hoped Miss Bond would pop in to say hello. She didn't like the tone of Jamaal's voice or the way he had told Braxton to hush, like he could really help himself. "He doesn't know you. That's why he's crying."

"He don't know me just 'cause his mama done messed up."

"Please don't talk bad about Georgia. She did the right thing."

Sarah didn't want to argue with Jamaal. She really didn't want to be at the agency alone with him either, but Miss Bond had pleaded with her to supervise the visit. *You're a nurse. If he has a seizure or something, you'll know what to do,* she'd said.

She leaned over and pulled Braxton's Elmo pacifier out of his diaper bag. She went to put it in his mouth, but Jamaal grabbed it from her and tossed it on the couch. "My son doesn't need that thing."

Braxton continued to cry, and at times, he'd turn his head to Sarah to see if she were still there.

Fifteen minutes later, Miss Bond entered. "I wanted to pop in and let you know that the next court date is set for the second week in May. I can't remember the exact day, but you'll be getting a letter in the mail. And I received the report from your psychiatrist."

"That's good." Jamaal bounced Braxton on his knee. "You gonna come home to Daddy."

Sarah cringed.

"Did you bring your rent receipts and earning statements?" Miss Bond asked.

Jamaal reached in his back pocket, supporting the baby with his big hand, then handed the receipts to Miss Bond.

Miss Bond tucked them into the file. To Sarah she said, "We need to talk."

Braxton wailed again.

"Hush, boy."

Miss Bond turned the handle on the horizontal blinds in the room to open them before she stepped into the hallway. Through the window, she viewed Jamaal holding Braxton.

Sarah paced. "I can't believe the judge would send Braxton home to him."

"I know, but in all fairness, he did complete his case plan."

Sarah couldn't argue that statement, but she feared for the baby's safety. "Did you hear how he talked to Braxton? He told him to hush like he was a ten-year-old child who needed to be scolded."

"I heard. And I'm not comfortable with it either, but I can't go into the court on a gut feeling that the father may not be the best fit for the child. The judge won't accept that."

Sarah quit pacing. "So it's pretty much set in stone that Braxton will go home with his dad?"

"I'm afraid so."

Sarah peered through the glass. Braxton continued to cry. "When?"

"I knew you'd ask me that." Miss Bond's eyes showed concern. "Probably the same day we go to court."

Sarah drew in a deep breath. "Wow. I wasn't expecting that. I was truly praying that he'd get to go home with Shirley. I mean . . . she's doing a great job. She's learned everything required to take care of him."

Miss Bond tucked a strand of hair behind her ear. "I know. I wish things could be different, but I don't make the decisions. However, I'm going to recommend some overnight stays to make sure the transition goes smooth."

Sarah latched on to a strand of hope. Maybe the overnight visits would be dragged out long enough for Jamaal to show his true colors. "How many overnight visits?"

"Probably every weekend, for at least two months. I know this isn't the news you'd hoped for."

Sarah fought against the constricted tightness of her throat. "I'm going back in the room. I'll see you soon."

"I'll call you as we get closer to the court date," Miss Bond said before walking away.

Sarah reentered the room and paced. Her nerves were shot. The more Jamaal scolded Braxton, the angrier she became.

"You don't trust me do you, Sarah?"

Sarah rubbed her hot cheeks. The question had left her off balance. No one had ever asked her if she trusted them, not even Josh. "No, I don't."

"Well that's too bad. Even his grandmother didn't want him, but I do."

She was not about to spill the beans and tell Jamaal that Shirley had spent the past two weeks in her home learning all of his care.

"She had every chance to get my boy when her own daughter messed up. She didn't bother."

Sarah quit pacing. "Maybe she was scared that she wouldn't know how to take care of him."

Jamaal's eyes widened. "Do you think you're the only person who can take care of my boy?"

"I didn't say that."

Jamaal shifted a wailing Braxton to his other arm. "I stand by what I said. His mama should've never put him in the system."

Sarah wanted to be compassionate toward Jamaal, but she couldn't get past the thought of him hurting Braxton. "Georgia agreed to it because she lost Jaron and needed to get herself together. She did the right thing by asking for help."

"Not Georgia. That woman couldn't do nuttin' right."

A moment of silence slipped between them. Sarah was glad Jamaal had quit talking. She didn't want to hear any more negative remarks about Georgia.

Jamaal didn't take his eyes off Sarah, making her feel uncomfortable. "You know what else Georgia told me?"

Sarah drew in a deep breath. "What?"

"That I'd never get social security benefits for our son."

"When did she say that?"

"The day she died."

Sarah shivered. "You talked to her the day she died?"

"Yeah. I told her that my attorney said that since Braxton is disabled, you know, born with problems, that I can get benefits for him. She told me I would never get my son. Ha. Proved her wrong again."

Sarah sat down on the edge of the couch and cupped her face with her hands. "What time did you talk to her?"

"We just hung up. Then she got herself run over by a car."

She sat up straight. "So you're the one she was talking to?"

"You mean arguing with. Don't be gettin' all tied up in a knot. It ain't my fault she didn't know how to cross a street."

Sarah couldn't believe what she was hearing. The Jamaal who had kissed her hand, thanking her for taking good care of his son, this didn't seem like the same person. *You're too trusting, Sarah.* Josh was right.

She was too trusting.

"Will you let me see Braxton when he goes home?" she asked, feeling the weight of how parents felt when they lost a child to the system.

"Depends. It shouldn't be a problem. Big Mama's gonna watch him when I work."

"Who?"

"We call her Big Mama. She's not really big, just a friend of mine. Actually my ex-girl."

"You mean the one you busted up before you went to prison?"

Jamaal laughed. "Yeah. That's her."

Sarah glanced at the wall clock. Five more minutes and the visit would be over. In two months or less, Braxton would have a stranger caring for him—a woman who had been abused by Braxton's dad.

"What about Shirley? Will you let her see Braxton when he goes home?"

"NO!" the answer came out harsh. "She had her chance and blew it."

Sarah felt it be best at this point to not ask any more questions. She glanced at the clock. "Time's up."

"Can I ask you a question? Are you gettin' social security for my son?"

"No. Children Services gets that money. Why?"

"You think you could lend me a couple of bucks to take the bus home?"

Sarah considered telling him to walk, but instead opened her purse. "Here." She handed him a five.

"Yeah, I get my son home and get that check, money won't be so tight."

Sarah didn't react. She took Braxton from Jamaal and put his jacket on. She didn't wait for Jamaal as she headed toward the door, but he followed her. At the SUV he said, "I'll see ya next week."

On the drive home, she glanced in the rear-view mirror. Braxton looked peaceful, both eyes closed. *Is that why he wants Braxton, for the money?* She'd been told not to judge others, but in this instance she couldn't help it—the baby's life could be at stake. She plunged a hand through her hair. *Money, abuse, busting up his ex-girl, Big Mama.* Her worry consumed her. *Please, God. Help Braxton.*

That evening, while Josh rocked Braxton to sleep, Sarah sat outside in an Adirondack chair, staring up at the sky. The clouds shifted, causing the moon to fade in and out, and the scent of the fire filled her nostrils.

Josh stepped onto the deck. "Want some company?"

"Sure."

He sat down in a chair beside her.

"Did Braxton finally go to sleep?"

He took her hand into his. "He fell asleep before I finished the story."

"That's sweet."

"Luke seemed to be pretty down tonight at the game," Josh said.

"He's definitely got a lot on his mind."

Even though Luke couldn't play, he showed up with Josh to cheer his team on. Unfortunately, they got beat with a final score of 6-5—the team's second loss of the season. In the past two weeks, he'd studied hard for his upcoming finals. Soon, he would know if he'd be permitted to walk with his class on the day of graduation. His high school years would boil down to one grade—English. He'd told Sarah and Josh, "It doesn't matter. I'll get my credit for English whether it is at school or online." But when he said those words, Sarah could tell by the sad look in his eyes that it did matter.

Josh squeezed her hand. "What ya worrying about?"

She wished she could lie to him right now and tell him she was just enjoying sitting there, listening to the hum of the hot tub filter, but that's what it would be—a big fat lie. So she asked, "Do you think Luke will graduate?"

"I think he will, but he might not get the credit he needs in time to walk with his class. Either way, he'll be fine. Our life is actually getting back to normal, whatever that is for us." he chuckled.

"What about Braxton?"

"I'll miss him if he goes home."

Sarah stared at the sky. A light winded shifted, causing her to shiver. She pulled her knees to her chest, wrapped her arms around them.

"Can you do me a favor?" he asked.

"What?"

"Can you not worry so we can have some quality time?" Josh got out of his chair and pulled her out of hers. He slipped his arms around her waist. Then he covered her mouth with his, not giving her the chance to say anything.

CHAPTER TWENTY-SEVEN

Sarah tilted the stroller to avoid a bump in the sidewalk, causing Braxton to giggle.

"Is that funny, big boy?" she asked, pausing to look at him. He had kicked the blanket off his legs and was waving his hands back and forth, obviously enjoying their outing under a warm sun and denim-blue sky. She turned the stroller into the driveway and parked it in the carport. He squirmed as she gathered him into her arms, then his droopy eyes closed.

In the living room, "Local on the Eights" blared on the TV. She sat Braxton's carrier beside the couch, then glanced at Josh. His eyes closed, mouth slightly parted. *Like father, like son.*

She decided to use the quiet time before the boys got home to her advantage. Stretched out on the loveseat, she closed her eyes. In the distance, the sound of barking dogs and kids squealing in excitement filtered through the living room windows. The noise was beginning to lure her into sleep when a screaming ambulance whisked by.

She felt a tap on her shoulder. "Mama?" Luke said. "I'm home."

"Hey." She sat up and rubbed her eyes. "Where's Zack?"

He exhaled a big sigh. "I'll go get him." He slipped his feet back into his tennis shoes, laces tied. "Sorry. I stayed over to talk to Mrs. Frenchie and got sidetracked with Thomas. He was telling me about last night's game." He opened the front door.

"Wait, Luke. I'll drive." She slipped into her pink clogs.

The phone rang and Luke went to answer it, leaving the door wide open. "Kiser residence."

Sarah leaned against the banister, waiting for him to get off the phone. But she could tell by the look on his face, it wasn't good.

"Is he okay?" Luke asked.

She took the phone from Luke. "This is Sarah Kiser."

"This is River Stone hospital. An ambulance brought in your son, Zack. You need to come to the hospital."

Sarah hung up, not giving them a chance to finish. "Josh! Get up! We have to go to the hospital, *now*. It's Zack!"

"What happened?" he asked groggily.

She didn't know what happened. The adrenaline flushed the grogginess from her system. "Josh, get up."

"I'm sorry, Mama. I didn't mean to forget him," Luke interrupted.

Sarah saw the concern in his eyes. "Don't. I need you to stay calm for Braxton."

"I'm coming with you."

"No, stay here. Braxton will be waking up any minute and he'll want a bottle."

Josh put on his shoes. "And don't worry; once I find out how he's doing, I'll come back home."

While Josh went to get the keys, Sarah finished giving Luke heads up on Braxton. They hugged Luke before they stepped outside.

❧

Luke watched his parents back out of the drive, then he picked up the phone and punched in the numbers to the hospital. "Come on. Answer the phone."

"River Stone hospital, how may I help you?" asked the receptionist.

"I need the ER."

A woman answered. "This is Jules, ER, can I help you?"

"I'm Luke Kiser. An ambulance brought in my brother Zack. What's wrong with him? How is he doing?" Luke drummed his fingers on the desk while he spoke.

"Hold, please."

The woman came back on the line. "I'm sorry. We're not allowed to give out information on the phone, sweetie. Are your parents on their way?"

"Yes. Did he get beat up?"

"I'm sorry. Your mom or dad will have to give you that information."

Luke hung up the phone. It had to be one of two things. Either Zack had an asthma attack, or he got in a fight with Tommy. Glancing down, he noticed the baby was still napping. *God? If you're listening, please let Zack be okay.*

⧽⧼

Sarah and Josh walked quickly to the metal swooshing doors of the ER, then rushed to the desk and waited for the receptionist to quit talking. She had her back to them, laughing with a woman who appeared to be a volunteer.

"Excuse me," Sarah interrupted.

The receptionist turned.

"Our son, Zack Kiser, was brought to the ER. What room is he in?"

The receptionist eased out of her seat. "Follow me."

The heavy yellow door shut behind them.

"Hey, Jules. This is the Kiser family," the receptionist said to a nurse who was talking with a doctor.

The nurse put her finger in the air, signaling for them to wait. Sarah took off down the hall, looking in every room. *Where are you, Zack?* She passed by a trauma room and spotted a little boy getting his lower lip stitched. The curtain on the other side was drawn. "Zack?"

"Mrs. Kiser?"

Sarah turned.

"Hi. I'm Jules, Zack's nurse. He's over in radiology getting a CT scan."

Sarah felt her heart skip a beat. "Josh." She waved him over.

"The doctor would like to talk to you," Jules said.

"Can't you tell me what happened?" Sarah asked, feeling her face flush.

"The doctor will tell you what is going on. Please, follow me."

They were ushered into a small room to the left of the ER. Josh seated himself at the long brown table, but Sarah couldn't relax. She paced, waiting for the doctor. "Josh this has to be bad."

"Honey, let's not get worked up until we hear what the doctor has to say."

Thirty minutes later, the oak stained door opened, and Dr. Palmer entered. Sarah knew him well. He'd taken care of Jordan in the past and was very passionate about his patients.

Josh extended his hand. "Good to see you again."

"Thanks, you, too." To Sarah, "Mrs. Kiser, would you like to sit?"

Sarah pulled out a brown padded chair and sat down on the edge of her seat. "What's going on with Zack?"

Dr. Palmer's expression was sympathetic. "Zack was beaten. We're doing everything in our power to make sure . . ."

"That he doesn't die?" Sarah interrupted.

Josh latched on to her hand. "Honey, calm down and let him finish."

Dr. Palmer placed Zack's scan on the white plastic flat board. When he flipped on the switch, Zack's facial skeleton appeared. Dr. Palmer pointed and said, "This is Zack's upper jaw. This is his lower, and it's been fractured. What has us more concerned is that he pauses in his breathing while asleep." The doctor paused for a few heartbeats, then said, "We're transferring him to another hospital because I suspect he has underdeveloped jaws. I can honestly say there isn't a surgeon here who I would trust to operate on him."

Josh held tight to Sarah's hand. "What kind of surgery are we anticipating, Dr. Palmer?"

"I would prefer you talk with Dr. Hendi. Have you noticed any pauses when he sleeps?"

Sarah held tight to her chest. Yes, she'd seen Zack lie on his back like a corpse, hands folded when he slept, and at times she'd lie her hands on his chest to make sure he was taking in a deep breath. She was a nurse by trade. *What did I miss?* At that moment, she felt like an irresponsible parent. "It's my fault."

Josh squeezed her hand. "Honey, this is not your fault. Stop trying to take the blame for everything."

Hot tears leaked down her cheeks. "I should've known. I'm his mother!"

"Mrs. Kiser, sometimes when bad things happen, and I'm not excusing what these young men did to Zack, but something good happens. It's good that we found this."

Someone knocked at the door.

"Come in," Dr. Palmer said.

Two officers approached. One held a clipboard.

Josh stood, but Sarah couldn't move. Panic swept through her. She tried to draw in a deep breath, but failed. She opened her purse and pulled an antianxiety pill out of the Sunday–Saturday plastic container. She placed it on her tongue and swallowed it without water. As if through a fog, she heard the officer say, "We're going over to Tommy and Jason's home. Zack was alert enough when they brought him in to tell who did this to him."

Alert. That was all Sarah needed to hear. Zack was alert and alive. But that didn't take away her feelings of being irresponsible.

"You will press charges, I presume," the officer said.

"Yes. We'll be pressing charges," Josh assured.

"Doctor Palmer," said Jules, stepping into the room. "The ambulance is here to transport Zack."

The doctor slid the paper to Josh. "Please sign this consent form."

"I want to see him," Sarah said.

Dr. Palmer directed an assistant to print directions to the hospital they were transferring Zack. Sarah followed the still-talking crew into the hall.

Jules took Sarah by the hand. "Follow me."

When Jules pulled back the drawn curtain in Zack's room, Sarah gasped. He looked like he had fought Rocky Balboa.

She reached out to him. "You're going to be okay, sweetie." She tried to keep her tears at bay, but the harder she tried, the more they flowed.

Zack's lips were dry, swollen, and cracked. Blackish-blue bruising circled his eyes, his left eyelid had begun to swell, and even though the hospital had cleaned him up, dried blood remained in the creases of his eyes.

"I'm going home to pack my bags, and I'll meet you at the hospital. Don't be scared. I'll be right there with you," she said.

After Josh wrapped it up with the officer, he came to Zack's bedside, and placed a kiss on his forehead. "I love you," was all Josh could muster.

Tears escaped Zack's eyes. He put a thumb into the air.

Sarah and Josh followed alongside his bed as far as staff would allow, and then went to the parking lot.

On the drive home, Sarah said, "What can we do about Braxton? Luke will want to go with us to the hospital."

"I'll call Pauline to see if she'll watch him."

Sarah hadn't thought that far ahead. She didn't want to leave Braxton, especially since he might be leaving her family soon, but she realized there were no options. "You know what I think is sad, Josh?"

"What?"

"We've come this far in life and neither of us have any family who can help us in a time of crisis."

"We have our church family. They're always there."

Pauline had sat with her at the hospital during the late nights when Jordan was alive. She'd squeezed her hand numerous times, and lent her shoulder for Sarah to weep on. She had also cared for Zack the night Sarah had to rush Luke to the hospital for an appendicitis attack. Other church members helped by bringing food to their home, picking up Zack after school, and taking him to his basketball games on Saturdays. "Yes, call Pauline." Sarah agreed.

Josh whipped the SUV into the drive, just as Luke poured out the door. "How is he?"

Sarah clipped the door shut. "He's not doing well, sweetie. We'll discuss it inside. How's Braxton?"

"He's fine. I fed him and he's in his swing. What's up with Zack?"

She followed him in the house. "We'll talk when your dad gets in here."

Sarah wound the handle on Braxton's swing, then collapsed on the couch. Where would she begin? Luke had been under enormous amounts of stress already worrying if he'd pass his English final.

"Pauline said she'd watch him." Josh closed the lid on his cell phone, and plunked down beside Luke's feet. "You have to understand that what I'm about to tell you isn't your fault."

"Is Zack okay?"

"He was beat up today after school by Tommy and Jason." Josh's voice registered calmness. Though, Sarah knew that inside he was falling apart.

Luke smacked his fist on his right thigh. "That's it, I'm goin' over there."

Josh grabbed his hand. "The police officers are going. Please let them handle this. Your mother has to pack her overnight bag and get to the other hospital."

Luke hopped up, pulling away from his dad's grasp. "Other hospital?"

"They had to transfer him."

Luke clenched his teeth. "How. Bad. Is. He?"

Sarah grimaced. How could they tell him that Zack's face was battered in bruises?

"He . . ." Sarah tried to say, is in bad shape, but she couldn't form the words.

"He's not doing well," Josh said. "We need you to be strong. Our family has been through a lot, but God has always been with us. Now, go get an overnight bag packed so you can go along with your mom. I won't be able to come down until Pauline arrives to watch Braxton."

"Josh, what about Children Services? Will they have a problem with Pauline watching Braxton, since she hasn't been fingerprinted?"

"Honey, at a time like this, we're not going to worry about that. Pauline's brother has a seizure disorder, so if Braxton has one, she'll know what to do. Besides, he hasn't had one in a long time, and hopefully, I won't be gone long."

⋙⋘

At the hospital, Sarah paused at the information desk and waited for an elderly woman to hang up the phone. On the drive there, Luke had only responded to questions Sarah had asked. How was school? Are you ready for your finals? He gave the same answer twice, "Fine."

"May I help you?" the woman asked, interrupting her thoughts.

"I'm Zack Kiser's mom, and this is his brother, Luke. He was transferred here."

The woman typed Zack's name into the computer, then said, "Take the elevator over there to the fifth floor. He's in room 526."

When they exited the elevator onto the fifth floor, Luke pointed to the sign posted on the wall. An arrow pointed to the right for rooms 526–535. "This way, Mama."

They turned the corner. Luke didn't even pause at Zack's bedroom door; instead, he brushed past the two doctors who were standing beside the bed.

"Mrs. Kiser?" a doctor said.

Luke froze. "No, Zack, no—" He plunged his hand through his hair and took a deep breath.

Zack's face had swollen more since Sarah had seen him last. He could barely open his eyelids. Sarah cringed. *God, please help him.*

"I promise you, Zack, they'll pay for this, if it's the last thing I do." Luke patted his brother's hand.

The nurse entered the room, her clogs squeaking against the tiled floor, and hung another bag of fluid.

"Mrs. Kiser, please come with us. There are a few things we need to discuss," the doctor said.

Sarah nodded.

"Mama? I'm not leaving." Luke sat down in a rocker.

Sarah followed Dr. Shoemaker—she'd seen his name embroidered on his lab coat— to a conference room down the hall.

"I've ordered an overnight PSG for your son." The doctor seated himself at the head of the conference table. "We'll be conducting an MRI at the same time. We know his jaws are undeveloped but we're trying to figure out how many times his breathing pauses in an hour."

Sarah tried to take in the information. She held tight to her chair and allowed herself to feel the rise and fall of her chest. "Then what?"

"I've contacted Dr. Hendi. If Zack has underdeveloped jaws, he'll need to undergo a major operation to correct his breathing issues. Dr. Hendi is the best surgeon around for this operation. Highly recommended."

Hearing the news that he was the best surgeon didn't make Sarah stop hurting, but it did offer a tinge of relief. The last thing she wanted was for Zack to be neglected like Jordan. "I see. What about his broken jaw?"

"Dr. Hendi will fix that, too, and the swelling around his eyes and nose will subside. If you have any further questions, I'll be in and out of the OR till midnight."

After he left, Sarah didn't move. She just sat there. Suddenly, the pain in her hip had taken a backseat to her broken heart. She inhaled deeply, as the emotions rose in her throat. Tears slipped down her cheeks; she didn't bother to wipe them away. She could taste the salty liquid. Finally, she placed her elbows on the table and clasped her hands under her chin. "God, you said you'd give me no more than I could bear. Well, I can't bear it anymore." She slowly pushed back her chair and stood. There was nothing she could do or say now. She shouldered her purse and walked slowly back to Zack's room, feeling like the load she carried would be too heavy for a mule to carry.

CHAPTER TWENTY-EIGHT

Luke sat by Zack's bed, his mom in the rocker on the opposite side, and his dad had gone for coffee. In one hour, they would take Zack for his overnight sleep study.

Luke couldn't take his eyes off Zack. The more he looked at him, the angrier he became. His fingers twitched at the thought, and he grabbed one hand in the other, and squeezed it. *Mouse and Tommy will pay for this. Bam! It'll all be over. His dad could only contain him for so long. In less than two weeks, he'd be eighteen, and then no one could tell him he couldn't leave the house.*

A man wearing a white coat approached. "I'll be taking Zack over to the A tower for the night. Tomorrow morning, he'll be brought back to his room. Will you be staying the night with him?"

"Yes," Sarah responded.

After the orderly pushed Zack's bed into the corridor, Luke watched them disappear around the corner.

Josh entered with two cups of coffee.

"Dad. If you go fast they just turned the corner."

After Josh left the room, Luke rested his head against the softness of the chair. He had to admit the furniture was way more comfortable then the stuff at the other hospital, and he had to believe that Zack would get good care. At this point, he had to believe in something. A headache was beginning to form. He closed his eyes for a brief second, then opened them and stared at the pocked ceiling.

His thoughts shifted to his school situation. He'd be forced to take the online English class. He shrugged. It didn't matter how he got his credit, the only thing that mattered was Zack. No way was he leaving the hospital until he knew Zack would be okay. It'd take a security officer hauling him off in cuffs before he'd leave. He was staying with the only brother he had left, and no one was denying him that right. After Zack had his surgery, he'd go do what he'd put off doing for a long time. Visit Jordan.

❧❧

Sarah, Josh, and Luke sat in the waiting room. Zack had been in surgery for three hours. They'd been informed the surgery would take five. Dr. Hendi had explained he would be performing a surgery called "LeForte," which they understood to be massive reconstruction. The MRI results showed underdevelopment of the jaws as suspected. The sleep study showed severe obstructive sleep apnea. Because of the jaw issue, Zack's tongue fell to the back of his throat when he slept, obstructing his airway, and his upper facial bones had to be advanced to allow the airway to open. They'd been assured by Dr. Hendi that even though Zack had been beaten, this was a *blessing in disguise.* He had not been getting enough oxygen into his bloodstream and his carbon dioxide levels were high.

"What did you find out about Tommy and Jason?" Sarah asked Josh.

"They're being detained at the Juvenile Detention Center. Let's pray that's where they stay until they get the help they need."

"What about Mouse?" Luke asked.

"I've been told he wasn't involved."

Luke rolled his eyes. "I find that hard to believe."

Josh leaned over and softly said, "The Warden told me to take as much time as I need."

"That's good." Sarah pulled her cell phone out of her purse and dialed home. "Hey, Shirley. How's Braxton?"

Although it was against foster care rules, Sarah and Josh agreed that Shirley was trustworthy. In the event something happened to Braxton while they were away, Sarah had instructed Shirley to call Miss Bond. If she received a write-up for a rule violation, she didn't care.

"He's doing well," Shirley answered. "And I'm praying for Zack."

"I appreciate that. Give Brax a kiss for me."

After Sarah clicked off her cell phone, she smiled, realizing that

212

even if Braxton had a seizure while she was away and Shirley had to call Miss Bond, at least she'd given Shirley what she rightfully deserved—time alone with her grandchild.

She tapped the top of Josh's sports magazine. "Shirley said Braxton's doing well, and don't forget he has a visit this Friday at the agency."

Josh closed the magazine, and laid it on the table. "You think Jamaal will actually show up?"

Sarah hoped he wouldn't show. He'd cancelled the last two visits because he'd found a new job. She had seen Luke go into the lounge when she had been on the phone with Shirley. "I'm going to get me another cup of coffee."

Luke sat at a table near the vending machines, his English book open. She sat down. "When did you start drinking coffee?"

He extended his arms toward the ceiling. "I'll be eighteen next week, Mama. I don't think I need a permit to drink coffee."

She smiled at his sarcasm. "We'll have you a party when Zack gets home."

He sighed. "I don't care about a party."

That reply shocked Sarah. Of course he cared, she cared. For the past seventeen years, she'd trailed him through the house, asking him what he wanted for his birthday. Later, he'd given her a mile-long list.

"But me and your father care. You only graduate high school once. And we're proud."

"I appreciate it, but let's just get Zack home first."

"Was Mrs. Frenchie okay with your decision about taking the online English class?"

"She understands." Luke guzzled the rest of his coffee like it was Hawaiian Punch.

"What about the other final exams?"

"I'll take them, while I'm studying for the English course."

She patted his hand. "Mrs. Frenchie told me they have another ceremony in August if you'd like to go."

"I wanted to be there with the majority of my class, but I'm cool with it. As long as I get my English credit and diploma, that's all that matters."

"Your party will be fun."

Luke grinned. "Like we haven't had enough excitement in the past year?"

Sarah laughed. "Hey. Our family has learned to take the good with the bad, right?"

"I hear that."

The hand-held pager Sarah had been lugging around since Zack went to the OR vibrated. Luke followed Sarah to the desk. She motioned for Josh.

"The doctor will see you in conference room two," the receptionist said.

Sarah, Josh, and Luke followed her into the small room. Josh and Luke sat on the couch while Sarah peered through the small window on the door. "Here he comes."

Dr. Hendi entered. His gray hair was damp at the edges, his scrubs rolled at the hem. "Everything went well."

Sarah stood on her toes and wrapped her arms around his shoulders. "Thank you so much."

"Following a major reconstructive surgery such as this, he'll need to spend a few days in ICU. He's on a vent, so don't be alarmed. This is necessary in case his airway swells. It'll be at least an hour before you can see him."

"Thanks, Doc." Luke hugged him.

Josh extended his hand. "Yes, we appreciate it."

They filed out of the conference room.

"You guys hungry?" Josh asked.

"Starving." Luke rubbed his stomach.

In the cafeteria, they took their seats. Josh blessed the food, and they raised their heads.

Sarah watched Luke swipe at a tear. She took a bite of her sandwich then swallowed. "So you're going back home with your dad tonight, right?"

"I plan to see Zack first."

"We figured that." Josh laughed.

"How long do you think he'll be in ICU, Mama?"

"A couple of days, I presume."

"After he goes to the floor why don't you let me stay with him, so you can go home and see Braxton?"

Leave Zack? She wasn't sure she could. She never left Jordan's bedside for one minute, but before she could refuse, Josh spoke up. "I think that's a nice gesture, bud. Rest would do your mom good."

The pager vibrated. "Let's go."

"Honey, finish eating."

"I'm not hungry."

Josh put the sandwich back into the wrapper and placed it in a white carryout bag. They took the elevators to ICU. Sarah walked to the window and waited for the receptionist to slide open the glass door. "We're Zack Kiser's family. Can we see him now?"

The receptionist pushed the buzzer and activated the door, allowing them access to ICU. Zack's room was across from the nurse's station. When they entered, Luke went directly to his bedside. Sarah saw a sheen of tears in Luke's eyes, and she mouthed, "Be strong."

"Hey, Zack," Luke said in a low tone.

Zack moved, but couldn't speak because of the vent tubing. Blood oozed slowly out of the sides of his eyes. Dr. Hendi had made a slit under each eyelid to access to his upper jaws. Zack's face had to be broken in half from the outer orbit of the left eye, extending across the nose, to the outer edge of the right eye. A Barney-purple halo surrounded his face. Attached to the front of it were the screws Sarah would be taught to turn daily.

"Hi, sweetie." Although Sarah had told Luke to be strong, she fought against the tears. She hoped her fragile voice wasn't obvious. Zack held tight to a button he could push if he needed a dose of pain medication; although, doses were limited.

The dark haired, brown-eyed nurse that charted at a station outside his door entered to hang another bag of fluid. "I'm Katie. I'll be Zack's nurse for the next twelve hours. Do you have any questions?"

Luke tucked his hands into his jeans pockets. "Is he in a lot of pain?"

Katie checked the bags hanging on the IV pole. "He has the pain pump, and every three to four hours we can give him extra medication. But you have to remember, this surgery is not a walk in the park. I've heard it is one of the most painful that anyone can endure."

Sarah cringed.

Josh patted Zack's hand. "We're here, buddy. I know you're hurting, but try to get some rest. Luke and I are going home, but Mom will be here all night."

Zack nodded and a tear escaped his eye.

Luke didn't move. "I love you, Zack. If you need anything, you know Mom will make sure you get it."

Josh hugged Sarah. "We're gonna get going. If you step outside later, give me a call."

Sarah walked them to the elevator. "I love you, Luke."

He put his strong arms around her and whispered in her ear. "Take care, Mama. I love you, too."

ৡ৵ঌ

The next morning, Mike honked. Luke went out the front door, locking it behind him. Earlier his dad had warned him not to worry about Tommy or Jason. This time Luke didn't open his mouth to dispute him. He was happy that Tommy and Jason were in the detention center until the court date. What they'd done to Zack, and Luke was sure Mouse had a hand in it, had left him livid. The only consolation he had was that he'd heard the juvenile judge didn't take kindly to kids being out of control. So, he'd decided to wait and see what the judge handed down for discipline.

Luke paused at the porch swing, picked up the bag of items he'd purchased at Lowes with his left hand, and with his right, the tray of flowers.

Mike poked his head out of his window. "Need help?"

"Yeah. Unlock the trunk."

Mike opened the trunk and Luke slid the items inside, then he opened the car door, slid into a seat, and strapped himself in.

Mike grinned. "Long time no see."

Luke gave him a high-five.

Mike backed the car onto the street, then jammed the gearshift into drive. "Check this out." He slid Dustin's latest CD into the player and cranked up the volume. "Hammered" blared through the speakers. "So you're not gonna walk the aisle with me on graduation?" he shouted over the music.

Luke turned down the volume. "No can do, bro."

"Man, I hate that you can't be there. We've been together since third grade, but I understand. You gonna have a graduation party?"

Although Sarah had told him she was giving him one, the celebration he looked forward to was when Zack would return home. "Said she was."

"So Zack quits breathing seventy-eight times a night?"

"That's what the sleep test showed, but he's better now."

While Mike updated him about Section Eight, Luke reached into his pocket and pulled out the Lowe's receipt, glanced over it, hoping he didn't forget anything.

"I might work for my aunt at Pet Groomer till I can find a job," Mike said.

"That's cool." Luke put the receipt back in his pocket and lowered the sun visor.

"Man. You're mama's gonna be surprised you went to Jordan's grave."

Luke's lips turned upward. "Hope so."

Mike whipped the Sunbird into the cemetery entrance and drove over the bridge. Creeping phlox had replaced the melted snow. Luke grinned as ducks waddled across the parking lot, causing Mike to slow and honk. After the ducks made their way to the other side, Mike drove up a little farther, then pulled his car to the curb, and turned off the ignition.

"Need some help, dude?" Mike asked.

"Nah. I got it."

"Take all the time ya need." Mike climbed out of the car, shut the door, and walked two lots over to visit his mama.

Luke went to the back of the car, leaving his door open. He lifted the bag and flowers out of the trunk. At the tombstone, he set the items on the grass and knelt in front of Jordan's picture. Then swiping his finger over it, he said, "Hey, buddy. Hope you're having a real nice day." The same words he'd said to Jordan when he was alive.

He stood up and busied himself, tossing faded flowers into an empty bag. Then he placed a polyresin golden retriever and a baseball flowerpot at the base of the tombstone. He worked the soil around the stone with the garden tools he'd brought along, tossing overgrown weeds into a bag, then carefully spaced the petunia's and begonia's in the front. Unsure if he was doing it exactly the way his mama had, but he grinned, satisfied with his work as he tapped the soil with his tool.

He repainted the stone borders slate-blue —something he'd heard his mama tell his dad she needed to do this year. Then he sat down, picked a blade of grass, and put it in the side of his mouth.

"Guess you know Zack's in the hospital?" At that moment, he remembered what Mike had told him before about going to the grave. *It's like it's final or something.* But he had to get it out. "After you died, I lost my sense of direction. I saw how quick death could come and swallow you up, and even though I didn't die with you, a part of me did."

He picked up the toy fire truck and drove it over the dirt. *"V-room. V-room."* Then he continued, "I'm flunking English, but I'm gonna get my credit online. I wanted to walk with my class really bad 'cause I wanted to prove to everyone that just 'cause I had the worse year of my life . . ." He swallowed. "Yep, your straight A, reach-for- the-stars brother messed up big time. At least in heaven, no one can hurt you. Chalk that up as a blessing."

He grinned, remembering Jordan's angelic smile, his chocolate-chip eyes. "At first I thought Mama was trying to replace you when she took Braxton, but even if she was, it don't matter, 'cause he's pretty cool."

Luke twisted his lips, then wiped his nose on the sleeve of his shirt. "The other day when I showed the baby Mr. Monkey, he cooed." Luke had to stop talking. He thought he'd flood the flowers he'd just planted, but he had to go on, or he never would. "Anyway, Braxton's brother died, too, and then his mama got hit by a car. And she was pregnant . . ." He choked then drew in a deep breath. He sat there a few minutes collecting himself, picking at the hangnail on his thumb. "Anyway, when I pushed the lever on your phone, "I just called to say I love you" played. And I lost it. When I looked at Braxton he stared at me like, you know, he understood." Luke leaned over, grabbed the golden retriever, and held it in his lap. "After I graduate, I know what I'm gonna do, but I'm afraid it'll break Mama's heart."

For the next twenty minutes, Luke talked, he laughed and he cried, occasionally wiping a tear from his eye.

"Looks nice." Mike took a seat beside him and handed him a tissue. "Thought you'd need one."

Luke blew his nose, replaced the golden retriever, and stood, wiping off the back of his khaki shorts. He pulled the throw-away camera out of his side pocket and snapped several pictures. He planted a kiss on Jordan's picture. "Just know wherever I go, buddy, you'll always be in my heart. No one can ever take away the memories, well, maybe Alzheimer's disease, but by then, I'll pretty much be on my way to see you . . . if I get to the Isle of Faith."

CHAPTER TWENTY-NINE

Luke was glad his mom had decided to go home and get some rest. They had left after Dr. Hendi had stopped by on morning rounds and said if Zack continued to improve, he'd be discharged in about three days.

On the drive to the hospital, his dad had said he was proud of him, and he could see the glimmer of approval in his dad's eyes when he'd said those words.

He hoped Zack would feel the same way when he shared the events of the past few days with him. Without a doubt, Zack had been through the mill, and Luke almost dreaded going back to his room. He knew his recent life decision would break Zack's heart, but even more, it would definitely break his mama's heart.

When he entered the room, he found Zack sleeping soundly. Luke sat down in the chair and blew out a long breath. The yellowish-green bruising on Zack's face was a reminder of what Tommy and Jason had done to him. Although Luke wanted desperately to intervene, like he'd always done in the past and give those two boys the exact same treatment they'd dished out to Zack, he'd made up his mind they weren't worth the effort. For once he'd let the officials do their job without running interference.

He squeezed his eyes shut. The day before, he'd gone to church with his dad and managed to stay for the whole service. He couldn't deny the heaviness in his heart any longer. Yesterday, he should've gone to the altar to pray, but he'd held back for fear someone might laugh at him.

He'd taken away from the service good thoughts to ponder on. Truman had said, "I've been in the same place you're at right now, needing the Lord, and all you have to do is wave your little white flag and surrender."

Luke had held tight to his seat to keep from going to the altar when a girl named Hannah and her family sang "Impending Storm." It was a relief when the service ended.

Pauline's testimony helped him the most. She'd talked about how she'd knelt on her knees in her bedroom late one night and accepted the Lord into her heart. "It doesn't matter where you're at," she'd said. "You can accept Him on a railroad track, in a cornfield, or on the side of the road. The most important thing to remember is when God is calling, you need to heed to his voice."

Luke took her testimony to heart. He was tired of running from God. He wanted what his family and his counselor had—peace that could only come from above. If they survived all their tragedies by leaning on God, then surely he could, too.

A blue-eyed nurse entered Zack's room. "I'm Tina, and I'll be Zack's nurse for the evening. Do you need anything?"

Luke stretched his arms to the ceiling and stood up. "No, thanks. I'm going downstairs to get me a cup of coffee. If Zack wakes up, tell him I'll be back."

"Take your time, sweetie."

Luke exited the elevator and walked past the gift shop. He stopped and stared at the steps that led to the chapel. He saw a set of freshly stained wooden doors. *You can accept the Lord on a railroad track, in a cornfield, or by the side of the road.*

He felt so brokenhearted; he took the steps to the top landing. He opened the door, walked in slowly, and looked around. Glancing to his right, he noticed two stained-glassed windows. The first one showed Jesus sitting with Mary and Martha in their home, the second pictured Mary Magdalene when she had seen the Risen Lord.

He walked down the center aisle to the second row, and knelt between the pews. He placed his elbows on the padded bench and clasped his hands together to pray. "Hey, Lord. It's me, Luke. I've made a mess of things. I ain't gonna tell ya all my troubles 'cause you already know, but I do believe that Jesus died for my sins and . . ."

The next several minutes, Luke poured his heart out to the Lord. When he finished, he couldn't remember everything he'd said, he just knew a peace came over him, he felt alive—the heaviness of his heart was gone. *Whew!* He sat down on the pew.

He heard the door gently close behind him, but he didn't bother to look back to see who had come in. He felt a hand touch his shoulder and he turned. "Hey, Truman. What are you doing here?"

He no longer wondered what Pastor Truman had that he didn't. They both had the Lord and that was all that mattered.

"Well, buddy," Truman began. "A little nudge in my heart told me to come up here. How's Zack?"

"He's doing better."

"How're you?"

Luke turned around in his seat to face Truman and a smile lit his face. "I'm doing great. I got saved."

Truman's grin widened. "Ya did?"

"I needed to come to the altar this past Sunday, but I didn't."

"That's good news, buddy." Truman patted Luke's shoulder.

"What do I have to do now?" Luke asked.

"When you're ready, you'll give a profession of faith, and then we'll baptize you into the church."

"Okay."

"I want to leave you with one more thought. Just because you're saved don't mean you won't suffer in this life. Many people don't know this about me, but I lost a brother. A man shot him in the back, killed him in cold blood." Truman's forehead creased and he shook his head. "If I hadn't had the Lord on my side, Luke, I would've never been able to withstand that kind of pain."

"You're the most trusting person I've ever met. That must've been hard."

"Well, yeah, it's something you never get over. Just hang in there, buddy. Okay?" Truman patted him on his back this time.

Luke stood. "I'm going to get a cup of coffee. Would you like one? I'll buy, then I gotta get back to Zack's room."

Truman grinned. "Boy, I'm proud of you."

They walked out the door and down the steps. Luke paused and gazed back at the stained doors. *Thanks, God, for not giving up on me.*

Luke came to Zack's bedside, and gently patted his shoulder. "You okay?"

Zack opened his eyes. "Hey."

"How ya feeling?" Luke could barely contain his grin.

Zack peered at him through his halo. "You're happy. Whadyado? Give Mouse a black eye?"

"Nope." Luke grinned. "I accepted the Lord."

Tears slipped down Zack's face as he edged himself up farther into the bed. He reached for Luke's hand.

"It's okay, Zack. I know you're happy, but don't get too emotional. I don't want you hurting or having an asthma attack."

Zack snickered, his halo bopping up and down. "Only you."

"What?"

Zack placed his hands over his ribs. "You crack me up."

Luke's tone turned serious. "I'm glad you never gave up on me. And I'm sorry for all the times I treated you bad."

"I forgive you. I suspected it wouldn't be long till you surrendered."

Luke's eyebrows raised. "How?"

"'Cause you were miserable. And you were asking a lot of questions. I prayed for God to show you the way."

Luke's heart melted. The brother he'd treated like the enemy for the past year had prayed for him. Tears squeezed past his eyelids. "I love you, Zack."

Zack grinned then pushed the button on the side of his bed, raising his head. "What you going to do after you get your online credit for English?"

"I found out they have another ceremony in August if I want to go, but I won't be here."

Even though Zack's face lit up when Luke told him the good news, he feared the news he was about to share might hamper his high spirits.

"Why? Did you change your mind about college?"

"No." Luke cleared his throat. I joined the, um . . . army."

Zack turned abruptly and then cringed, holding his ribcage. "Ouch! That hurt!"

"Take it easy, buddy." Luke patted his hand.

Zack wrapped his hand around Luke's hands. "I'm proud of you. And I'm thankful God blessed me to have a brother like you."

Luke look puzzled. "You mean that? I mean, I haven't exactly treated you nice."

Zack put his hand in the air to silence Luke. "Do you remember when we used to snoop around the house to find our Christmas presents before Mom could wrap them?"

Luke grinned. "Yeah. Do you remember when we used to dress up and play cops and robbers?"

Zack's halo bobbed up and down as he laughed. "I remember when you ate the entire batch of cookies Mom just baked and put the empty plate on the floor, making her think the dog ate them."

Luke chuckled. "Those were the good old days. Weren't they?"

For a moment, the only sound came from the IV machine, pumping meds into Zack's veins.

"Luke?" Zack's tone turned serious. "You'll be back. We're gonna grow old together and get married and have a bunch of grandkids for Mom to watch. And . . ." Zack's tears began to flow.

Luke slightly squeezed his hand. "Don't worry, I'll be back."

"But what if you have to go to Iraq or Afghanistan?"

"God will watch over me. And you'll pray for me. What more could a brother want?"

Then they talked about their childhood days—playing with Tonka trucks in mounds of dirt, riding their bikes pretending they were school bus drivers, pestering the cat until it clawed them, and pretending Zack was the preacher baptizing Luke in the bathtub. They talked and laughed until Zack drifted off to sleep.

Luke pulled the thick white blanket up around his brother's shoulders. *And thank you, God, for giving me a special, loving, brother.*

CHAPTER-THIRTY

Sarah lay awake, staring out the window, until at last, the sun came to brush away the night. She was thankful Zack was home from the hospital; although, they needed to return for a follow-up visit with the doctor and for weekly x-rays of his jaws.

She could still see Luke's smiling face as he'd said the words to her. "Mama, I accepted the Lord in the Chapel at the hospital." The day he shared the news, his face glowed. Sarah's heart had jumped for joy when he'd said those words.

Miss Bond had called earlier in the week to say she'd spoken with Jamaal's attorney, and Braxton's Guardian Ad Litem. They said Braxton should be returned home to the father, and that she'd be getting a paper with the court date.

Sarah made her way down the steps. The smell of freshly brewed coffee lured her into the kitchen.

"How's my lovely wife?"

"Fine." Sarah sat down in a barstool at the counter.

Josh carried two steaming mugs of coffee and set them down on the countertop, then took a seat beside her. "You look worried."

She sighed. "I can't quit thinking about what Georgia said—that Jamaal would hurt Braxton. I can't believe the judge would send him home."

"What did Shirley say last night?"

"She's worried, too. And she plans to fight Jamaal for grandparent rights. I'm just thankful that we're going to keep on being friends."

"Try not to worry about Braxton. The table could turn at any time," Josh said.

They stared at each other with an understanding—why worry when you can pray.

"Our life is like a merry-go-round that never stops." Sarah traced her fingers around the rim of her cup. She thought about Zack's medical issues, Luke's problems over the past few months, Braxton's health issues, the loss of his mom, and his current situation—that any day he would go home to be with his dad. She knew that life could be unfair, that love could break your heart, and that nothing was worse than being left behind when a family member passed away, or in this case, when Braxton would go home. "We'll miss him."

"Yes, we will."

She swallowed the lump in her throat. "I miss Georgia, too."

Josh's eyes were deep, thoughtful. "I believe God will use Georgia's life as a testament. We might not see it, but somewhere down the road, he will."

Sarah remembered the book, *Stand Still*, that Luke's counselor had given him. The husband who died had lived his life where others could see Christ living in him. His wife had gotten saved after he passed away, and Luke got saved after he'd read the book.

"I don't mean to change the subject, but have you given anymore thought to Luke's party?" Josh asked.

"I think we should combine his graduation and birthday, and have the party the Saturday after he gets his English credit," Sarah said.

"I agree."

She made a mental note to go shopping later that afternoon. "I was thinking that since Luke turned eighteen, we should buy him a car. He'll be getting a job soon, and well, it's time."

"We'll see how things go."

"You don't seem very upbeat today. Is something bothering you?"

"Not really. I meant to tell you that Truman called last night, and this coming Sunday they're going to baptize Luke," Josh said.

"That's good. I'm happy he finally accepted the Lord."

"Prayer changes things, doesn't it?"

"Yes it does, but it makes it easier when the person you pray for heeds God's word."

For the next few minutes, they nursed their coffee. For some reason, Josh appeared to be sad today. Sarah couldn't shake the feeling that something didn't see quite right.

"Who will you invite to Luke's party?" Josh interrupted her thought.

Sarah planned ahead. Always. She intended to invite all of the church members, Mrs.Frenchie, Mike, and Dustin. "I'll get the guest list ready and show it to you. You know what else I think would be fun?"

"What?"

"Okay. Check this out. We need to get a huge box and put Hollister shirts, shorts, a new wallet, and a Michigan ball cap in it. Then I'll write clues on index cards as to where he can find his other presents, like his favorite cologne and whatever else he needs. Wouldn't that be cool? I mean for Luke?"

Josh leaned back, folding his hands in his lap. "You're getting into this. I like that, but I know how you are Sarah, so don't get too carried away."

"I won't."

Over the next two weeks, Luke received his English credit, passed his final exams, and picked up his diploma. Sarah and Josh prepared for his belated birthday and graduation party. At any minute, the guests would arrive, along with five dozen balloons from the flower shop.

Luke entered the kitchen. "Mama. You shouldn't have."

She glanced over at the spread of food. Potato salad, baked beans, coleslaw, corn on the cob, three crock-pots of chicken salad, mac-n-cheese, and chicken and dumplings, Luke's favorite, hid the countertops.

Luke linked his arms around her neck. "You're the best, Mama. I love you so much. Thanks for everything."

"You're very welcome, sweetie. I'd take a bullet for my kids."

Luke grinned. "I don't doubt that for a minute."

When the doorbell rang, Zack ran to answer it. Luke joined Josh on the deck where he was grilling the last pack of hamburgers and hotdogs. Sarah finished washing the dishes, dried them, and put them into the cupboard. When she glanced through the kitchen window, she spotted Josh hugging Luke and patting his back.

Through the cracked window, Sarah heard Josh say, "Don't worry about it, Son. It'll be alright."

Of course it would be alright, she thought. She knew that any kid would be nervous worrying about their future, or was he worrying about getting a car?

"Mom, look who's here," Zack said.

Sarah towel-dried her hands and turned. "Hey, Pauline, L.D. Thanks for coming, and for the cake."

Zack pulled the cake from Pauline's hands. "I'll put this on top of the freezer that way it'll stay cool." Before Zack walked away, he paused to show it to Sarah.

She smiled. "Luke will love it."

The sheet cake was layered with shells of yellow-gold icing and turf-green centered the top with yellow yard lines. A Michigan winged-helmet lay in the middle of the field. It read MICHIGAN in frosted letters. Pauline had made goal posts out of drinking straws and placed one on each end of the zone.

Minutes later, the kitchen and outside deck filled with church members, Mrs. Frenchie, Shirley, Mike, and Dustin. Josh called out, "Time to eat."

After the plates were cleared and tossed into the plastic liner of the trashcan, Zack stepped out on the deck. "It's time to cut the cake."

Sarah decided to let Luke have the honors. She handed him the knife.

"Wow." His eyes danced. "Check it out, Zack. Michigan."

"Duh? Nerd herd." Zack teased.

"Hey, don't be stealin' my lines." Luke cut the cake and put each piece on a small paper plate. Zack and Mike passed them to each guest.

"Is this where the party's at?" Truman asked through the screen door.

"This is the par-tae," Zack said, grinning.

Luke licked his fingers. "Hey, Truman, come on out."

Truman slid open the screen door, stepped out on the deck. "This is my buddy." He slipped his arm around Luke.

"You hungry?" Luke asked.

Truman rubbed his stomach. "Nah . . . Joyce fed me pinto beans and cornbread."

Luke chuckled.

Zack popped several balloons to get everyone's attention. "Present time."

Luke opened his presents and thanked everyone for their gifts. Next, he lifted the present Mike and Dustin gave him and shook it. "Hmm?" He tore off the paper, opened the box, and grinned. A pair of baby-blue tennis shoes stared at him, pleading to be tried on. Luke kicked off his flip-flops, then slid his feet into the shoes. "Yeah, baby, yeah." He pranced around on the deck.

"You got one more." Zack handed him a huge box, wrapped in gold paper. A navy-blue bow sat on top.

Luke lifted the lid. "What's this?" He pulled out a rubber chicken—a clothespin clipped six index cards to its gill. He held the chicken in the air. *"Cluck, cluck, cluck."* Then he read the index cards, following each clue until he found a bottle of cologne, Hollister shirts, shorts, and a wallet. The last clue he read aloud. "When I came into your life, you have to admit, you needed me. Now I know You Love Me. You'll find your next clue near my diaper, but be careful."

Everyone laughed and clapped.

Luke walked over to Shirley and lifted Braxton out of her arms. Sarah felt her heart speed up when he kissed his tiny cheek and said, "I love you, too, Brax." He pulled the envelope out of the front of Braxton's pants and read it aloud, "We'll go car shopping, Monday. We love you, Son. Dad and Mom."

Sarah, Josh, and Zack formed a circle around Luke, embracing him. For a moment, nothing else mattered in the world to Sarah, but this moment—a perfect snapshot of her family that she'd never forget. When Sarah opened her eyes, she glanced at Shirley, who had tears streaming down her cheeks.

Luke marched over to Shirley, handed Braxton back. Then he turned and said, "Everyone here has played an important role in my life. You, like my parents, reared me in church. You prayed for me and cheered me on, even when I could be very bad. I'm sorry for the times I stuffed the mops into the toilet and wrote bad words in the song books."

"I suspected that was you," Zack said, grinning.

"After Jordan died, I thought I'd never see the light at the end of the tunnel. Then my family decided to take a baby named Braxton." He tickled Braxton's ribcage, causing him to squirm. "At first, I was afraid of him, but I've learned that everything in life is a process. If I spend the rest of my life running from . . ." Luke couldn't finish his sentence. He sobbed like a baby.

The guests applauded. Sarah placed her arms around Luke.

"Oh, Mama, I love you."

"Honey, what you said was wonderful."

"Mama." Luke cleared his throat. "I have to finish my speech."

Zack tapped his plastic fork on his cup. "Luke has something else to say."

Luke, slung his arm around Sarah's shoulder, drew in a breath.

"Go ahead, Luke," Josh said.

"I joined the army. I'll be leaving in two weeks." Luke immediately turned to Sarah. "We'll go car shopping when I get back from boot camp." His gaze held hers for a heartbeat, then she began to clap. The yard filled the sound of laughter and applause.

Sarah felt like she could fly away. The little baby boy who'd turned into a toddler and muddled through adolescence and teen years, had emerged into a fine young man—no longer the confused, defiant, scared teenager she'd seen over the past year.

"Are you proud of me, Mama?"

Sarah latched hold of his biceps and gazed into his dark-brown eyes. "I'm so proud of you, Luke. I always was."

Truman approached them. "I'm glad you finally got your horse in the right stable, buddy."

Luke grinned. "I know what that means."

"Tell ya what," Truman said, "I think we should all give Luke a big hug and let him know we'll be praying for him."

And just like at church, they formed a line on the deck that extended into the grass. Sarah stood in the line next to Mike, Dustin, and Pauline.

Sarah tapped Mike on the shoulder. "Did you know Luke joined the army?"

Mike lowered his head. "Guilty."

She patted his back. "Luke loves you, Mike. Our whole family does."

Mike flashed his million-dollar grin. "Thanks, Mama."

"You think we should put on some rap music?" Dustin asked, humming his lyrics to "Brains" and moving his feet around.

Pauline giggled.

Zack opened his mouth and started to sing "Amazing Grace," and the crowd joined in.

"Ain't never been to a party like this," Dustin said, and got back in line.

Mike rolled his eyes and grinned.

Sarah felt overjoyed, sad, and blessed, all at the same time. She looked to the bright blue sky. *Thank you, God, for your Amazing Grace, and tell my mama thanks for teaching me that nothing is ever lost.*

CHAPTER THIRTY-ONE

Sarah sat on the floor with Braxton doing his morning therapies. When she finished, she pulled him into her arms. His face had taken on new curves and characteristics. She planted a kiss on his chubby cheek. "I love you, Brax."

The phone rang. She picked up Braxton and went to answer it. "Kiser residence."

"Good gravy. How have you been?" her therapist asked.

Sarah shifted Braxton to the other hip. "I'm fine. And you?"

"You haven't called me, and you missed your last appointment. Are you sure you're fine?"

"I'm sorry. Zack was in the hospital and it totally slipped my mind." Sarah said.

"Tell me what's going on."

Sarah updated her on Zack, Luke, Braxton, Georgia, and Jamaal, but left out the part about the baby going home to Jamaal. She hoped that wouldn't happen.

"That's all?" Toni huffed. "Girl, you do need a counselor."

"I got the best."

"I take it you're not talking about me," Toni said.

Toni was right. Although she had been a godsend, Sarah couldn't deny the fact that God was her best counselor. "You'll always be a good friend, though."

"I'd like us to get together soon if you have the time. We can catch up over a cup of coffee, and I'd love to meet Braxton of course, free of charge."

Sarah loved the idea—miles could be covered over a cup of coffee. "Are you sure it'll be a free session?" she teased. "I mean, Josh and I could've paid cash for our dream boat, a Chaparral, for what you've been charging me for therapy."

"Now don't be getting carried away, honey. Dream all you want, but with a new baby, I don't foresee boating anytime soon in your forecast."

Sarah laughed. "Call me when you're ready and we'll get together."

"Are you coming to my class at the agency in August?"

Sarah laughed. "I could probably help you teach it."

"I bet you could." Toni laughed, too. "I'll call you back when I have an off day."

Sarah hung up. I could teach a class, she thought, perhaps one on saying goodbye to your foster child, and your biological child. She sat down on the couch, supporting Braxton with a stack of pillows. She latched on to his hand. "What will we do without you, Brax?"

He rubbed his head back and forth against the couch. Finally, his gaze met hers. "Ewe, oo," he babbled, waiting for her response.

"Once upon a time there was a little baby named Braxton, and he . . ."

Sarah told Braxton the story of how he had given her family a new meaning in life. She wrapped it up by saying what a wonderful mom he'd had who went on to be with the Lord. Lifting his shirt, she put her lips to his tummy and kissed it. Braxton wiggled and laughed out loud.

The door swung open and Luke walked in. "Hey, Mama."

"Hi. How did it go with the recruiter?"

"Fine. I took him my diploma and a few other documents. I need Dad to drive me to Columbus next week. I'll be flying out from there. I'll take my basic training at Fort Sill, Oklahoma."

"I took my training at Fort Jackson, South Carolina."

"Was it hard?"

"Trust me on this when I say that just because I'm a woman they didn't cut me any breaks."

"I bet they didn't. You're one tough bird, Mama."

She smiled.

"And I scored pretty high on my ASVAP test, so my recruiter showed me the fields I'd get to choose from. I think I'm going into field artillery. And I want to be a Ranger."

"I'm proud of you. Does that mean—"

"I doubt I'll be deployed to Iraq or Afghanistan, but if I do, I'm ready to fight for my country," Luke interrupted.

Sarah couldn't believe that the Luke she had lost many nights sleep over the past months was the same person she was talking to now.

"And if I do go to Iraq, I know you'll be praying for me."

Sarah swallowed the lump in her throat. "You know it."

Josh entered. "How's my beautiful wife?" He pecked her cheek with a kiss.

"Fine. How was work?"

"Busy. Today we got another bus load of inmates."

The phone rang. "Can you make sure Brax doesn't roll off the couch?" she said to Josh, and went to answer it. "Hello."

"Sarah. It's Miss Bond."

She swallowed hard, afraid to ask what she wanted. Miss Bond didn't usually call unless there was a problem, such as a cancelled visit, and since this wasn't Friday, she knew that wouldn't be the case.

After she hung up, Sarah sat on the floor next to Josh's feet and waited for Luke to finish.

"I think I'll get into field artillery."

Josh nodded. "So if you have to go to war that means you'll be dealing with bombs and weapons?"

"I'll be leading and controlling field artillery troops and combined armed forces during land combat."

"Who was that on the phone?" Luke asked.

Sarah swallowed, unable to digest the news given to her. "Miss Bond."

"What'd she have to say?" Josh asked.

"She said there would be no more visits because Jamaal got arrested last night."

Josh's eyes narrowed. "For what?"

"According to Miss Bond, he had a stable of girls, and went from one to the next. Last night, he assaulted one of them. He then proceeded to run from an officer on a high-speed chase which ended when he ran his car into a concrete wall."

"Is he okay?" Luke asked, eyes wide.

"Yes. Just a few bumps and bruises, but he hit the officer before he was arrested."

"Guess anger management didn't do him any good," Josh said.

"And you'll never believe who he assaulted."

Josh sighed. "Who?"

"Big Mama. Apparently, last week on the Maury show, Big Mama told Jamaal he was not the father of her oldest son, Melvin. Well after the show, Jamaal wouldn't leave it alone. He kept calling her on the phone, calling her names I'm not going to repeat, and then he showed up at her house last night and beat her up. Miss Bond hadn't known Big Mama had a restraining order in place and he wasn't allowed to be within fifty feet of her."

"Wow." Josh leaned back and placed his hands behind his head. "What about Braxton?"

Sarah lifted him from the couch and placed him in her lap. "Looks like you're going home with your granny."

"When?" Josh asked.

"Probably within the week."

⤜⧫⤛

Sarah wiped the cereal off Braxton's cheeks. Over the course of the week, she and Josh had sent carloads of Braxton's belongings home with Shirley whenever she visited. In less than two days, he'd be leaving them, but Shirley had kept her promise—Sarah would be permitted to have Braxton two weeks out of the summer, every other weekend, and they'd alternate the holidays. In addition, whenever Shirley needed someone to watch Braxton while she worked, Sarah would be the fill-in sitter.

In less than one hour, Luke would be leaving for boot camp. Last night, she and Josh had sat out back after Luke had gone to bed. They talked until the wee hours of the morning, until only smoldering embers were left in the fire pit. Josh had said it best. 'We'll get through this Sarah, just like everything else, by clinging to our faith and allowing God to help us.'

Luke came downstairs. "Mama? Have you seen my watch?"

"It's on the hutch. Dad found it outside last night."

Luke reached up, found it, and placed it on his wrist. "Hey, Zack. You wanta go to the airport with me and Dad?"

"Yeah, I'm going." Tears leaked down Zack's face.

Luke wrapped his arms around Zack. "Remember our talk at the hospital? We're gonna grow old together and have a ton of babies that Mama can babysit. Right?"

"Uh-um." Sarah laughed, swallowing the lump in her throat. She didn't want to break down; she wanted to be strong for Luke. Besides, last night Josh had held her and let her cry an ocean of tears.

Josh came to stand beside her and patted her back. She looked up at him and forced a smile. "Our oldest one is leaving for the army."

"Yep."

"You okay?" Sarah asked.

"We'll be fine. I told you last night how we'll get through this, and we will. You about ready, Luke?"

"Yeah. I just gotta grab one more thing." Luke fled up the stairs.

"Zack, I know it hurts, but we'll help you through this," Josh assured him.

"I know, Dad." The rims of Zack's eyes were red and swollen.

When Luke came back into the kitchen, Josh said, "Oh. I meant to tell you that Officer Michaels called the prison yesterday when I was out doing fence checks. When I called him back, he said that Tommy and Jason would be serving four months at the juvenile detention center. And when school goes back into session, they're expelled for the first three months." Josh coughed, then he added, "The judge ordered the parents and kids go to counseling."

"That's good." Luke said. "I wonder if Mouse will go to college?"

"Nope. He got arrested for drugs," Josh said.

Luke eyes narrowed. "How do you know that?"

"Officer Michaels told me."

"Josh. These are important things you keep forgetting to share," Sarah said.

"Honey, with the load we've had to carry, I'm lucky if I can remember to clock in at work."

Sarah giggled.

Luke glanced at his watch. "We better go."

Sarah held tight to Braxton and before they filed out the door, the phone rang. "I'll get it." She handed Braxton to Luke, and answered it.

"Mrs. Kiser, the reason for my call is that we have a baby in the ICU at River Stone hospital," Miss Johnson said, and continued to explain the baby's issues. "She was born full term, but has been placed on ECMO, which is heart and lung bypass. She was born drug and alcohol exposed."

Sarah swallowed hard, listening, and wondering why this happened.

"She's very fragile right now. Would you be interested in caring for this child? I mean—it would be awhile before she's discharged due to her critical status, but since Braxton's going home in a day or so, I figured you might be up for another placement."

"Can you hold for just a sec?"

Sarah put the phone down and shifted her gaze to Luke and Zack. Her eyes finally settled on Josh. "Miss Johnson is on the phone and wants to know if we'll take a baby who was born drug and alcohol exposed?"

She said the words with much more ease than she'd expected. Josh tucked his hands into his pockets. "Are you sure you're ready for this? I mean, I'll help you all that I can, but the decision is up to you."

"I'll help, too," Zack said.

Sarah's gaze met Luke's. "What do you think?"She wanted his opinion even if he was leaving.

Luke glanced at Braxton, then slowly lifted his head and looked at Sarah. "Yeah, we have room for another one in our little tribe."

After the family filed out the front door, Sarah picked up the receiver to give Miss Johnson the news. When she hung up, she joined the others on the front porch and cupped her hand to Luke's face. For a moment, all the years of raising him rushed through her mind: She saw him sitting on the floor banging her pots and pans with wooden ladles, and chasing her through the yard, tripping over Josh's shoes he'd placed on his own feet.

"Don't worry about me, Mama." Luke put Braxton back into her arms.

"I won't." She lied. She was the warrior of worry.

Their gazes held. "I'll see you out in Oklahoma. You can watch me graduate boot camp."

Sarah held back the tears. "Okay."

"Oh here," he said, pulling Mr. Monkey out of his bag. "This is for you, Braxton."

Sarah took it, holding it in the crook of her arm. "Tell Lukie goodbye, Brax."

"Come here, Mama."

Sarah took a step toward Luke. He placed his arms around her and Braxton, holding them tight. "I hope that someday God blesses me with a woman like you. I love you so much, Mama."

"Ah. Luke, I love you, too." She cupped her free arm around his waist.

Luke pulled out of her embrace and trotted to the SUV. He paused, hand on the door handle, looked back, and clenched his right hand in the air. "I did it. Yeah, baby."

Josh and Zack laughed.

Sarah stood on the front porch and watched the SUV fade. An emptiness inside made her want to cry, but instead she looked at Braxton and smiled. "Life goes on."

Inside, she went up stairs and laid Braxton in his crib. She leaned over and gave him a kiss, tucking Mr. Monkey beside him. And although she smiled at him, the feeling didn't reach her heart. She was happy Luke had made all the right decisions, but now the emptiness she felt was just like when she had lost Jordan. *But they're not really lost,* she assured herself.

She slowly made her way out of Braxton's room and paused at Luke's open door. A picture on his dresser caught her eye. She remembered when she'd taken the snapshot of him. He was sitting by her flowerbed, knees bent, a smile plastered to his face. He'd had the picture enlarged to a five-by- seven and had put it in a plastic golden frame. She walked in his room, lifted it off the dresser, and traced her fingers over the glass. When she went to put it back, her fingers accidentally brushed against the lower frame.

A sound so sweet filled the air. "Mama, Dad, Zack, and Brax, by the time you find this, I'll be gone. When you miss me, push the button so you can hear my voice. When I come back, I'll be a changed man. Keep me in your prayers."

Sarah placed her hand over her chest and turned toward his bed. On his pillowcase, there was a five-by-seven picture, unframed. She picked it up, tears slipping down her cheeks. On the front of the picture, she saw Jordan's tombstone and felt immediate guilt for having not gone over there to decorate. She brought the picture into focus and laughed. *Only you, Luke.* Petunias and begonias lined the front of the tombstone, and the rock edge had been freshly painted.

For the next few minutes, she allowed herself to be immersed in the good times of when Luke had nestled his nose into Jordan's neck and made his funny monkey sounds. Then, she turned the picture over. SHMILY was written at the top with Luke's handwriting. Underneath, it read, SEE HOW MUCH I LOVE YOU. LUV, LUKE.

ABOUT THE AUTHOR

 **PAMELA KLOPFENSTEIN** writes, reads, and lives in a large brick community with her husband, daughter, three sons, and a dog named Sawyer. Her days are filled with sunshine smiles, driving her kids to endless activities, and a never ending stream of words that try to find their way to her laptop. She loves hanging out with her kids playing games, having friends over, fishing, gardening, hiking, boating, and almost any outside activity. Before becoming a full time mom, she worked as a nurse. She writes devotionals, articles, and books. Some of her work has been published in magazines and other publications, including *Christian Devotions, Angels on Earth, and Inspire a Fire.* Her passion is sharing so others can open their hearts for life changing experiences. Oh, and when she laughs, she snorts.